BLOOD, MAGIC & MERCY

ROBERT SANBORN

BY ROBERT SANBORN

League of the Moon

In Your Dreams

The Red Witch

Blood, Magic & Mercy

Black Magick & Envy

Soul of the Witch

This one is for Sandy. Thank you for being a light when things were darkest. I will never forget.

Vinci Books

vinci-books.com

Published by Vinci Books Ltd in 2025

1

Copyright © Robert Sanborn - 2022

The author has asserted their moral right to be identified as the author of this work in accordance with the Copyright, Designs and Patents Act 1988. This work is a work of fiction. Names, characters, places and incidents are the product of the author's imagination or are used fictitiously. Any resemblance to actual persons, living or dead, places and incidents is entirely coincidental.

All rights reserved. No part of this publication may be copied, reproduced, distributed, stored in any retrieval system, or transmitted in any form or by any means, including photocopying, recording, or other electronic or mechanical methods, nor used as a source for any form of machine learning including AI datasets, without the prior written permission of the publisher.

The publisher and the author have made every effort to obtain permissions for any third party material used in this book and to comply with copyright law. Any queries in this respect should be brought to the attention of the publisher and any omissions will be corrected in future editions.

A CIP catalogue record for this book is available from the British Library.

Paperback ISBN: 9781036705442

Printed and bound in Great Britain by Clays Ltd, Elcograf S.p.A.

CHAPTER 1
PREPARING THE STAGE

The area was ready. He'd chosen it long ago, before they'd named it. Few knew its history. The name of the area, in historical terms, had existed for less than the blink of an eye. In mortal terms, it was almost a hundred years old. The irony of the name was timeless.

What would take place here, a few short days from now, was inevitable; he'd made certain.

Even when you could see the future, you never really knew for sure. You made your best guesses and planned accordingly. The future *was* predictable—to a point. Still, people reacted in ways you couldn't predict.

He'd always seen well beyond time's horizon, but it was like seeing a vast forest from far away. A huge green blob that loomed in the distance. Individual trees emerged only when the distance was closed. It had taken almost nine hundred years for the first trees to separate from the pack—the first hint of their soul grouping coalescing. Souls he'd need to get the job done.

Everything went according to plan until two days ago,

when someone who wasn't *supposed* to know what was happening stuck his nose in where it didn't belong. He'd have to watch him now. Guide him. Arranging it so those who knew and loved him played their parts. There was much to do and scant time to do it.

The Red Witch looked out from the bell tower's opening. She couldn't see him, of course, but he ducked back into the forest all the same.

As he eased into the tree line, he backed himself against the enormous trunk of a maple. He noticed the missing arms of the crucifixes atop the twin spires at the front of the church and wondered why they were missing. Then dismissed it as simple vandalism.

It would begin tonight. The guardian would be the first sacrifice. But not the last.

CHAPTER 2
DREAMS OF DECEPTION

It was 3:13 in the morning. The sound seemed to come from outside. In a place like this, you could never be sure. When there was a manhunt going on, and you were the focal point, it was *good* to be sure.

The room in the church's bell tower glowed a dim orange, the fire all but spent. Naked, she slipped out of bed. Aaron, asleep next to her after another athletic night together, snored the snores of the well-laid.

The nights were colder now. Her robe remained on the floor in the spot Aaron had peeled it off of her. She swung her legs from the bed, picked it up and threw it over her shoulders, cinching it tight at the waist.

Under one of four openings in the topmost room sat a rickety wooden bench. Mondra mounted it, then leaned through the opening as far as gravity would allow. Bats flitted about, hunting for their night's meal. Pinched sonar squeaks bounced off brick, tickling her eardrums.

It was one of *them*. How a guardian found their location, she hadn't a clue, and it wasn't important at the moment.

Dealing with the guardian scaling the outside wall was priority one. When she saw glowing red eyes closing fast behind, she breathed a sigh of relief. The demon's eyes used to frighten her. Now, she considered those eyes, and the spirit animating them, her salvation.

Inanis scaled the wall silently behind the gray-cloaked guardian, letting her gain altitude—and confidence. Allowing her so close would make it that much sweeter when he watched her fall.

As the woman drew her sword, inches from the Red Witch, the demon sank his talons into the guardian's calf. A scream of agony pierced the night. As she was ripped from the church tower's wall and flailing, back-first, to the forest floor, her parting vision was a pair of glowing red eyes, and a bright, hideous smile. Then, nothing.

HENRY WOKE WITH A START. The digital clock on the dresser read 3:13 a.m. Sweat covered him. His heart pounded in his chest. *Why the hell does weird shit always happen at 3:13 in the morning?*

He rubbed his eyes, ran a hand through his hair, and slipped quietly from the bed—careful not to wake Joanne after the night she'd had getting Delilah to sleep.

Images from the dream were fading fast, and he struggled to hold on to them. The last thing he remembered was someone falling from some place very high, and then the figure of a woman—he was almost positive it was a woman—lying dead on a dirty floor. The shape of the body didn't resemble Joanne, at least as far as he could tell, but he'd heard Jo's screaming voice echoing in his mind when he snapped awake.

He crept to the bathroom, where he filled a glass with cold water and drank it down in one long gulp. His shift at Massachusetts General Hospital started at seven and he usually left for work at five—less than two hours. Going back to bed was pointless. He'd never needed that much sleep, anyway.

More than a month had passed since things went down between the League of the Moon and the Red Witch. Mondra Tibbets (aka Mondra Sticla), Aaron Hendricks, and a now demon-possessed Salem Police Officer named Raul Martinez were on the run. Raul was not a willing participant. He was, for all intents and purposes, along for the ride.

Chief Byron Miller of the Salem Police Department had issued an all-points bulletin in the early morning hours following the events at Wanda's Wicca'd Emporium. Police departments across the Commonwealth of Massachusetts and the neighboring New England states, as well as New York, had received the bulletin. Knowing a brother officer was involved added extra urgency. Byron mentioned in the bulletin they'd kidnapped Raul; no sense putting the bizzaro-land truth out there. Who'd believe it, anyway?

Since then, there'd been zero news about the trio of fugitives. They were last seen in north central Massachusetts in a town called Athol, where they'd stolen a car and taken off for parts unknown.

Henry wracked his brains for the last month trying to figure out where they were hiding, and also why they'd headed west. What was out there for them? Had this been part of Mondra's plan all along?

Byron called Henry a week or two after that night, asking

if he wanted to head out to Athol and start a search of their own. He didn't need to ask twice.

They'd driven back and forth on Route 2, stopping at every exit heading west and then coming back east, scoping out towns Henry'd heard of once or twice—Orange, Greenfield, Templeton, Baldwinville—but never actually been to.

The first and only sighting happened in Orange. The attentive station manager recognized the car from the news and called the number flashed on-screen. It didn't hurt that he was also a car nut, mechanic, and the station's owner.

When they arrived, Byron flashed his badge. The station manager promptly brought up the file on his office monitor. In the video's replay, Aaron Hendricks got out on the driver's side to fill the tank while Mondra went inside to grab supplies.

If they hadn't known what they were looking for, they would have missed the subtle glow of the eyes in the back seat. Raul Martinez stared into the camera, a slight smile on his face. He pretended his nose was itchy and scratched it, quite intentionally, with his middle finger, sending them a signal that was part taunt, part victory celebration.

Henry cast aside the frustrating memory—a new morning ritual since then—and turned on the shower. He loved their apartment, but the fucking hot water took forever to get going.

He brushed his teeth, rinsed, and gargled as the steam in the room built. Last night had been warm, and Joanne opened all the windows to air the place out. Mother Nature had shaved a good twenty degrees from the temperature overnight, and the steam in the bathroom billowed like the cloud cover at the top of Mount Washington.

Henry finished his shower and was toweling off when he

saw it. He'd left the door open—the vent fan had died a while back—to let the mist run out of the bathroom faster. As it had, the writing on the mirror emerged from the steam like the silver belly of a fish in dark water—strange symbols of a type he'd never encountered. But maybe Jo had.

He whirled and ran back into the bedroom, gently shaking Joanne awake. It was a risky proposition. She would either pop wide awake and give him a ration of shit for waking her, or she would be half asleep and rising from a dream that, depending upon what it was, had the potential to result in serious bodily injury to her husband.

"I will take this banana and ram it straight up your furry, purple dinosaur ass if I hear that song one more time..."

Henry stifled a laugh. "Jo... Jo, it's me. Barney's gone, now. It's okay."

Jo blinked, her eyes focusing on Henry as the undoubtedly disturbing dream faded.

"Wha? Henry, wassamatter?" She rubbed her eyes and opened and closed her mouth, trying to bring the desert floor of her tongue some much needed moisture.

"You need to see something in the bathroom before it's gone!"

"Aww, did you make a nice boom boom, Henry?" she asked, smirking. She rolled from bed and followed Henry across the room, then leaned on the door frame and yawned.

He was laughing as he re-entered the bathroom, despite his fears about the message in the mirror.

Jo rubbed the sleep from her eyes. When she pulled her fists away, Henry was pointing at the message. "What do you think this means?"

Instinctively protecting her husband, Jo feigned ignorance, knowing full well what it said. For now, she played dumb. The purple, pain-in-the-ass dinosaur hadn't been her only dream. "What the hell language is that?"

"I have no idea. I thought *you* might know. You've been at this witchcraft thing longer than I have."

Jo shook her head. "Nope. I got nothing. Maybe Archie or Wanda might know."

Henry nodded, pulled out his cell phone, and snapped a picture of the symbols in the mirror before they faded. "I'll send it to them later today."

ON THE OTHER side of Salem, Wanda Heinze awoke at the exact same time as Henry. A dream of someone falling from some place high and the sound of shattered glass awoke her. She snapped her eyes closed again, trying to capture the fading images, but they dissolved into the place where dreams go to die.

The white witch swung her legs over the edge of the bed, planted her feet in a pair of fur-covered, leopard-print slippers, and creaked herself upright.

"The old grey mare ain't what she used to be," sang Wanda as she made her way to the bathroom. Unlike Henry, she needed all the sleep she could get. A quick pee, then hit the sheets for about four or five more hours.

The hot water was running. When she flipped on the light, clouds of steam danced lazily before her eyes. She walked over to the faucet and turned it off.

Running water in the bathroom was hardly something to set Wanda's heart atwitter. Uninvited, un–bodied guests had visited her since she was old enough to remember. More than a few of them took to running the tap to get her attention.

As Wanda took care of business, the steam dissipated. She flushed the toilet and was about to douse the light when the message in the mirror caught her eye.

One simple word. Written in a language seldom used today, and complete gibberish to the uninitiated. Though she recognized the language—or more accurately, the code—she was out of practice, and unable to decipher the message.

Wanda suspected it related to the events leading up to the escape of Inanis the demon, Mondra the Red Witch, and the threatening letter from the Council of the Realms.

Someone, somehow, had observed Joanne using powers that, before Mercy Glass, had been invisible to the outside world. Jo had always possessed powerful magical abilities. And a powerful temper to match.

Each of the members of the League of the Moon, save for Archie, had received some sort of boost from Mercy Glass. So much so that the magic they were capable of, though usually invisible to the naked eye, was suddenly manifest. A link between dimensions had formed, bringing power from beyond the veil into the three-dimensional world.

Jo's incident on the storm-swept streets of Salem had drawn the attention, and ire, of a higher authority. Said authority, until the delivery of the letter, had remained a secret to Wanda.

She'd thought about the letter often over the last month. When she'd received it, Mercy Glass, her young employee, and (as the League of the Moon quickly found out) a powerful witch in her own right, reacted in a way which completely surprised Wanda. The conversation replayed in her mind as she sat on the edge of her bed.

"We need to talk," said Mercy.

Wanda blinked. "About this?" She held up the letter.

Mercy nodded. "I didn't remember it until now, but seeing that letter brought it back."

Wanda waited. Mercy continued. "About a month before the 'accident' at the quarry, I was at the University filling out financial aid forms. Some guy approached me as I sat at the tables, dotting the i's and crossing the t's. I'd never seen him before. He asked if he could sit down. I never looked up. I was concentrating, and I didn't want to screw up any paperwork up, you know?"

Wanda nodded and stayed silent.

"Well, it got quiet for a bit. Too quiet. It felt like he was watching me, waiting to say something. So I looked up, and he was just staring at me. I asked what I could help him with. He said nothing. Just kept staring. It creeped the hell outta me. So, I gathered my things to move to another table when he finally spoke. 'I dreamed about you, Mercy,' he said."

Wanda leaned forward, resting her forearms on her knees.

Mercy said, "I'm getting nervous now, thinking 'total nut-job.' So I asked what he meant. Then, he says, 'I've dreamed about you since the day you were born. There's something special about you. I can help you'."

"Strange," said Wanda.

"I know, right? So I asked why the hell he would dream about me, and why I needed help."

"And?" asked Wanda.

"You know, he never came right out and said it. Only

that I needed to come with him and find out. Well, I told him I wasn't in the habit of just walking off with complete strangers."

"You didn't—?" Wanda asked.

"Of course not. In fact, I asked him to leave. And if he hadn't gotten up to go, I told him my next stop was campus security. The creepy bastard got the hint."

"Did you ever find out what he wanted?"

"No. But he told me to watch my back. I asked why, and he said, 'They're coming for you. Beware those pretending to love you when they never have. Seek the white witch and her coven. They can protect you. You belong with them.' He was talking about you, Wanda. So I guess it's no surprise I ended up working here. Thank God for that."

Wanda nodded. "But I don't understand. What does this have to do with the letter?"

Mercy reached into the back pocket of her jeans and produced a small, rectangular piece of paper about the size of a business card. She handed it to Wanda.

"I've carried it with me since that day."

There was no writing on the card, only a symbol. On a field of red, the symbol for infinity stood out in raised gold. Two swords crossed at the nexus of the symbol; it was identical to the one topping the mysterious letter.

"Would you recognize him if you saw him again?" asked Wanda.

"Definitely," said Mercy.

Wanda slipped under the covers, thinking about how her coven had changed since Mercy's arrival.

When Mercy first applied to work at her store, Wanda hadn't gotten much of a vibe from her—positive or negative. It was a face-value hire of a college kid looking for a job to pay her share of the off-campus rent. Nothing more. She chuckled and told the empty room, "It's always something more."

When Mercy showed up for work that first day, the only thing remarkable about her was her work ethic. The girl kicked ass and had to be guided little, if at all. It was only a few months later, when a malevolent entity began stalking the store, looking for a way past its magical barriers, she realized how special Mercy was. In the end, it saved their lives.

Joanne showed the first overt signs of Mercy's influence. Looking back on it now, it shouldn't have surprised Wanda. Together, Wanda and Jo had opened a portal to 1692, searching for the items needed to defeat Inanis. The magic they'd used that night was visible to the world, of course, but a large part of what made that possible was the energy of the land the shop sat on, and the supernatural nature of All Hallows' Eve.

Wanda had known from the moment she met Joanne there was a raw power within her. A warrior's spirit with magical potential that, for years—and much like her own powers—had been suppressed with drugs and alcohol. When confronted by the hooded entity who tried to kidnap her daughter, Jo lost her shit and almost killed him. As Jo recounted to Wanda, 'Some green crap flew from my hands and almost lit the bastard on fire. I'm just sorry I missed.'

Henry was now so adept—thanks to the augmentation imparted him by Mercy—at traveling the astral plane, he no longer required hypnotherapy to cross the veil. He'd merely close his eyes, stow his body in a safe place, and was good to go.

Wanda thought about her own powers. In her entire

existence, be it this incarnation or others, she'd never had the power to see through the eyes of another. All that changed the night the entity had stalked the store, and she'd taken Mercy's hand into her own.

It was a power she knew would be invaluable to the League, but also one she had to be careful and virtuous in applying. It was hard to resist slipping behind the eyes of another without their knowledge. The temptation to eavesdrop on another person's life was a heady power to have, and the desire to use it was a constant temptation.

That left Archie. Though not a witch or a warlock, he was still a member of the League of the Moon. It was more out of friendship and a close working relationship between parapsychology and witchcraft that Wanda thought it best he became part of the coven.

Penny, Archie's sister, and Henry's aunt—surprise, surprise—had the same powers as Henry. But, as far as Wanda could tell, Archie didn't have any type of magical ability. Or did he? As she drifted toward sleep, Wanda made a mental note to call her best friend tomorrow morning.

CHAPTER 3
THE DARK AND THE LIGHT

Henry was late for work. Driving into Boston from the north shore area sucked. On a good day, it sucked. It sucked more on a rainy day. It absolutely blew chunks when it snowed. And it monumentally sucked when one of an endless supply of careless drivers on I-95 South decided the rules of the road didn't apply, and his skills as a motorist rivaled those of the cast of Fast and Furious. So, when this genius decided he could safely cut across three lanes and make it to the I-93 South exit, the predictable pile-up ensued.

Crawling along until he reached the accident scene, he glimpsed this Mensa candidate being lifted into the ambulance. Bloodstained bandages surrounded the man's head, and a marine-blue New England Patriots hoodie lay draped across the white, blood-speckled sheet covering him.

The guy was in rough shape, and Henry wondered if he might end up knowing this fine motorist on a first name basis by the end of the day. There was no doubt in his mind they were taking him to the Massachusetts General Hospital ER.

Thirty minutes later, Henry pulled into the Fruit Street garage. From there, it was a short walk to the receiving area and through the doors on the left side of the front of the building. Henry showed his badge to Louis from security.

"How's it going today, Louis?"

"Just another day in paradise, Henry," Louis said. "Have a good one."

Henry shot him a salute and stepped inside.

The ER buzzed with activity. Beds lined the hallways, most of them filled, and Henry took mental notes of what he thought each person suffered from as he passed them. He got to the nurse's station and checked in with the head nurse, Marla Branch.

"What's the good word today, Marla?"

His boss stopped typing, raising her eyes over the frame of her readers. "Well, look who decided to show up, finally."

Marla never passed on an opportunity to bust Henry's balls. But it was always good-natured.

"I'm sorry, boss-lady. Some guy pretending to be Vin Diesel fucked up everyone's commute."

Marla pulled off her readers and ran a hand through her wavy blonde hair. She winced when she stood, and both knees popped like firecrackers inside a coffee can. "I gotta lose some weight before my knees explode one day."

"That was loud!" Henry said.

She waved it off. "I'm going on a diet for New Year's."

Henry had only been working at MGH for a little over a year, so he kept his trap shut. But others in the ER always gave Marla shit about her annual New Year's weight loss proclamation. Another six months, at the least, would earn him that privilege. Everyone had to earn their stripes.

"Speaking of Vin Diesel, guess where you're going right now?" Marla wiggled her eyebrows.

"You're shittin' me." Henry said, mildly surprised. His ability to see things coming before they happened was growing. The feeling he got when he saw the guy on the highway, had it been a couple of years earlier, he would have chalked up to coincidence. He'd learned coincidence and precognition were sometimes members of the same family by a different name.

Marla shook her head. "Nope. Luck of the draw, I guess. He's in seven. Out cold. Check his vites. Start with him and make the rounds."

Henry gave her a thumbs up over his shoulder as he headed toward bay seven.

True to her word, the guy was out cold. Henry pulled a chart from the pocket at the front of the bed and read the rundown on the guy's condition. Concussion. No surprise there. Lucky for him, there was no internal bleeding. Broken collarbone, three cracked ribs, and a broken arm—all on the left side of his body. Henry recalled the accident scene in his mind. It made sense. The car had rolled over on the driver's side.

He felt pity for the man's condition, but not a lot. The stupid bastard had done it to himself and he could have gotten others killed. It amazed him people took chances like this guy had. Why not just go one exit down and turn around if you missed one?

He dropped the chart back in its pocket and made his way to the right side of the bed. Henry was about to add morphine to the intravenous drip line when the man moaned.

"Hey, you okay, buddy?" Henry asked. "I can up your dose if the pain's too much."

The man whispered something low. Henry couldn't hear it. He whispered again, and Henry leaned down, trying to catch the man's words but still unable to decipher them. The man tried a third time, and Henry leaned in as close as he could, tilting his right ear until it hung just above the man's mouth. Silence. He watched the rise and fall of the man's chest.

Henry hovered over the man, his left arm arched over the guy's body, bracing himself to hear his whisper. Without warning, the patient's right arm shot out. Pain flared in Henry's left forearm as the man clamped his fully functioning right hand over it. For all the trauma he'd suffered, it shouldn't have been possible to keep Henry rooted to the bed, but he was. Henry pulled for all he was worth and could not break free.

The lights went out inside bay seven. The privacy curtain hid the drama within. Henry's cry for help died in his throat when the overhead fluorescents faded to black. Darkness swallowed the entire bay, save for the heart monitor. Its glow cast an eerie blue light across the bed, but no further. The light ceased where the sheets trailed over the sides. A precipice to a lightless and silent void.

When the man suddenly released his arm, Henry shot upright and scrambled back from the bed, never taking his eyes from the patient. Blue light from the monitor painted the man's face grey, and the blood on his bandages black. It matched the blood in his eyes, where vessels had burst from the impact of the accident.

"Hello, Henry. Long time, no see." He spoke slowly, his voice a thin rasp. Vapor twisted upward from his mouth like a gray snake seeking prey in the darkness. In his terror, Henry failed to notice the dip in temperature.

"Who are you?"

"A child of the void," he whispered, then smiled. Malignant teeth glowed grey in the blue light. Along with the reflection of the monitor in his blackened eyes, they were the only features discernable within the frame of the bandages.

As frightened as Henry was, the statement still registered as 'off' in his mind. There could be no 'children' of the void. The void was a place where obliterated souls went when they ceased to exist. Neither light nor sound, pleasure nor pain existed there.

"That's not possible," said Henry. "The void is the absence of all."

The man chuckled low. "Even God had to start somewhere, Henry. Let there be light... and there was light," he mocked.

Henry fought an insane urge to tell him Bon Scott had sung that line in "Let There be Rock" by AC/DC and said, simply, "Creation started somewhere. God has always been."

It still astounded Henry how much his own beliefs had changed over the past year.

"But what is God without creation? Who can know Him without first being?" hissed the man.

Henry had no answer for that.

"The void has light now. Souls once vanished now stir. The Red Witch brought the light to us, and we are coming!"

On cue, light flooded the room, blinding Henry. As the fluorescents flashed to life, the man's body flopped down on the bed, bounced once, then went still. Henry watched, horrified, as the same message from his bathroom mirror rose in lumpy relief onto the man's forehead. It glowed red, as if the guy was being branded from the inside out, then faded as the skin of his forehead smoothed. Henry was still staring at him when the curtain to bay seven flew back. Marla saw Henry standing in the corner, ashen-faced.

"Henry? Are you okay?"

He jumped at her voice, swallowed hard, and said, "I think so."

"You don't look too good. You look like you've seen a ghost."

Henry resisted the urge to tell her she wasn't too far from the mark. Instead, he said, "Sorry, just thinking about a problem we've got at home. I didn't sleep well last night, either."

It sounded lame to his own ears, and Marla's face only confirmed it.

"Let's head down to the caff. Get some coffee. Sound good?"

Henry nodded and followed Marla out of the ER and downstairs to the cafeteria.

Dr. Archibald Love couldn't get the dream out of his head. He ran it backward through his mind, from the moment his eyes had popped open and spied the digital alarm clock on the dresser reading 3:13 a.m., to the moment he saw a hazy figure bleeding out on a dirty floor in a place he didn't recognize. Then, right before the dream had winked out, he saw two brilliant diamonds twinkling in a field of red.

Though he didn't know it, Henry, Wanda, and Joanne

had endured a similar dream, with only one difference; they couldn't hear anyone's thoughts. Archie was hearing them, thanks to the spell Mondra had tried, and failed, to pull off at Wanda's Wicca'd Emporium. So he knew what might be coming. He'd known for some time now, but feared telling the others. He couldn't say for sure who it was bleeding out on that floor. And to guess might lead to disaster.

He showered quickly, dressed quicker, and was in his VW microbus and on the road out of Salem before most people were rubbing the Sandman's gift from their eyes.

Archie drove at a steady seventy-five miles per hour, as fast as he thought he could get away with, and made it to the Route 2 exit marked Leominster in less than thirty minutes. He took the exit, barely slowing down or even looking as he merged into sparse, early morning traffic, and headed west. Though the place in his dreams wasn't a place he recognized, the unincorporated area of Northfield, Massachusetts, had plucked the strings of intuition.

Archie's iPhone sat in its cradle on the dashboard, the screensaver's dim glow morphing from one color to the next. He pecked it, bringing up the app interface, then swiped down to check his notifications. Nothing. Relieved, he let out a breath he hadn't realized he'd been holding. He held down the power button on the phone, waiting for the bitten apple icon to appear, then go black. The phone was off, severing electronic ties to family and friends. The isolation he felt was immediate. But he didn't want them following him.

At least with the phone off, it would buy him some time. How much? Who knew? What he *did* know was Wanda would find him, phone or no phone. Once she realized he was missing, and then figured out *why* he was missing, she would move heaven and earth. He was counting on it. But there was something he needed to find out for himself before she did. Who was the one bleeding out on the floor in that hideous church? For all he knew, it could be Wanda.

Archie looked in the rear-view mirror, stealing glances at the miraculous sunrise taking place behind him, hoping it wasn't his last.

CHAPTER 4
A STORY OF WITCHES

It was eleven-thirty a.m. when they sat down with their coffee. The cafeteria was starting to fill up as noon approached. Marla had chosen a booth in the least occupied area.

"What happened to you up there? And don't give me the bullshit line you gave me earlier, either."

This surprised Henry. He wasn't sure what she'd seen, so he took his time answering. It was one thing to convince Byron he was in the middle of something supernatural when he, in fact, *was* in the middle of it. It was quite another when you were considering how to tell your boss roughly the same thing and not be worried about losing your job.

Henry wasn't sure, but he had the feeling an ER nurse who reported a supernatural event to his boss, no matter how open-minded she might be, would probably be considered unreliable at best, or fucking nuts and in need of a leave of absence for stress, at worst.

"Henry, what was it?" asked Marla. "I'm not gonna judge you. But I have to send you home if you can't get your shit together. This isn't the place to be when your mind is somewhere else."

He squirmed a bit in his seat, then said, "I told you I saw the accident on the way in, right?"

Marla nodded.

"Well, what I didn't tell you was, as I went by the accident, I had the feeling I'd be the one taking care of that guy later today."

Marla shrugged and said, "So?"

"Soooo, don't you think it's kinda weird how that came true?" asked Henry.

"Not really. I mean, the chance of you being the one taking care of him is slim, but it ain't exactly 'winning Powerball slim' Henry."

When she put it that way, it was hard to argue. He was thinking maybe all that had happened to him over the last year-plus might be tipping his thinking too far in the other direction—that maybe his new readiness to believe in all things spiritual had crossed some line, tainting his rational mind. And then he thought about the scene in bay seven. That was real. He may have been the only one to witness it, but he knew it had happened. He rubbed his sore arm as a reminder.

With these thoughts in mind, he decided to see where Marla stood on things unexplained. It might be valuable to know down the line, if only to protect himself from unforeseen consequences.

Magic was as real to him now as the chair he was sitting in, but most of the rest of the world didn't share that belief. It was risky, he thought. But he'd gone through enough in recent times to make a risk of this nature something he was willing to take.

"Marla, what's the strangest thing you've ever seen happen? I don't mean just at work, but in your entire life?"

Marla considered the question. "I don't know. When you say strangest, are you talking about something like a guy walking naked through one of the red-line subway cars, or are you talking more like Twilight Zone shit?"

"Twilight Zone shit."

She stroked her chin with her left hand and looked out across the cafeteria. A few moments passed. "You'll think this is nuts."

"Try me," said Henry.

Marla focused on Henry then, seeming to weigh in her mind if she could trust him, then shrugged. "What the hell. If you tell anyone I told you this, I'll stick you with morphine and you'll wake up without balls."

"Seems fair."

"Okay." She shook her head. "I've never told anyone about this before. When I was about, ohhh, six, maybe seven, there was this homeless guy who used to walk around town mumbling to himself. It was cruel. Kids can be cruel at that age, but we used to call him Crazy Eddie.

"Well, I woke up in the middle of the night. I think it was close to Christmas... maybe even Christmas Eve. Yeah, had to be Christmas Eve cuz I couldn't stay asleep. I was too excited. Anyway, Eddie would cut through the back alley of our building now and then, looking through the trash for bottles and cans to redeem. Sometimes he would score and find a pizza box thrown away with a slice in it.

"That night, I heard noises coming from the alley. I was curious, but not *that* curious. I knew it had to be Eddie. And it was. But Eddie wasn't doing 'Eddie' things. He was hunched over something in the alley. Our apartment was on the second floor, so I couldn't really see what it was. It crossed my mind that he might be taking a dump out there, crouched over like that, but thankfully that wasn't it at all."

Henry leaned forward but kept silent—subliminal encouragement for Marla to keep going as she was almost whispering now.

"He held his hands over something lying in the middle of the alley. Against the snow, from two floors up and about thirty feet away, it looked like it might be a black bag. You know, like a lawn and leaf bag?"

Henry nodded.

"Well, it wasn't. All of a sudden, around Eddie, there was this blue haze—kinda dull, at first. It got brighter and brighter. There were little flashes of light inside the haze, just a few here and there. The entire alley, by this point, was glowing with soft blue light. It turned the snow, the fence, and the entire side of the apartment complex blue. The little flashes of light picked up until it looked like a thousand Fourth of July sparklers going off all at once.

"Then it wound down. Henry, when my eyes readjusted to the night, Eddie was standing and bent over. He was petting a dog. It *wasn't* a black bag. I watched him bring a *dog* back to *life*. Poor thing probably starved and froze to death."

"The next day, I went down there. In the snow was the outline of the dog, among other things."

"What other things?" asked Henry.

Marla shrugged. "Who knows? Just some trinket that probably fell outta Eddie's pocket. I scooped it up anyway, just to remind myself down the road what I actually saw really happened. I carry it around with me now. It reminds me, when life gets too serious, there's more to all this than working and paying bills."

Henry smiled. "A Christmas miracle."

Marla seemed surprised at his reaction. "I didn't expect you'd believe me so easily."

Henry considered this for a moment. Believing her was one thing. Telling her exactly what happened in bay seven was quite another. But, he thought, what was the point of asking her to open up if he wasn't going to return the favor? He was the one who'd asked her for 'Twilight Zone' stuff.

"I asked you about the strangest thing that ever happened to you for a very specific reason, Marla."

"And that is?"

"Because, if you really want to know what happened up in seven, I need to know you have an open mind. I think the Eddie story is proof enough for me."

"So tell me what happened," said Marla

Henry recounted the entire story from the time he'd pulled the curtain closed until Marla found him in the shaken state he was. He held nothing back.

Marla said nothing at first. Henry watched her face as her mind processed what had to be, for her, almost as shocking as what she'd seen Eddie do on Christmas Eve.

"I believe you Henry. No one wanting to keep working here would come out with a story like that. Unless they were bat-shit crazy. You're obviously not."

Henry laughed. "That's what they call damning with faint praise, but I'll take it."

"Now, what I don't get, Henry, is all the stuff surrounding this. What's all this stuff about the Red Witch and bringing light to the void? That *almost* sounds crazier than what happened up in seven."

This, for Henry, was the tricky part. How in the world could he tell her about the Red Witch and the void and how it connected to his life away from work?

Part of him enjoyed having a secret life away from work. A mystery that he, and a handful of others he cared for deeply, had all to themselves. It made him realize how profoundly his life had changed, and it was a change he guarded jealously without realizing it. Like a kid with a secret fort in the woods only he and a few other close friends knew about. He didn't want to spill the beans. But he had to tell her something now. That ship had sailed.

"Did you hear that news story about the three fugitives up in Salem? You know, the ones wanted for attempted kidnapping?"

Her eyes lit up, and her head tilted slightly. "You mean the one's that tried to take that Salem couple's baby?"

Henry nodded.

"What about it... wait, didn't they describe one of them as a redheaded woman?" asked Marla.

"They did."

"I don't remember much about the other two," said Marla, "but I'm pretty sure one was a cop. That right?"

"It is." Henry said, keeping silent and letting her work toward the answer.

Marla tapped her fingers on the cafeteria table while she rested her chin in her left hand, working through the connections.

"So, you're telling me this 'Red Witch' is what? The redhead from the news story?"

Henry nodded.

Marla looked at him suspiciously. "There's something else you're not telling me."

"In the news story, do you remember the couple's name?" Henry asked.

"No. But they never mentioned—" Her eyes went wide again. "They took *your* baby?"

Henry closed his eyes and nodded.

"Holy fuck, Henry! Why didn't you ever tell me? I would have given you a paid leave of absence to find her! Or them!"

"I was told not to mention it to anyone not already in the know. And we got her from them the same night, thankfully."

"She was okay?" Marla asked. The concern on her face made Henry like his boss even more than he already did.

"She's fine. Thanks for asking, Marla."

"Why did this psycho bitch kidnap your daughter?"

This was where Henry knew, despite the Twilight Zone conversation from earlier, he could still come off as a nut in his boss's eyes. But he was already deep in the woods, and the trail of breadcrumbs had been blown from the path a while ago. The only way out was through.

"It's true. The redhead from the story and the Red Witch are one and the same. She put a spell on my daughter the day she was born."

"A spell? You mean like some abracadabra-type stuff?" asked Marla.

"It's a bit more complicated. This woman is crazy, as you might have noticed. But she's powerful. She's an actual witch, Marla. Her spells aren't just words. They work. They have real-world consequences."

Marla stayed silent. The look on her face, for the moment, was unreadable to Henry.

He continued, "Her name is Mondra Tibbets. My father used to date her. Well, *date* is a bit misleading. She seduced him and put a love spell on him, forcing him to love her against his will. It was black magic.

"My friend Wanda was the one who figured it all out and broke the spell. Mondra didn't take too kindly to that. She swore she would get revenge against Wanda and that she would never let my father go. And, apparently, she's extremely patient. When my baby was born, she'd already been waiting—God knows how many years—for her chance to get him back. The day Delilah was born, she showed up at the hospital dressed in a nurse's uniform and took the baby from the on-duty nurse. That's when she put the spell on her."

"What was the purpose of the spell?" asked Marla.

"To bind my father to my daughter. That way, Mondra could force him to do what she wanted. If he didn't, the baby would die."

Marla shook her head and whispered, "Holy shit."

"I told you, she's fucking nuts. And she's still out there."

"What about the cop and the other guy? They still with her?"

"Yeah. The kid is her boy-toy. Mondra *loves* to ride the old hobby horse. The cop's possessed by a demon. Anything he's doing right now is against his will," said Henry. If she was gonna bail on the conversation, this is when it would happen, he thought.

Marla's eyebrows shot up. "Come again?"

Henry nodded, "It's true. I won't bother trying to convince you. All I can tell you is I know the guy through my uncle. The Chief of the Salem Police is married to my aunt. Raul is a solid guy who was in the wrong place at the wrong time. They've put out a story they kidnapped him."

"Well, after seeing what I saw Eddie do that night, I

guess I can't say I don't believe it. That poor cop," said Marla. "What about the other one? He was a college kid, right?"

"Yeah. Aaron Hendricks is his name. Apparently, he's her new 'boyfriend.' His mother was sick. Mondra and the others promised to make her well again. And they did, apparently. At first, we thought the kid was innocent. That they forced him to help them get to my baby through my father. When they escaped that night, I watched him plant a juicy one on her as the car took off."

"A May-December wacko's romance. Wonderful!" said Marla. "So you still haven't been able to find them yet?"

Henry shook his head.

"How long they been hiding out now?"

"A little more than a month. My uncle and I went looking for them a couple weeks after the trail ran dry out in Athol. They dumped the police cruiser and stole a car. I don't know why, but I have a feeling they're still in that general area."

"What makes you think that?" asked Marla.

"Just the way Mondra is. Her ego won't let her accept defeat. She'll be back. And then there's the demon. As long as we live, he won't stop trying to get rid of us. We'll always be a threat to him."

"Who's we?"

"What?" Henry asked.

"You said 'we.'"

Henry cleared his throat. "My coven."

"Coven? As in a bunch of witches?" asked Marla.

Henry smiled. Marla was the third person, including himself and Byron, who had asked that *exact same* question, and in *those* words. He answered Marla as Joanne had answered him, "Yes. A bunch of witches."

"So you're a witch, then?"

"Yes. Well, technically speaking, a warlock. But no one really goes by that title too much these days. More of a male witch thing, now. Or just witch. Kinda how no one uses actress much anymore, it's just actor."

Marla was staring hard at Henry now. It made him uncomfortable.

"What's the matter, Marla?" he asked. The feeling he may have gone further than he should made him nervous, and the fear he began the conversation with stole over him again.

Marla squinted, scanning Henry from the top of his head, down to his elbows resting on the cafeteria table top. She said, "That explains it. All this time I had suspicions, but now I know what I've been seeing isn't my imagination."

In a shaky voice, Henry asked, "What do you mean?"

"Your aura, Henry. It's tinged with gold and emerald green. It's something I've not seen in a long time."

Henry's eyes bugged. "You're a witch?"

She smiled. "Who do you think recruited you to work here?"

CHAPTER 5
LEAVE A MESSAGE

Wanda was worried. Archie wasn't answering his phone. This, for Archie, was way out of the ordinary. He was a first ring kinda guy. She wondered if maybe he was counseling a student over at the University? Though it was early in the year for something like that, she couldn't rule it out. Archie was accessible to his students, which was one of the many reasons his class was popular and his students adored him.

She put her worries on the back-burner, showered, dressed, made her way out of the second-floor apartment on Derby Street, and over to her shop. Mercy Glass awaited her, a smile plastered on her face.

"Good morning, Wanda!"

Wanda smiled. "Hi, sweetie. Ready for another crazy day?"

"I'd be disappointed if it wasn't a little crazy. That's why I love this job."

Wanda pulled her keys from the pocket of her purple

cloak and unlocked the door. When they were both inside, Mercy asked, "What's the matter, Wanda? You look like something's bothering you."

It startled Wanda. She'd thought she was putting on a good show of not worrying about Archie. Mercy had sniffed it out with ease. "Is it that obvious?"

"Your aura is a mess. And, judging by the colors swirling around in it, you're worried about something. It's mild, but there all the same."

"You're amazing, honey."

Wanda had known Mercy for barely six months, but in their short time together, the bond they'd formed seemed forged from lifetimes. Which, when she thought about it, wasn't too far from the truth.

Mercy had been a part of Wanda's life in her last incarnation. Though the connection, when first revealed, was not clear. After what had happened with Mondra the Red Witch, the ties had revealed themselves. And the power Mercy possessed became obvious.

Mercy had been a powerful white witch in her past life, and the only witch Wanda knew to've had direct contact with Hecate, the goddess of the three realms.

"It's Archie. He didn't answer my call this morning. It's just got me a tad worried. I'm sure there's a good reason for it. But it's so unlike him not to answer."

Mercy seemed puzzled by her worry, and it showed on her face.

"He's the kinda guy that almost always answers on the first ring, honey. And if he doesn't, it's not long after that he'll get back to me."

"How long's it been?" Mercy asked.

"A few hours now," said Wanda.

"I can head over to the U and see if he's there, if you'd like."

Wanda smiled. "Would you mind, sweetie? It would take a load off my mind."

Mercy turned and headed for the door. "If I see him, I'll tell him to call you first chance he gets."

MERCY ARRIVED at the University after a twenty-minute walk along Lafayette Street. Finding Archie's office was easy enough; she'd been in it a few times since taking his class.

Annie, Archie's receptionist, sat at her desk, squinting at the monitor in front of her. Her mouth moved as she glanced from the monitor to a notepad and back again, each time jotting something on a legal pad.

"Hi Annie," said Mercy.

Annie jumped at the sound of her voice. "Bah!" She held her left hand over her heart. "You scared the shit outta me!"

Mercy winced. "Sorry."

"It's okay, just a little warning next time, doll. What brings you here?" asked Annie.

"Wanda's looking for Archie. Have you seen him today?"

"Did she try calling him?"

"More than once, according to her. And he hasn't gotten back to her, either. Wanda said that's way out of the ordinary for him?" asked Mercy.

Annie nodded, her brow creased with concern, and tapped a button on her office phone. She put it on speaker so Mercy could hear. Archie's voice mail played through it, telling anyone listening he would get back to them "...as soon as possible. Leave a brief message."

"Arch, it's Annie. Where the hell are you? Call me back as soon as you get this."

Annie tapped the call closed.

"When was the last time you saw him, Annie?"

Annie tilted her head sideways, pursed her lips, and looked at the ceiling. "Friday, I think. Yeah, he was here then. Come to think of it, he wasn't acting himself that day. You know him, Mr. Sunshine and Lollipops. He didn't even tell me to have a nice weekend, which he always does. Just put his head down and headed out. When I told him to have a good weekend, he just waved over his shoulder."

"I hate to ask this, but would you mind if I had a look in his office, I—"

Annie was up and out of her seat, fishing the keys from her pocket before Mercy could finish the sentence.

Both women stood at the darkened, frosted glass of Archie's door as Annie worked the lock.

"It sticks a little." Annie jiggled the keys, twisting them back and forth in the lock. When she heard the lock snap, she kicked the bottom of the door, rattling the glass in its frame, and the door finally gave up its fight.

"No matter how many times I tell him to get that damned door fixed, he never does it."

Annie reached to her right and slapped the light switch on. The overhead fluorescents blinked to life.

To Annie's eyes, nothing appeared out of the ordinary. Mercy had been in Archie's office twice, and nothing hit *her* as out of place at first, either.

Annie walked over to his desk and stood to the right of

the leather office chair. The faint scent of spent Dragon's Blood incense hit her nose. The ashes sat in a bowl on Archie's desk next to his statue of Hecate. They were the only things on a desk that was usually a disaster area.

Mercy made her way over to the erasable white board hanging above and to the right of a model globe of earth suspended in a polished wooden stand. There was writing on the board—a series of what appeared to be random letters and numbers. Mercy stared at them for a while, trying to discern their meaning.

"Annie? Do these mean anything to you?" asked Mercy

Annie came out from behind the desk and walked over to Mercy. She tilted her head back, reading the letters and numbers aloud. "SK? 2W-NFLD. Beats the hell outta me."

Mercy pulled her phone from the back pocket of her jeans and snapped a picture of the whiteboard. "Thanks, Annie. Maybe Wanda will know."

Annie nodded. "Let me know if she comes up with anything. And tell that sweetheart Annie says hi."

WANDA STUDIED the photo Mercy had taken of Archie's whiteboard. "I'm stumped. I haven't the first friggin' clue what this could mean."

Mercy took the phone back, placed it on the counter, and stared at it—willing the code to confess. As powerful as both Mercy and Wanda were, they couldn't make the curious code give up its secret.

Wanda took out her phone.

"Who are you calling?"

She was about to answer Mercy when Archie's sister

answered on the other end. "Penny, it's Wanda. Have you seen or heard from Archie today?"

"No. But I wasn't exactly expecting to. What's up?" asked Penny.

"I tried calling him this morning. He still hasn't gotten back to me. I'm worried."

"I can see why. I know how he is. When was the last time you talked to him?"

"A few days ago. Friday morning, I think."

"What did you two talk about?" asked Penny.

Wanda thought on that, "Nothing out of the ordinary, I think. He told me he was looking into something on where Inanis might have taken Mondra and Raul, but he's been doing that since the night everything went down. He didn't mention any new developments. But there was something strange on his whiteboard at the university office. I'll send it to your phone as soon as we hang up."

Penny stayed silent on the other end, thinking. Then she said, "Do that. I'll forward it to Byron and see what he comes up with, and have him call you soon. Okay?"

"Thanks, sweetie." Wanda hung up.

Penny hung up on her end. She wasn't telling the entire truth to Wanda. The part about not talking to Archie lately *was* the truth. But what she *didn't* tell Wanda (because she wasn't sure why herself) was that her usual connection to Archie was silent. She didn't want to panic Wanda, though panicked was the way Penny felt at the moment. And something told her to hold back the information from Byron, too. At least for now.

Penny had a habit of keeping tabs on her brother, her husband Byron, and their children and grandchildren, by sneaking a peek here and there over their shoulders from the astral plane. It was her way of looking out for those she loved. What they didn't know couldn't hurt them. On more than one occasion, it had kept her brother and her husband alive.

Since last Friday, Penny hadn't been able to connect with Archie. It was as if he'd dropped from the face of the earth... like a dark and silent void had consumed him.

These were the thoughts running through her mind when the iPhone in her hand rang. The caller ID showed the name 'Jo.' She tapped the green 'answer' button.

"Hey, Jo. What's up?"

"I need to talk to you about a dream I had last night," said Jo.

"If it's about Barney again, I told you, it gets better," she said with a smile.

"I wish it was. And yes, I dreamed about that purple motherfucker again. But it's about Henry. I think he's in trouble, Penny."

"How so?"

"In my dream, last night, I saw a message written in blood, carved into his forehead. And it was written in the Theban alphabet. When he woke me up this morning, just after 3 a.m., the same message was written on our bathroom mirror—you could read it through the steam from his shower. It translated into a Romanian word. I don't want to tell you what I think it means, I want you to confirm it on your own first."

Penny breathed in sharply. "Romanian? As in crazy, redheaded, psycho bitch Romanian?"

"My thoughts exactly," said Jo.

"What are you thinking about doing?" asked Penny.

"You still got that pineal gland from Zachary?" Jo asked.

"Yep."

"Give me a couple hours. I need to bring Delilah some place safe. You ready to take a ride when I get back?"

"Where to?" asked Penny.

"West."

CHAPTER 6
ON THE MOVE

Joanne studied the bathroom mirror photo. Playing dumb about it with Henry was the only way she could protect him. If she'd told him what it meant, he might try playing the hero and screw things up. And that was the last thing anyone needed right now.

The message made no sense to him, thank God, because it was in a language few modern witches used. Though, in recent years, it had made a bit of a comeback.

The Theban Alphabet, more commonly known as the Witch's Alphabet, is a cipher—a coded way for witches in the know to communicate secretly when the times call for it. It was highly preferable to being hanged or burned at the stake.

Though the dream she'd had varied somewhat from Henry's, the carving on his forehead had scared the living shit out of her. Getting out in front of it, before Henry could even consider making a move, seemed the safest bet.

It was an instinct buried deep in her soul. In her last incarnation, she'd been a powerful hunter named David. His failure to protect Madeleine—Henry's previous incarnation as David's wife—had left a deep scar stretching into this lifetime. It would not happen again.

Jo believed in her heart the message had Mondra's fingerprints all over it. And though, at the end of her dream, she hadn't actually seen the figure bleeding out all over the floor of the abandoned church, there was no doubt in her mind it was Henry. Mondra was going to get back at Jo by killing the man she loved.

∽

"You knew what I was before I started working here?" Henry asked. The shock hadn't worn off yet.

Marla nodded. "Yeah. Word travels fast. My old boss was your old boss. Dr. Heath up in Portland ER."

Henry's eyes went wide. "No shit?"

"No shit, compadre." Marla smiled and said, "He'd just made the opposite move you were making. Said he wanted out of Boston, wanted to lessen his workload. I asked him about you. Well, not you specifically, but if he knew anyone up there with abilities beyond the norm. Someone whose patients seemed to heal much faster when they were around them. And he mentioned your name."

Henry remembered the day Dr. Heath approached him. Timmy Allen, a head-trauma patient Henry was working with, made an almost miraculous recovery. Dr. Heath pulled Henry aside after he'd finished checking on Timmy for that day and told him of the opportunity at Massachusetts General Hospital. Henry was ecstatic and jumped at the opportunity, but only agreed to go after he was sure Timmy would leave the hospital without complications. Doctor

Heath said that would be fine, and he was glad Henry wanted to see it through.

Henry now saw that time in his life with fresh eyes. He'd always wondered how someone as badly injured as Timmy could have recovered so fast. The kid's skull had practically caved in the day before, but the next morning he was up, watching TV, and telling Henry about seeing the nurse on the roof smoking a cigarette. That Timmy was dead as Rebecca smoked on the roof wasn't lost on Henry. But he never in a million years would have believed his own proximity to Timmy played any part in the kid's recovery. Even now, it made him feel a little uncomfortable.

"I don't think I had much to do with patients healing faster, Marla. Other than their own desire to live and modern medicine applied correctly."

Marla waved that away. "Don't sell yourself short, Henry. You've been here a while now. I've seen enough to know I made the right call. The things you've told me today only confirm it."

Henry blushed a little.

"No need to feel embarrassed, Henry. Witches have been healing others for centuries. And, mostly, a lot more effectively and safely than supposed 'Men of Medicine' have been doing since the first idiot decided bloodletting was a good idea."

Henry was about to say something when his phone rang. He tapped its face. "Hello?"

"Henry, it's me," said Wanda. He smiled at her innocence with modern technology. She'd never gotten used to the concept of caller ID. "Have you talked to Archie at all today?"

"No. But I've been at work since early this morning. I

don't normally even hear from him until the weekend. If that. What's up?"

"I can't reach him. And no one's heard from him at all. It's like he's dropped from the face of the earth."

The hairs on Henry's neck stood up. Intuition screamed at him Archie's disappearance had to do with the events in bay seven. "When's the last time you heard from him?"

"Last Friday. But there's more, Henry. I sent Mercy over to the U to see if he was there. He wasn't, but there was some kind of coded message on his whiteboard. Mercy snapped a picture. I'm sending it to you now."

Henry heard his phone ding. He put Wanda on speaker while he checked it out.

"Do you know what it means?" asked Wanda.

Henry expected to see the same message he'd seen in his steamy bathroom mirror, and the one branded on the accident victim's forehead. But this was nothing like that. He told Wanda he didn't know what it meant.

"When do you get off from work, Henry?" Wanda asked. "I'm worried about him. I want to find him sooner rather than later. Something bad is happening. I can feel it in my bones."

"Hi Wanda. This is Henry's boss, Marla. He's leaving right now."

Wanda uttered an audible sigh of relief. "Thank you, Marla. See you soon, Henry." Wanda hung up.

"Thanks," Henry said.

"You're welcome. Let's go."

"You're coming with me?" asked Henry.

"You bet your ass. After what you just told me, you think I'm sittin' around here today?"

Henry smiled. Witches were pretty chill. But when they

knew one of their own might be in trouble, they didn't fuck around.

~

ARCHIE HAD DRIVEN for almost two hours. He'd passed Athol, where the two lanes of Route 2 dropped to one. He was closer—the pain in his head confirmed it. The odometer told him he still had fifty-plus miles to go. If it felt this bad so far out from his destination, he realized he was going to need stronger stuff for the pain.

He reached into the glove box and shook two Tylenol from the bottle he kept there. A few minutes and a few miles later, the headache subsided, but not much. The pills allowed him to get closer and keep the pain at a bearable level. They would stop working altogether the closer he got.

He pulled the baggie from his pocket. The weed was strong enough to smell through the plastic. Hopefully, it would be enough to cut through the fog.

~

JOANNE PULLED up in front of Penny Miller's house at 3:00 p.m. sharp. Penny was watching from behind her front door, praying Byron didn't decide to come home from the police station for some unforeseen reason. The minute Jo's car stopped out front, Penny was down the steps, across the lawn, and pulling the passenger door of the orange Jeep Wrangler open.

"You got that baggy with the thingy in it?" Jo asked.

"Yep. We're gonna have to drink this thing down eventually."

Jo wrinkled her nose. "Don't remind me."

"So, where are we headed?" Penny asked.

"Athol seems like the best place to start. At least, that's what I recall from the night you guys came to the Cauldron. Once we get past there, we'll need to drink that nastiness. It should draw us toward Arch."

"Friggin' Archie! I love him, but my brother can be a pain in the ass sometimes," said Penny.

Jo smiled, put the Jeep in drive, and pulled out. "Look on the bright side, Penny. Life with Archie is never boring."

Penny rolled her eyes. "I could use a little boring in my life right now. By the way, where is Delilah?"

"I brought her to Maine early this morning. She's with Henry's parents."

"Does Henry know?" asked Penny.

Jo winced. "No. I couldn't risk telling him. I don't want him in on this. At least, not yet."

"He won't be too thrilled with that, I would imagine."

Jo nodded. "Nope. He will definitely be all kinds of pissed off. But I don't see where I have a choice at the moment."

"You know, he and Byron will probably figure out what we're doing pretty quickly and come looking for us. Right?"

"Yeah." Jo turned to lock eyes with Penny. "I'm counting on it."

ARCHIE PULLED into the spot he'd mapped out back in his office. It was deep within the woods, about a mile or so from the closest road. The last time he'd been out this way, about a week ago, he'd sat in his VW microbus for several long, boring hours and watched the road. Making sure there was little to no traffic (on foot or otherwise) passing through the area. He would need to be 'under' for a long, uninterrupted time.

He was positive no one in the League of the Moon knew what he was up to. There was no way they'd let him do what he was about to do. Not even Mercy knew, and she was the reason he had this newfound ability. Whatever power was buried within that young woman's soul was beyond his understanding. But, like many things in life, you didn't need to understand something in order to use it. People used electricity every day and didn't give one thought to how it worked. Archie considered this no different. He had the power now, and he would use it to set things right.

CHAPTER 7
QUESTIONS

Henry pulled up to his apartment on Lafayette Street at 4:00 p.m. and told Marla he'd be right back out. He wanted to let Joanne know what was going on and get her opinion on the situation. When he got to the top of the stairs, Mrs. Greenblatt was waiting for him—arms crossed and a stern look on her face.

"Good afternoon, Henry," said Mrs. G.

"Hi Mrs. G, how are you?"

"Oh, fine. Fine. Everything okay, Henry?"

Henry tilted his head and looked at Mrs. G. Something in her voice sounded... off. "Um, I think so. Why do you ask?"

"Oh, I don't know. I saw Mrs. Henry leave here this morning with little Dee, and come back without her. Then leave again. I don't know about you, Henry, but to me, that's a wee bit strange, don't ya think?"

A bolt of fear shot through Henry. He whirled and headed for his apartment, fumbled with his keys, finally steadying his hands enough to get the key in the lock, and pushed open the door.

"Jo?"

Nothing.

"Jo, are you here?"

Nada.

The apartment was small, and Henry didn't bother searching for Jo and Delilah. If she didn't answer, she wasn't there. He tried her cell. It went straight to voice mail.

"Jo, where are you? Call me, I'm worried."

He hung up, left the apartment, and locked the door behind him.

Mrs. G. stood her post.

"Did you talk with Jo on her way out, Mrs. G.?"

"Nope. I went to say something, but you know her. She held up a hand and said 'not now.'"

Joanne wasn't Mrs. G's biggest fan. If something was up, there was no way Jo was going to let the town crier know about it.

"The only thing I can tell you is she hopped in that orange deathtrap of hers and took off," said Mrs. G.

"How long ago?" Henry asked. Desperation crept into his voice. He took a deep breath and tamped it down.

"About an hour ago, Henry."

Henry took off at a run. Mrs. G. yelled, "What the hell is going on, Henry? I wanna—" Her last words were cut off when the lobby door slammed closed.

"What's wrong?" asked Marla as Henry plopped into his seat and yanked the Camry door closed.

"Joanne's not home. My neighbor said she left with Delilah and came back without her this morning. Then Jo took off in her Jeep. I tried calling her, but it went straight to voice mail."

Marla put a hand on Henry's arm before he could put the car in drive. "Wait, Henry."

"For what?!" Henry shouted.

Marla flinched at the outburst, but held his gaze. "You need to stop and think. Take a deep breath and think."

Henry fought instinct. He nodded, put his head back, and sank into the headrest—taking a deep breath, letting it out, and repeating the process three times. It helped.

"Now, why would she leave the baby with someone and go out?"

"I don't know," said Henry.

Marla nodded. "Who does she trust with your daughter?"

The list was short, and at the top of it was Wanda, Archie, and his parents. He immediately ruled out Archie, for obvious reasons, and he doubted Jo asked Wanda to babysit, especially on a workday. That left his parents. Could she have driven to Portland and come back so fast? He thought about Jo and her lead foot, and reached for his cell phone. He tapped the front and waited.

"Hello?" asked Jeanne Trank.

"Mom. Is Delilah there with you?"

"Yes, honey. Joanne dropped her off this morning. She said she had something she needed to do and she might pick her up later, or would call if she needed to leave her overnight. What's up?"

Henry didn't want to alarm his mother. "Nothing. She must've forgotten to mention it. Or, you know me, I forgot she told me."

"Is everything okay, Henry? You sound a little worried."

"No, it's fine, Mom. It just took me by surprise."

There was a pause on the other end of the line and Henry could almost hear his mother thinking.

Jeanne Trank was nobody's fool. Henry, when he lived under her roof, never bothered lying to his mother. It invariably ended up with him grounded. She was scary observant.

"Uh-huh. Well, like Jeff Goldblum said in Jurassic Park, 'That is one big pile of shit.'"

So much for that *secret*, he thought. "I don't know what Jo's up to, but something strange happened at work today."

"I figured *that* much out, Henry."

This surprised him, and he held the phone away from his face. Shaking his head, he put the phone back to his ear. "How?"

Jeanne snorted. "Let's see. Jo is missing, you're worried about it. You obviously can't reach her on the phone, since you called me. And, according to the app you put on my phone, you're sitting in front of your house right now in the middle of a workday. So, wanna try again, Henry?"

He marveled at her perceptiveness.

"Henry?"

"Do you still have any of that paint Wanda gave you, mom? The stuff that was blessed?" asked Henry.

He heard his mother gasp.

WANDA AND MERCY were getting ready to end the workday early at Wanda's Wicca'd Emporium. Mercy was at the front of the shop and about to flip the sign hanging on a clear, plastic suction cup on the front door from open to closed, when a man across the street waved at her. He looked both ways before crossing, then trotted up to the front door of the shop.

Mercy thought he looked familiar.

"I'm sorry, sir. We're closing early today," said Mercy. She was about to shut the door politely in his face when he put a hand up.

"I'm not here to shop, Miss Glass. I'm here to talk to both Wanda Heinze and you."

Immediately, Mercy was wary. "I'm sorry, and you are?"

"Armand Moreland."

The name was no mystery to Mercy. She recognized it from the signature on the letter Wanda had received the day after Mondra had escaped. The day after Joanne had used magical power she'd never realized she had, trying to kill the entity who'd kidnapped her baby. Power that, Mercy knew, directly resulted from her own near-death experience and some mysterious quality she'd returned with from beyond the grave.

Anyone with innate magical ability Mercy came into contact with became, for lack of a better term, enhanced. What Joanne had done on the streets of Salem that night had triggered a threatening letter from this supposed 'higher' authority. It pissed Mercy off. The look on her face made it plain to the man in the doorway. She pulled the door closed behind her and stepped onto the landing, getting right in the guy's grill.

Mercy made a fist and jabbed a finger in the man's chest. "I remember you. You're the creep from the University. Who the hell do you people think you are?"

Moreland seemed genuinely stunned at Mercy's outburst, and that she recognized him. So much for that disguise, he thought.

He put up both hands. "Please, Miss Glass. I come in peace."

"My ass. You don't send a letter like that and expect to be welcomed with open arms. I ought to—"

The door behind Mercy swung open. "Is there a problem here, Mercy? Do I need to call Byron?"

Moreland leaned to the right, looking desperately over Mercy's shoulder. "Miss Heinze! Nice to finally meet you. I'm Armand Moreland. The man who sent you the letter."

Wanda's eyes narrowed. "Really? No wonder Mercy looks ready to rip your balls off. Maybe I should go back inside and pretend not to notice what's going on out here."

Armand Moreland's eyes went wide. "No! Please. I just want to have a word with both of you. I promise it's to your benefit. *Both* of your benefit."

Mercy stood in front of him, arms crossed. Her right foot tapped the bricks impatiently.

"I don't know, Mercy. What do you think?" asked Wanda.

"I think I should kick his ass first, then call Byron."

Wanda mulled the idea over, just for effect. She was curious about what this guy offered, but unconvinced he'd come here on truly peaceful terms. The letter he'd sent wasn't exactly warm and fuzzy.

Curiosity got the better of her. "Let him pass, Mercy. But keep your guard up."

Mercy stood aside, but her eyes never left Moreland's as he cautiously slipped by her and into the shop. She flipped the sign on the door to closed, walked around Moreland, and stood to Wanda's right. Both witches faced him and waited.

Moreland was speechless at first. He gazed around the shop, appearing to take in Wanda's wares. Bright blue eyes scanned the walls while bushy grey eyebrows rose and fell beneath a black bowler perched on a wiry mat of thick, wavy salt and pepper hair. His mouth hung open, and he seemed to be on the verge of speaking, but with each turn of his head, the words died on his tongue.

To Wanda and Mercy, he looked like a child the first time they pass through the gates of Disneyland. When he found his voice, he said, "Remarkable."

Mercy turned to Wanda. Tilting her head, she prompted Wanda to find out what the hell this guy's deal was. Wanda got the hint. She cleared her throat and asked, "Mr. Moreland, what do you want?"

He snapped back to reality, "I've never seen such amazing sigil work. My compliments."

Wanda raised an eyebrow, but said nothing.

Moreland didn't expect that. To Wanda, he seemed like a man used to being fawned over. *If that's his deal,* she thought, *he's got a long wait.*

After a few awkward moments, Moreland said, "I see. You want to know why I'm here and, of course, why I sent the letter."

"No. I don't really care why you're here. And as far as the letter is concerned, when you take to threatening people, you really ought to find out all the facts first," said Wanda.

"I'm sorry. Was I wrong about what happened that night? Did, or did not, one of your coven use overt magical power on the streets of Salem?" asked Moreland.

Wanda took a step forward, getting into his space. She was a foot and a half shorter than Armand Moreland, but he stepped back.

"You seem to be under the assumption, Mr. Moreland, that I have an obligation to answer your questions. I don't know who you are, or who you *think* you are, but if threatening people with consequences for something they had no idea was wrong is the way you and whatever *'Council'* you claim to represent like to operate, then you can turn right the fuck around and waddle your arrogant ass out of my shop."

Mercy's cheeks ballooned with stifled laughter. She tilted her head toward the floor to hide it.

Moreland gaped, and it was obvious (and infinitely satisfying to Wanda) that few spoke so plainly and directly to this guy. When he gained some composure, he said, "I've clearly offended both of you. I apologize. The letter, as written, may have been a bit of an overreaction."

"Ya think?" asked Mercy.

Moreland ignored the jab. "It has come to my attention we share a mutual problem. Dr. Archibald Love is missing. Has gone off the grid, so to speak."

"And how do you know that?" asked Wanda. Her eyes narrowed. The lilt of suspicion in her question was obvious.

Moreland cleared his throat. His face flushed a few shades. "Because, until this morning, we were watching him. Surveilling him, if you will."

Wanda's face turned beet red, and she was about to give it to Moreland with both barrels when he held his hands up, palms out. "I know what you're going to say and I one hundred percent agree with you. If there was another way to do what we've been doing, we would. Spying on your friend is, without question, wrong and reprehensible, but it has also, unfortunately, become necessary."

"How in the world has it become 'necessary?'" Wanda shouted as both she and Mercy took a step closer to Moreland.

Moreland was babbling now, spurred by the white-hot

anger of two extremely powerful witches. "I know Dr. Love is skilled in past-life regression. And, as we all know, coming into contact with Miss Glass, if you have any magical ability at all, will magnify that ability to the nth degree."

Wanda waved him off. "That's a load of BS. Archie doesn't have any magical ability. I would have seen it years ago."

Moreland looked stunned. He tilted his head. "You don't get it. I just assumed you were hiding it from us to protect your friend. But I see it now. You don't know."

Wanda was almost at the point of exasperation and ready to throw him out of the shop. She asked, "What, exactly, don't I know?"

"When the Red Witch pulled him into her spell, was it complete? Was it successful?" asked Moreland.

"No. We stopped her," said Wanda.

He nodded. "It's as we thought, then."

Wanda stood with her hands on her hips, waiting.

"Had the Red Witch completed her spell, your friend could not do what he's doing now."

"He'd also be a drooling mass of nothing, parked in a nursing home for the rest of his life." Wanda shot back.

Moreland nodded in concession. "I can't argue with that. An incomplete ritual can be a dangerous, if not deadly, event. But the unfortunate side effect is what's happened to your friend."

Wanda threw her hands in the air. "What happened?"

CHAPTER 8
WATCHED AND WAITING

She stood at the top of the bell tower, watching the buttery orb of the sun sink into the dark claws of leafless October trees. It was colder at night now, and she wondered how long they'd be here. And when the League of the Moon would show up. They were coming. She felt it already.

Hardly a soul darkened the ground for miles around, making it so safe for them it was almost boring. Except for the other night. No, *that* wasn't boring at all.

The demon had dealt with the problem, though. She had to admit that. And since he'd killed the guardian, no doubt sent by the Council of the Realms, she knew they'd be safe for at least a little while longer.

Their 'guardians' went out on assignments lasting weeks on end. Mondra knew—hoped—it was a routine patrol and not one sent because they'd been discovered.

The Council were the self-appointed watchdogs of the magical world. They sent 'guardians' into towns where the vibration levels were just right, and the concentration of those with magical ability was at its highest. It made sense the guardian had located her—she was undoubtedly one of the few magical people in the area and probably for miles around.

Salem was one of those towns, too. You didn't have to be a witch, a warlock, a vampire, or a shapeshifter to feel it. There was something special about the place. Something in the air that even the 'muggles' could feel. Except it wasn't relegated to a private area for witches and wizards to learn spells and practice magic, like Hogwarts. It was an entire fucking city.

Things would be different now. Mercy's survival of Mondra's attempt on her life had seen to that. Mondra wanted Mercy's power for herself. In the worst way. She'd spent the better part of a year setting things up. Zachary Villitz, an entity animated by a shard of the demon Inanis's soul and the consumption of pineal glands, (human or otherwise), was to capture Mercy's soul before it ascended either to eternity, or into its next incarnation. One never *really* knew the intentions of the universe.

The EMTs revived her faster than seemed possible. This had thrown the proverbial 'wrench' into her plans, but she was nothing, if not adaptable. She'd promised to make Zachary whole again by combining the 'barely there' body he'd inhabited with that of her former boyfriend, Dr. Archibald Love. It would have been a much simpler process, had Mercy cooperated and died. When that didn't happen, she'd needed something else. That's when she'd remembered the demon.

Twenty-six years earlier, she'd begun dabbling in dark magic, and things began happening to residents of Salem: an accident here, an illness there, a wealthy family losing everything they'd worked for, a marriage broken up by a cheating spouse suddenly smitten by a new love. Of course, these things happened all the time, and magic would be the last thing anyone would point a finger towards. But the frequency of these events seemed to tick up at an unnatural pace. A fact noticed by one of the wealthiest, most connected men in town.

Solomon Dobson dropped by for a visit one night. When she answered the door, she could tell right away there was something different about him. Mondra didn't say a word as she held the door open, ushering him inside. He followed her into the living room. The ingredients for what he needed rested neatly on the table in the middle of the room.

"I believe this is what you're looking for?" she asked. A knowing smile crossed her face.

He arched an eyebrow. "Is it?"

"If what you're looking to do is breach the witch's shop, then yes."

Solomon tilted his head. "I'm curious. How did you know I was coming? And, for that matter, what I would need?"

"Everyone dreams. Not everyone dreams alone," she said.

He threw his head back and laughed. "Impressive. You've seen the dreams the witch has been having?"

"I've seen the dreams *everyone* has been having. Yours, hers, the child's. When you're tapped into the things I am, you pick up on *everything*! There are threads, Mr. Dobson. In this town, consciousness crisscrosses the night sky like the wires running through the walls of a house. You just have to know which ones you can touch, and which ones to stay away from. And I've got the house *wired*."

They were silent for a time as she put the ingredients together and completed the spell. She offered the vial to him, then pulled it back. "There's going to come a day when this will need to be repaid. How do I know you'll honor that?"

"You don't. But I have no interest in starting a war with you. We're on the same side, you and I. I'd be a fool not to leave my options open down the road. When you need me most, I'll be there."

"What about the Council?" she asked. "They're going to know something happened. It will be as obvious as a neon sign in the middle of a graveyard. They'll come after me."

"That's a chance we *all* take. Cover your tracks, and it shouldn't be a problem."

She'd been doing just that since. She was fucking tired of it. *Unfortunately*, she thought, *there isn't a thing I can do about it now.*

Aaron Hendricks slid his arms through hers from behind. "What are you thinking about?"

She whirled around in his embrace to face him. He was tall, as tall as her. They were eye to eye. She answered, "Just how I'd like to get away from here. How tired I am of this place."

Aaron nodded. "You and me both. I don't think it's happening anytime soon, though. Too much heat."

Mondra pouted. "Yeah. Cops! Magical and otherwise. I need a distraction." She slid her hand down his shirt, over his belt, and then lower.

Aaron smiled. "Looks like you found one."

∾

Three miles away, as Mondra and Aaron were distracting each other's brains out, Archie set up camp. The trailer he'd towed here with the VW microbus had few items in it. A rope hammock hung diagonally from the back driver's side corner to the top passenger's side tailgate. He had a GoPro camera set high in the trailer's corner, on the passenger's side, and aimed across the hammock and toward the tailgate. In the back corner, on the floor, he kept only essentials: water, food, and a small charcoal-burning grill. He wasn't sure how long he'd be out here, or how long it would take to find what, or more accurately, *when* he was looking for, but he'd brought just enough to last a week if required.

The GoPro was a precautionary measure to record anything he might say aloud, or not remember correctly from his astral travels. As it stood right now, someone was going to die. He'd seen that much already. It didn't mean it was certain to happen. It didn't even mean the visions were true. But they sure as hell felt that way.

The days since Mondra had almost pulled his soul from his body and placed it into Zachary Villitz had bubbled with visions. At first, he didn't know what they were. He figured maybe he hadn't come out of her little ceremony completely intact. That maybe Mondra had done something to him that was irreversible, and perhaps he might go slowly insane.

Then there was the vision of the void. The place where souls and spirits unfit to continue on, in either direction—good or bad—resided. It wasn't a place of torment, like the hell of the Bible, and it sure as shit wasn't heaven, or nirvana, or whatever one might call paradise, but it wasn't where you 'ceased' to exist, either. They'd all had it wrong. It was dark. It was silent. But it was far from the 'nothing' he'd assumed. It was a place of spiritual stasis, where things held within were neither alive nor dead, just 'there.'

Archie thought back on his conversation with Dr. Darren Biltmore the night before he'd come out here. They'd been discussing quantum mechanics and how it related to the spiritual world.

"You know, Archie, how skeptical I've always been about the things you talk about in your course," Biltmore had said. "And I know it's always bugged the hell out of you, too. But a part of me *was* just a tad curious. Of course, given what's happened since, my curiosity has only ballooned into outright fascination, but it's also led me to consider things from an entirely new angle."

"I'm all ears, Darren," said Archie. He still couldn't get used to the idea he was having a conversation about these things with a man he used to refer to as 'douche bag.' DB for short. A nickname that conveniently lined up with Darren's initials. *Life can throw you some serious curve balls,* he thought.

"One train of thought in quantum mechanics is that by observing something in one location, you unavoidably affect the outcome in another."

Archie tilted his head, not quite understanding the concept.

Biltmore saw his confusion. "There was an experiment a while back called the 'double slit experiment.' I won't go into all the technical mumbo-jumbo, but I'll boil it down to its essence. What they found was that electrons fired through a barrier with two vertical slits on its face, when unobserved, will split in two, leaving two impressions on the board behind it. But, when the electron is *observed* by someone, it will behave as expected. In other words, it will act like a golf ball fired through the barrier. It will leave only one impression on the wall. It has *duality*. The electron behaves like a wave when unobserved, causing two impressions, but like a particle when observed, only causing one. It somehow *knows* it's being watched, and acts accordingly."

Now it was Archie's turn to be fascinated. The first thought he had was that QM wasn't all that far removed from appearing, for all intents and purposes, as nothing short of supernatural. Then his thoughts turned darker. Something in the information Darren had presented to him rang a faintly disturbing bell in his mind. Mondra's ceremony pricked his consciousness. A vision contained within the visions.

In the days after Mondra's failed ceremony, when he'd been recovering mentally and physically, memories rose unbidden. The intertwining of Zachary Villitz's soul with his own came roaring back. Most of it made a twisted sort of sense. But hidden within the visions, and because there were *four* souls linked during the ceremony, he'd seen something not meant for his eyes.

It was a moment of complete darkness, and then it wasn't. A pinprick of light shone in the middle of his field of vision, and much like the example Darren had given him, that tiny dot of light had landed somewhere else. And something in the pitch-black void had observed it.

Stasis was altered.

Light had leaked into the void, activating things meant to remain dormant forever. It was like information stored on some supernatural hard drive had suddenly been fed electricity and its programs were springing to life.

Archie shivered at the thought. He'd condemned entities to that dark place and was terrified by the thought of their return.

After their conversation that night, Archie decided the time to act was at hand. In the days preceding the conversation with Darren, other visions tormented him. Visions of friends in danger, or dying. Visions of the streets of Salem roamed by the dark beings released from the void. Visions of someone he knew but couldn't see, dying on a stony floor... their cold, vaporous breath trailing toward a ceiling covered by a stained-glass dome.

It never occurred to him that these visions were only of *potential* outcomes, and that maybe the actions he was about to undertake would be the very *cause* of those outcomes. At least, it hadn't occurred to him until this very moment, out in the woods and setting up for God knew what. But he couldn't *not* do anything. If something from his visions came to pass, if someone he loved *died*, and he hadn't lifted a finger to stop it, he'd be unable to live with himself.

Archie killed the engine of the VW microbus, plunging his campsite into complete darkness. A soft symphony of night sounds filled his ears. Frogs croaked en masse, and crickets harmonized just underneath. An owl supplied scant lyrics.

He pulled the trailer door shut and locked himself inside, muting the night music. For several moments, he did nothing but breathe—stilling and centering himself. And now, like the creatures outside, Archie got ready to do *his* thing. He climbed into the rope hammock, thinking to himself how odd it was he could climb into something like this with little trouble, but he almost always fell over backwards when he tried sitting in a beanbag chair at Wanda's shop. It made him smile as he closed his eyes and got ready to slip into the astral plane. Traveling to timelines he had no business being in.

CHAPTER 9
DRAWN OUT

Joanne pulled the orange Jeep Wrangler off Route 2 west as the last sliver of sunlight clung to the horizon, its color an almost perfect match to the shade of her own vehicle. She and Penny were now three quarters of the way across the entire state of Massachusetts, and heading north toward a spot where the borders of three states met. Vermont and New Hampshire were a short drive in either direction from their ultimate destination. But the road trip would stop just short of those states. In a town called Northfield.

Jo pulled over at the first safe spot she found so she and Penny could get out and stretch their legs. When finished, they sat on the Jeep's bumper. Jo pulled a sheet of paper from the front pocket of her hoodie, unfolded it, and handed it to Penny. "This is what I saw in the mirror this morning."

Penny looked it over, recognizing the obscure symbols scribbled on the paper. It had been a long time since she'd seen characters like these, and she strained her memory looking for the meaning of each.

"Do you know what they mean?" asked Penny.

"I do. But I don't want to tell you what I think they spell. Or what it translates to when it's figured out. I wanna see what you come up with, so I know for sure I'm right. And I hope I'm not." The look on her face said otherwise.

Penny pulled a pen from her back pocket and went through the symbols with deliberate slowness, only jotting down a letter underneath each symbol when she was absolutely sure it was the correct translation. Jo stood back from the truck and faced Penny, chewing a thumbnail and biding her time. It took about fifteen minutes and several re-checks before Penny felt she'd translated the message correctly. When done, she flipped it around to show Joanne. Their results matched.

"Okay, we've got the letters. But the word makes no sense. At least, it's not English as far as I know," said Penny.

She handed the paper back to Joanne. As Jo folded it and stuffed it back into the pocket of her hoodie, she said, "I know. But I found out what language it is—Romanian. Mondra is half Romanian."

Penny's eyebrows shot up. "What's it translate to?"

"Inviere in Romanian means resurrection," said Jo.

Penny tilted her head. "I don't get it. I mean, I know what resurrection means, obviously, but what does that have to do with why we're out here?"

"I don't know, for certain, but I have a theory... well, a couple. First, the message was sent in Theban, which means only people who know the meaning of the symbols were the ones intended to translate it. Henry didn't have a clue what it meant when he saw it in the bathroom mirror this morning. It's why I resisted telling him."

Penny nodded.

"Second. The message is in Romanian. We both know Mondra is half Romanian, but she was born in America—raised to speak English, as far as I know. That's beside the point. There's no way she sent it. Why tip us off?"

Penny nodded again, conceding the point. "True. But we don't know that for sure. So let's keep it open as a possibility. Who else?"

Jo shook her head. "I don't know, but I have a feeling it's got to do with the Council of the Realms. It's the only thing I can think of right now that makes any sense."

"I wish we knew more about them," said Penny.

"You and me both, since I'm the one that brought their attention down on us."

"You can't blame yourself, Jo. There is no way in the world you could have known what would happen."

Jo nodded, but didn't look convinced. "Anyway, we need to find out more about them when we get back, but for now... let's find Arch."

Penny pulled the Ziploc baggie from the pocket of her dark-blue windbreaker. "Did you bring a bottle of water?" she asked.

Jo went to the front of the truck, returning with a bottle of Poland Spring. Penny squeezed the baggie from the outside, grinding the dried-up pineal gland of Zachary Villitz into a fine powder. She did it within the bag to avoid losing any to a random gust of wind. Jo handed her the water bottle, uncapped, and Penny used the corner of the Ziploc to funnel the ingredients into the water. Penny capped the bottle and shook it until it dissolved. She drank down half and handed the bottle to Jo, hiding a gag until she watched Joanne finish her half.

"That is fucking disgusting!" yelled Joanne.

Penny couldn't answer. She was too busy bending over and gagging, trying like hell not to yack the vile potion back up. *It would supremely suck*, she thought, *to come to this point and puke away the only link we have to Archie... and Mondra.*

Jo was thinking the same thing as she covered her mouth with the inside of her elbow. After a few minutes, the urge to hurl faded for both of them. The potion took effect.

"Let's get somewhere safe," said Jo.

They hopped back in the Jeep. Jo flipped on the headlights and pulled from the side of the road. Stars poked through the silvery curtain of twilight and above rolling hills lined with trees reaching gnarled fingers into the sky.

The witches sat in silence... listening. But not for any earthly sound. Nothing came to them for a while, and the miles flowed by unnoticed—the knobby tires of the Jeep gobbling up the highway was the only sound for miles.

When it started, it was slow to come. Whispers dashed at them, swirling in the darkness, like a tornado stirring in a soup of grey-black clouds, whirring around but not quite formed. It holds your attention, but you're never quite sure if the danger will materialize. They drove on into the night, keeping a mind's eye on the gathering storm.

CHIEF BYRON MILLER of the Salem Police Department stood outside the back door of the station, a filtered cigar lit and glowing between the thumb and forefinger of his right hand and on its way to his mouth when he spotted headlights turning into the far end of the lot. He flipped the cigar as far away from himself as possible, praying he wasn't too late and that it wasn't Penny pulling into the lot. Byron swore to her he was going to give them up, but he loved the damned things. The chief drank little, and he didn't care for drugs, so his cigars were the *only* vice he had. Penny was the love of his life, *and* he loved his cigars. But the cigars wouldn't chew his ass out if he flung one or two away in fear, now and then. *It's the price you pay*, he thought.

When he saw the red Camry getting closer, he let out the breath he hadn't realized he was holding. Only to draw in another that would catch in his chest. *What the hell is Henry doing here?* Whatever the reason, it wasn't good.

Byron lit another cigar and walked over to the Camry. "What brings you here, Henry?"

"Have you talked to Penny at all today, Chief?" asked Henry.

"No. But my shift isn't even half over. I usually call her on my lunch hour. Why?"

"I tried calling her on the way over. It went straight to voicemail. I wanted to ask her if she'd seen Joanne at all today."

Byron looked at once confused, then worried. "Why would Penny have seen Joanne? And why are you looking for Jo in the first place?" asked Byron. "Shouldn't she be at the coffee shop with Delilah?"

"You'd think so, but no. I left work early today. Something happened to me in the ER. I came right home and checked the apartment. Jo wasn't there and Mrs. G.—"

"That nosy lady?" asked Byron.

Henry nodded. "That nosy lady. She said Jo took the baby out in the morning and came back without her. Turns out she dropped DeeDee with my mother up in Maine. I think Jo and Penny hooked up and took off. I think they know something we don't about our friends in the West.

And that's not the *only* wonderful bit of news today. Archie's gone off the grid. Wanda can't find him and no one's seen or heard from him since last Friday night."

Byron's face went pale. If Archie was missing, Penny would know. And she didn't need a *phone* to find him, either. Which, he realized, meant Archie was in some kind of trouble. He pulled his cell phone from his shirt pocket and tapped his wife's number. It went straight to voice mail.

Byron pointed to an open spot in the station parking lot. "Pull in there, Henry. I'll be right back out."

Henry pulled into the spot as Byron vaulted the three steps leading up to the station's back door. He ripped the door open, held it with one leg, grabbed a set of keys from the hooks hanging just inside, and ran over to the Camry. "Let's go."

Henry and Marla jumped out of the Camry and into the police-issue Ford Explorer. Henry sat up front with Byron, and Marla scooted to the middle of the back seat. She rested an arm on the backs of both front seats and leaned forward. Byron turned to look at her. "And you are?"

Marla smiled at him. "Marla. I'm Henry's boss."

Byron shot a look at Henry.

"I'll explain on the way, Chief."

With that, Byron flipped on his siren and lights and sped from the parking lot, racing out of Salem and onto 95 South, headed for Route 2 West and toward God knew what.

"You say your friend has no magical ability. Is that correct?" asked Moreland.

"I already told you that," Wanda said. Her patience was whittled to a toothpick.

"Has he always had the ability to travel the astral plane?" asked Moreland.

Wanda tilted her head back and forth, "Somewhat. With my help. Why?"

"Interesting. Since the failed ritual, he's gotten much more proficient. Indeed, he's gotten to where he needs little, if any, help getting there," said Moreland.

"How would you know that?" asked Wanda. "It's one thing keeping an eye on him in the real world. It's quite another to know when he's astral traveling."

"It came to our attention just last night. Which is why I've come to you today. It seems your friend has not only figured out how to travel the astral plane without your assistance, he's figured out how to travel to whatever *timeline* he chooses. He is attempting to change the past."

Wanda stared at him for a long time.

Moreland waited, returning her stare. Much of the cockiness he'd displayed earlier had returned.

Mercy held her breath, her eyes bouncing between the two.

Wanda spoke first. "I suppose you have proof?"

Moreland said nothing. He nodded and smiled one of those sad smiles that attempts to convey sympathy and regret, but comes off as pitying and condescending. Wanda wanted to punch him in the face. Instead she said, "Prove it."

"Oh, I intend to, Miss Heinze. But I'd need you to come with me for that."

"Come with you where, exactly?" asked Wanda.

"To where the Council resides in Salem, of course."

CHAPTER 10
DOORS

Byron piloted the Explorer down the same ramp Archie had several hours earlier, and onto Route 2. Henry worked the phone, trying to raise Penny or Joanne, but with zero luck. He hadn't *expected* to reach them, but you never knew.

"Why in the hell would they head out there on their own?" Henry wondered.

"I don't know, Henry. But I think I might need some details here. I'm a bit in the dark, you know? I can't help you if I don't know what's going on."

Henry told him everything. From the dream he'd awoken to, to the incident with the mirror in the bathroom and how Jo said she had no clue what it meant. He finished with the terrifying moments in bay seven at the MGH.

Byron listened without interruption, then went quiet as he tossed the facts around in his mind. Henry was used to this silent introspection from the chief, knowing the man was logical and perceptive and practically a savant with piecing together tidbits of information. Byron, when the shit was hitting the fan with the Red Witch, had figured out why she was after Henry's child... revealing the monstrosity hidden inside Delilah.

"So this message in the mirror, you say you couldn't understand the words?" asked Byron.

"They weren't even words. Just symbols. Nothing *I've* ever seen before, anyway," said Henry.

"And Jo said she didn't know what it meant?" asked Byron

"No. If she did, she did a great job of pretending otherwise. Jo wouldn't lie to me, but I got a funny feeling she knows *exactly* what it means. And she's trying to protect me from something—or someone." He shrugged and blew out a long breath.

"Henry, could I see that message in the mirror?" asked Marla.

"Sure." He handed the phone back to her.

Marla laid Henry's phone flat on her right leg, then pulled out her own iPhone. With her left hand, she tapped away on her own phone. With her right, she pinched her hand down on the open screen on Henry's phone, first expanding the photo and then drifting it from left to right. Her head flew back and forth from each screen, like a dealer at a blackjack table. After a few minutes of intense back and forth, she handed Henry's phone back.

Henry was about to ask her if she found anything interesting when she held up a finger. He zipped his lip and waited a few more minutes while Marla pecked furiously at her screen. When finished, she frowned.

"What is it?" asked Henry.

"Well, the symbols are definitely from the Theban alphabet," she said.

"What's that?" asked Byron.

"It's an old set of symbols witches used, way back when, to talk in code to each other. It's a secret language they used to keep alive while communicating under the noses of whatever authorities existed back then," said Marla.

"Were you able to figure it out?" asked Byron.

"Oh yeah. It's pretty straightforward. I figured out the letters, but the word they spell is something I've never seen before," said Marla.

"What's the word?" asked Henry

"Inviere." Marla spelled it out for them, then said, "There are a few languages that have the same word, with the *same* spelling, but each means something different."

Byron looked in the rear-view mirror and caught Marla's eye. "Any chance you have the Romanian translation on your screen?"

Marla looked down at her phone and swiped until the translation she was looking for appeared. "Found it. Why did you want that *particular* translation, Chief?"

Byron locked eyes with Henry. "There's a certain redhead of the Romanian persuasion I think might be behind the message. What does it translate to?" asked Byron.

"Resurrection," said Marla.

Henry's eyes bugged. The incident in bay seven instantly made sense to him now. And he understood why Jo had first moved Delilah as far away from the house—and herself and Henry—as soon as possible, and then taken off with Penny without letting himself or Byron know her reasoning. "She's protecting us from Chesrule. It all makes sense. What that guy in bay seven said to me about the Red Witch bringing the light to them; it's true. I didn't recognize the voice at first. Probably because it made no sense. At least, I didn't think it did. The void was supposed to be the place none can come back from. But what if we're wrong about that? What if they can?"

Byron was nodding, taking it all in. "I still don't understand something. Why go alone? I mean, wouldn't it be better being all together if this supposed badass demon is coming back for you, Henry?"

Henry was about to say something when Marla broke in. "Maybe they aren't trying to do it alone. Whatever *it* is."

"I'm not sure I follow," said Henry.

"Think about it. The only reason we're headed out west is because of what happened to you at the hospital, right?"

Henry nodded.

Marla continued. "Now, let's say the thing at the hospital never happens. You go about your day, you finish work, then you get home at about six or seven at night, considering traffic. Well, Jo's still gonna be gone, and you're still gonna make all the calls you did, and eventually find out your baby is in Maine with your mother. Jo and Penny would still be gone. You and Byron are going to take the exact same course of action, whether or not it had happened earlier."

Henry raised an eyebrow. "You sure you're not related to my friend Wanda? You think an awful lot like her."

"What are you getting at, Marla?" asked Byron.

Marla shook her head. "You don't see it? They know you're going to come after them. They know you guys will put two and two together and follow them out there. In fact, I'd bet they're counting on it."

"Why in the world would they do that?" asked Henry.

Marla smiled. "That, my friend, is the million dollar question.

It was getting easier. Archie was out of his body and on the astral plane mere minutes from the time he'd closed his eyes.

He ignored the lesser beings flitting about the strange realm. Henry'd always referred to them as *'the astral plane equivalent of squirrels hoarding nuts.'* They were interesting, but paying attention to them—to *any* beings roaming this realm—could distract someone as inexperienced as Archie from his mission. And the mission was a life and death errand.

When Archie had helped Henry on the astral plane, the circumstances were dire. They'd needed to get Henry back to the life he'd lived before his current incarnation. The first stop on that ride was a place called 'the in-between.' A place where souls went when between lives. It was a place of learning. A place where one absorbed the lessons from previous lives. It was also, Archie recalled, the place where Henry crossed from this life to his last.

Henry had connected with the consciousness from his last incarnation—a witch named Madeleine Tranch—and figured out a way to contact her through her dreams. In the end, though unable to affect events on that timeline, Henry discovered the item needed to defeat the demon Inanis.

Archie was in that place now. Ever since he'd figured out where Inanis, Mondra, and Aaron Hendricks had gone, he'd set about trying to anticipate their next move. He felt guilty not telling the others, but he also felt ultimately responsible for the trouble his ex-girlfriend had caused those he loved most in the world. If he could end all this, and do so without endangering his family, he'd move heaven and earth.

When Mondra and company had gone west, Archie

suspected there was more to the move than met the eye. And when considering why they'd made a dash toward the western part of the state, he thought hard about the things the Red Witch and the demon had in common. Number one on the list was narcissism. Both of them believed the sun rose and set for them alone.

Archie studied the map in that part of the state. Taking for granted they'd reached the area via Route 2, which ran close to the northern border of Massachusetts. The last place they'd been seen was at a gas station in Orange, Massachusetts. Archie circled out from that point on his map, looking for a town name or a geographic location that made sense when considering the personalities of Mondra and Inanis.

It didn't take long. The name of the place actually made Archie laugh out loud when he'd found it. It was close to the borders of Vermont, New Hampshire, and Massachusetts, and within the town of Northfield. It was called Satan's Kingdom—an unincorporated area of the state.

According to legend, a citizen of Northfield coined the name. When the parishioner had left church one Sunday, a forest fire raged across the Connecticut River. He was rumored to have remarked, "Satan's Kingdom is burning."

The ironic arrogance was not lost on Archie. Inanis coveted his own domain. What better way to declare independence than spitting in the eye of the dark forces that had spawned him?

Finding the three fugitives was not even half the battle. It was late when they'd fled in Raul's cruiser for parts unknown, and the League of the Moon's members decided it was best for Byron to put out an all-points bulletin and start the search for them after a good night's sleep.

Archie had driven Mercy home that night. He took no chances, walking Mercy right up to her front door. Mercy was overjoyed at having her job back and officially becoming a member of the League of the Moon coven. Wanda had made it happen before they said their goodnights. So when Archie turned to leave, Mercy gave him a long hug and a peck on the cheek. That was all it took.

The next morning, as Archie sat in his office, he'd felt strange. Not in a bad way. In fact, it was quite pleasant. When he thought back on it now, it reminded him of the clear-eyed, clear-mindedness he'd had as a child. That feeling when you wake up in the morning and your thoughts are still, the hopeful smell of the morning air fills your lungs, and the excitement of possibility fills the mind. The endless options of imagination stir, untethered to the cares of adulthood—totally *alive* and in the moment.

The *best* thing was, the feeling remained. What made it even *better* was the sharpening of his intuition. As if something or someone was alive inside him—a voice not his own. That voice told him he needed to find the Red Witch and the demon, and time was shorter than he knew. It was *very* insistent.

These were the thoughts swirling in his mind as he approached the doors lining the side of the never-ending room. When Henry had been here, he'd told Archie a few days later what the place was like. Henry, because of Archie's curiosity, went into great detail about how things worked in the in-between.

The part that interested Archie most was how things worked with the doors. Henry'd told him the doors were portals to different times along the path of a soul's journey. And when the powers-that-be deemed it necessary, the scrollwork labeling the door would suddenly clear, pointing the way forward.

It made Archie think about the name of one of his favorite bands. The Doors. Few people knew the band's name came from the title of a book by Aldous Huxley called "The Doors of Perception," a book about his psychedelic adventures under the influence of mescaline. *What are these doors if not that exact thing?* Archie thought. Maybe he was exploring the same ground as Huxley now?

He moved silently along the corridor, the doors to his right. Something was wrong. Henry had mentioned that the name on any door with the potential of passage, and *only* that door, would come clearly into focus, while the others remained blurred. Any door with blurred scrollwork was, as Henry understood it, 'off limits.'

For Archie, every single door he passed was clearly marked. He had his pick. It never occurred to him to wonder why this was the case, and that maybe there was something not quite right about the ease of passage through any door he chose.

He walked on until he found the one he was looking for; the one he'd been through at least half a dozen times before. Archie reached out his hand, turned the knob, and walked through the door labeled "Inviere."

CHAPTER II
XAVIER

Wanda, Mercy, and Moreland left Wanda's Wicca'd Emporium at exactly 8:13 p.m. The sun had called it a day, and a chill had settled in on the Witch City. Moreland led the way down the brick covered length of Essex Street and to the curb of the main drag of Washington Street. They waited out the light cycle, then crossed.

Wanda noticed Moreland heading straight toward the statue of Elizabeth Montgomery who played Samantha on the TV show "Bewitched." She'd always loved the statue. And the show. Samantha, frozen in time, sat on a broom, surrounded by a fingernail moon. Her left arm was held high and crooked at the elbow. The middle, ring, and pinkie fingers angled in toward her thumb, leaving the index finger loosely pointing out. The result was an empty hand that appeared ready to hold something. If you looked at it from just the right angle, standing to Samantha's direct left, you could see this.

"Are we going on a sightseeing tour of Salem today, Mr. Moreland?" asked Wanda.

He smiled, but it was purely reflexive. "If you care to notice, Miss Heinze, you'll see that Samantha is pointing in a certain direction. If you observe more carefully, you'll notice the shape of her hand. Almost as if you could fit something in it."

"Is there a point somewhere along the line here, Mr. Moreland?" asked Mercy.

The smile melted from his face. Moreland wanted to make this a grand exhibition, hoping to impress the two witches. They were having none of it.

"Fine," he said, like a petulant child. He pulled something from his coat and placed it in Samantha's hand.

To Wanda, it looked an awful lot like a magic wand. Though she'd always loved the statue, and had taken more than her fair share of pictures with friends and family beside it, she'd never noticed the obvious missing object from Samantha's hand. *How the hell did I miss that?*

After a moment, Wanda and Mercy watched in awe as a cone of blue light, laced with white sparkles popping like little flashbulbs, bloomed from the wand in Samantha's left hand. It lasted less than five seconds.

Moreland retrieved the wand and put it back into his coat pocket. Wanda and Mercy waited to see what would happen next. When several seconds passed and nothing did, Wanda turned to ask Moreland what the point of the exercise was. Before she could speak a syllable, he held up his hand, looking around the area. He nodded, as if he'd been waiting for something to happen. And then it did.

It was fast. If you blinked, you missed it. Which was the

point. Wanda and Mercy looked around the dark room in awe. Part of it was how they'd arrived here, part of it was the room itself. The floor was polished onyx. It gleamed under soft, buttery candlelight emanating from gold sconces trimmed with intricate silver scroll work. The sconces hung from marble pillars holding up the four corners of the room.

"What the hell just happened to us?" Wanda demanded.

Moreland's smile returned. It reached his eyes this time, and Wanda could tell he was quite pleased with himself.

"You are in the receiving area of the Council of the Realms. Welcome!"

"Didn't you just send me a letter chastising someone in our coven for using," Wanda put up quote fingers, "overt magic on the streets of Salem?"

"I assure you, Ms. Heinze, no one saw us," said Moreland.

"How is that possible?" Mercy asked.

"The cone of blue light was visible only to us. People without magical ability can't see it. And, until a couple of months ago, you and Miss Glass wouldn't have either. Also, there was one other there. You probably didn't see him, but he was there. He stood very close to Miss Glass. I think you intrigue him."

Mercy looked doubtful.

"I know it's hard to believe," said Moreland, "but there are more beings in Salem, with powers the two of you have never witnessed. And they will only make themselves known if *that* is their desire."

Mercy dismissed him with a wave of her hand. "If you say so."

"He does."

The whisper in Mercy's left ear made her almost jump out of her skin. And the man who materialized out of thin air caused both witches to jump back a step.

"I apologize. I didn't mean to startle you," said the man. His accent sounded familiar to Wanda. Something from the Baltic area was her guess.

He was tall. Mercy pegged him at about six feet. Maybe six-two. The first thing she noticed, aside from his height, was the way he smelled. It was like nothing she'd ever encountered before, reminding her of several things all at once: roses, earth, decay (but not in a bad way). Something similar to the smell leaves give off after a few days on the ground in autumn; it was a smell of both life and death coexisting. Her interest didn't escape him, but he said nothing.

The man reached out his hand in an offer of peace. Mercy took it in hers. It was cool and dry. Perfectly manicured nails complimented skin that was smooth, porcelain-white, and flawless. The hair on his arms was dark and just on the thick side, but neatly combed in one direction up to the cuff of the rolled-up sleeves of a crimson pullover sweater. Black dress pants with knifepoint creases flowed toward shiny, black loafers as polished as the onyx floor beneath them. But what pulled her in like iron filings to a magnet were his eyes. They were an unusual shade of blue, bordering on grey. The kind of eyes Mercy would have written off as cold and distant, but that were, in fact, irresistible. They possessed their own gravity. For a change, Mercy was on the receiving end of a handshake that felt like way more than what it was. When he let go, she felt an instant sense of loss, and smothered it with a smile she knew looked as real as false teeth.

He smiled back. Bright white teeth practically glowed

through a thick five o'clock shadow on a face framed by black, wavy, shoulder-length hair. "I'm pleased to finally meet you, Mercy. I've heard so much about you. Yes?"

Mercy's eyebrows shot up. "You have?"

He nodded. "Oh yes. It's the talk of the town. Well, to those in the know, at least."

Moreland seemed uncomfortable with what the man was revealing, and stepped forward to halt the conversation, stopping short when the man glared at him.

Wanda thought *that* was quite interesting. It was something she filed away in her mind for later reference. She said, "I didn't catch your name."

"I don't recall offering it up. But if you must know—"

"I must," said Wanda.

He paused for a moment, taking measure of Wanda. When she held his gaze, he realized this wasn't someone he wanted to quibble with over something so trivial. He bowed his head in apology. "I'm sorry. It was rude of me not to introduce myself. I am Xavier Saulis."

Moreland rolled his eyes, then hung his head.

"Come now, Armand. It's not a state secret." He turned back to Wanda. "Forgive my friend. With good reason, he likes to keep things close to the vest, but he sometimes gets carried away with all this cloak and dagger business."

"Yes," said Wanda, "he likes to write nasty letters and threaten people."

"In his defense, I was the one who suggested we contact you. He was against it," said Xavier. "Perhaps it could have been worded with a little more tact."

"Ya think?" asked Wanda

Xavier held up both hands. "No argument from either of

us, Miss Heinze. There is no excuse for the tone of the letter. But I just ask that you consider the circumstances under which it was written."

"Enlighten me," said Wanda.

Moreland and Xavier exchanged a quick glance, and Moreland nodded his approval.

"Since the night your coven exposed Solomon Dobson for what he truly was, and in doing so, opened a portal to the year 1692, there has been a ripple effect," said Xavier. "This is not a criticism. There was no other way to handle it. But we noticed immediately. Since that day, we hoped nothing would come of it. Unfortunately, that is not the case. As a result, we were already watching."

"You mean spying, right?" asked Wanda.

Xavier tilted his head back and forth. "More or less, yes. Though you never would have known had the incident with the green witch not happened. It was unfortunate—"

Wanda held up a hand. She was at a boiling point. "Okay, I've heard enough. Did it ever occur to you that what happened on the street that night was a mother trying to protect her child? Joanne Trank did not know what she was capable of. And Mercy couldn't possibly know her near-death experience would have the effect that it did on all of us. And for you two to sit there in judgement of us, and then send a letter threatening us! Who in the *fuck* do you think you are?"

Mercy was blown away. She'd never seen Wanda get this hot, and she was loving every minute.

Moreland went to say something, but Wanda was having none of it. "I'm not done!" She pointed a finger at both of them. "You two better get to the bottom of what's going on here. Like fucking yesterday!"

"Take my hand," Xavier said to Wanda.

She looked at it like he'd offered her a rotting fish.

"Please. I won't bite you," said Xavier. A faint smirk crossed his lips.

Wanda hesitated and then gave in. She took his hand, and he said, "Watch the floor."

As the last word passed his lips, the floor beneath Wanda's feet churned. Gleaming black onyx gave way to a stormy sea. They soared across giant waves and toward a ship rising and falling in the swells. The wind billowed massive sails, reminding Wanda of the fat pillows on her bed back home. As they approached the old ship, their momentum slowed. They floated gently downward and landed on the deck of the massive vessel.

"What's going on?" Wanda asked in a dreamlike voice.

"You'll see," said Xavier.

Rain flew in criss-cross patterns, driven by a fierce wind. Crimson colored water flowed across the ship's deck. Though she couldn't feel the rain, the wind, or the water as it sloshed over her feet, her gasp of disgust was no less real. When she recovered, she raised her head and stared the length of the deck. Bodies dotted its surface, lolling in time with the rise and fall of the ship. Lifeless arms flew in one direction and slapped down with a sickening splash in the other. Dead-puppet legs swayed with the tide. It was a scene of massive carnage. Her eyes followed the trail of bodies toward the helm of the ship.

"Let's move forward," said Xavier.

"Okay," said Wanda in a faraway voice.

They drew closer to the helm. On each side of a large, polished wooden wheel stood a man. To Wanda's left was a figure she recognized instantly as Solomon Dobson, back then known as Dobson Molonos. To the right was the same man who held her hand in the present. Blood covered both men.

"You see, Miss Heinze, we have a common enemy," said Xavier.

CHAPTER 12
PARTING SOULS

They were close now. Joanne could feel it. One look at Penny's face told her she felt it too. With that, Jo pulled the Jeep from the road, slowing to a crawl on the shoulder and searching for the optimal spot to enter the forest. After a minute or two, a trail wide enough for the Jeep presented itself, and she slapped the shift into four-wheel drive. The going would be a lot slower now, but that couldn't be helped. Snapping an axle because of impatience would do no good for anyone.

"What are we looking for, exactly?" asked Penny.

"Beats the shit outta me," said Jo. "But we'll know it when we get there. I can guarantee that."

"Well, if you think about it, Zachary's pineal had been around all of them. So we're going to find Archie, or them."

"True enough," said Jo. "Either way, we have to trust it. We can figure out the rest when we get there."

With that, they became quiet. The Jeep's headlights bounced up and down on the uneven terrain. Shadows danced wildly in front of their eyes as the light from the truck flashed from tree to tree. It was a dizzying display, and both witches felt as if they were seeing figures through the trees. Jo stopped the Jeep.

"Are you seeing the same things I'm seeing, Penny?" asked Jo.

"If you mean people, then yeah. But it's quick. Like I can't be sure if my mind is making it up or not. I think they call it pareidolia. Your mind fills in the blanks for you, creating a face or a form that might not be there. Still, it's freaking me the hell out!"

Jo nodded. "Same." She took a deep breath and crawled the Jeep forward, hoping to slow down or stop the forest phantoms from darting in and out between the trees. It was working, she thought. Five minutes passed, and the phantoms seemed to disappear, but it pained her to move at this pace, and anxiety gnawed at her patience. She couldn't help it. Jo was an aggressive driver, and in moments when she was honest with herself, she'd accepted Henry's diagnosis of her as a lead foot. When she had Delilah with her, she drove slower. Barely.

Without realizing it, she edged back into the danger zone. Moving even faster than before. When the eyes appeared in the forest, directly in front of her, she reacted on instinct, pulling the wheel hard to the left. At that exact moment, the Jeep's front passenger's side tire dipped into a ditch on the forest floor. The energy and momentum of the turn caused the Jeep to tilt on its axis.

Jo did her best to control the roll, but it was useless. Penny screamed as the truck tilted on the passenger's side. Jo reached out and grabbed Penny by the collar of her jacket and yanked her up and away, just in time to save her from being crushed by over two tons of vehicle.

The Jeep slid along the forest floor, coming to an abrupt stop with a hollow boom as the front end slammed into a bright white birch tree. Steam billowed from the shattered radiator, sending angry clouds rocketing through the headlight beams and into the starry sky above. When Jo regained her wits and composure, she shut the engine off. Silence descended, punctuated only by the sound of crickets and the low hiss of escaping radiator steam.

"It's okay, Jo. You can let go now."

Penny's voice startled Joanne into realizing she still had a death grip on Penny's collar. Penny braced herself against the passenger's side as Jo released her.

"Well, this fucking sucks," said Jo. "Did you see those eyes in the road?"

"Yep. I did. They were glowing too bright to miss."

"You think it was him?" asked Jo.

"Who, Inanis?"

Jo nodded.

"Not unless he's recently possessed Bambi," said Penny.

Jo's mouth hung open. "It was a fucking deer?"

Penny started giggling—and found she couldn't stop. Jo stared at her for a minute, trying not to laugh. *This was a serious situation, goddamnit!* And then she couldn't help herself.

The giggles were contagious, and within seconds, two witches from the city of Salem were laughing hysterically in the middle of a forest in northwestern Massachusetts.

Jo was wiping her eyes with the heels of her hands. "Stop! I'm going to piss myself."

This only made Penny laugh harder. "I think I did

already." Penny held her thumb and forefinger up for Joanne. "Just a wee bit!"

Jo, hanging sideways and held in her seat by the belt, started pounding the steering wheel because it hurt too much to laugh now.

Finally, after what had to be a solid five minutes, they calmed down. Their breathing and the sounds of the forest at night were the only noise.

"We need to get outta this thing," said Jo. She grabbed the *'oh shit!'* handle above the driver's side door, unlocked her seat belt, and hoisted herself through the window. Once out, she leaned back through and offered her hand to Penny. When they were both safely out, Jo went around to the back of the Jeep and grabbed a flashlight, a blanket, and pullover rain smocks for each of them.

"You always travel prepared for the apocalypse?" asked Penny.

"Thank God for Henry. Ever since the night things went down with Inanis, he's been on a prepper kick. Says you never know when we might have to hide out. I always busted his balls about it. So, if you tell him I admitted he was right, I'll have to kill you, of course."

Penny smiled. "Understood."

She handed the items to Penny. "What are you feeling right now?"

Penny pointed. "I'm being pulled that way."

Jo frowned, "Weird. Whatever this thing is doing, it's pulling me in the opposite direction."

"What do we do?" asked Penny.

"I'm not too thrilled with the idea, but I think we need to split up. I don't wanna take a chance and have both of us heading to the wrong place. And it feels like time is running out fast."

"Yeah," said Penny. "I don't like it either, but it feels right. You got your cell with you?" She held up her iPhone.

Jo pulled hers from the back pocket of her jeans. "I'm at forty percent. You?"

"Twenty-seven."

"Okay. Just in case, let's shut them off for now. Turn yours back on in about half an hour," said Jo. "And keep your flashlight use to a minimum. We don't know which of us is headed towards Archie. And we don't need those assholes getting a heads-up we're coming."

"Got it."

Jo reached out and hugged Penny. "Be careful."

"You too."

They turned and set off into the woods in opposite directions. Jo had only taken ten steps when she turned around to look for Penny. Even with the light from the half moon, she couldn't see her friend. The forest had swallowed her, and Jo felt very alone.

"ONE OF THEM is close now. I can feel it," said Mondra.

"Which one?" asked Inanis through the face of Raul Martinez.

"The green witch. Joanne."

"Are you afraid of her?" asked Inanis.

Mondra's personality wouldn't allow for the truth. She tilted her head down, raised her left eyebrow, and frowned. "Be serious."

"I was. I know what she's capable of. You'd be wise to be afraid."

"She's only capable of the things she is because of Mercy," said Mondra.

"Not true. I've dealt with her in two lifetimes now. It's true she's even more powerful now, but I mean *before* Mercy. I watched her slay six of my best men, when she was David. The *form* is different. The *soul* is the same."

"You're forgetting something, dear demon. I've come in contact with Mercy, too. I'm ready for her."

"How so?" asked Inanis.

She stared at the demon, holding his gaze. She said, "Aaron? Could you come in here?"

They could hear Aaron's footsteps as he shuffled across the dirt and debris in the other room. Years of neglect had caused parts of the old church to crumble, and pretty much any space on the upper levels announced whoever traipsed across its filthy, debris-strewn floors.

Aaron appeared in the doorway, his silhouette framed by alternating shades of orange, red, and yellow as firelight glowed behind him.

"Come, sweetheart. Show Inanis what I've created," said the Red Witch.

Aaron strode slowly across the room, the dirt on the floor grinding under his feet with each step. Mondra had lit her own fire in the middle of the room, and as Aaron stepped into its glow, his features changed. Not his body; that was similar in build, enough to appear as she needed. It was the face that mattered. When the firelight exposed her creation, Inanis fled his spot by the fire. The face of the man who'd almost sent him to the void stared back.

"Wait!" yelled Mondra. "If you leave now, you'll miss the best part."

Inanis stood by the open space in the bell tower, ready to jump out, and watched as Henry Trank split into two entities. On the left was Aaron Hendricks, looking around as if he didn't know where he was. On the right was a dark entity he knew well.

"What do you require of me now, masters?"

Chesrule had returned.

CHAPTER 13
JAZZ AND JEEVES

Essex Street was mostly deserted now. A few restaurants remained open, but Monday night wasn't exactly a party night in any town. Even Salem. Wanda turned the key, pulled the back door to Wanda's Wicca'd Emporium open, and stepped into her safe room. Mercy followed close behind.

"What did that guy show you, Wanda?" asked Mercy.

Wanda didn't answer at first. She was too busy gathering items they'd need for the trip, and the confrontation, ahead. She piled the items on top of the bar in the southern corner of the safe room. Once done, she said, "That man, whoever he is... *whatever* he is, came over on the ship with Inanis in 1692."

Mercy's eyebrows shot up. "He did?"

Wanda nodded. "The scene on the boat was a bloody massacre. I think Inanis killed everyone on the ship. My bet is someone on there recognized him for what he really is."

"That doesn't surprise me. What else did you see?" asked Mercy.

"It ended with the ship smashing into the rocks at the shore. They were both thrown into the water. As usual, the bastard got away."

"So, is Xavier some kind of immortal?"

Wanda tilted her head. "He said nothing to that effect. I'm assuming he was showing me a scene from a past life. Letting us know he's aware of what we're up against."

"What did he look like back then? Still as sexy?"

Wanda smiled at that. "He *was* pretty hot, wasn't he?"

"Oh yeah," said Mercy. Her cheeks reddened a bit.

"That's the funny thing, honey. He looked almost exactly the same. But if I'm being honest, he was soaked from the storm and bloody from the fight with Inanis. So it was kind of hard to tell. It wouldn't be *unusual* if he looked somewhat the same. In *my* last incarnation, I was a man, but the universe played a cruel joke on me; I've been exactly four feet, ten inches, and with almost the exact damned hairdo, the last *two* times. The gods owe me in the next life. Bigtime!"

Mercy laughed. "What are we doing now?"

Wanda was about to answer when her phone chirped. She reached into one of the giant pockets of her purple velvet robe, fished the phone from it, and tapped its face. "Henry, what have you heard?"

Mercy watched Wanda's face as she listened. The news didn't look good. Wanda listened for a few moments more, then said, "Alright sweetie, be safe. We'll see you soon."

"What's up?" asked Mercy.

"Henry and Byron are on their way out west. Joanne and Penny are already out there, but Henry can't get either of them to answer their phones. It's like an instant replay of Archie from this morning."

What the hell is going on? Wanda thought to herself.

"Are we going out there, too?" Mercy asked.

"As soon as Moreland pulls up out back," Wanda answered.

Mercy's eyebrows raised a bit at that. "You trust him?"

"Not as far as I can throw him. But I live by Vito Corleone's motto. 'Keep your friends close and your enemies closer.'"

Mercy smiled. "I like that. But who's Vito Corleone?"

MORELAND PULLED into the back parking lot of Wanda's shop. The two witches were waiting for him, each with a cardboard file box in their arms. Mercy went to the rear of the black Cadillac Escalade, popped the hatch, and stowed her box there, then grabbed Wanda's and repeated the process. She closed the hatch and hopped in the backseat with Wanda.

Moreland turned in his seat. "No takers for the front?"

Wanda pointed toward the windshield. "Jazz likes to ride up front."

Moreland seemed puzzled at first. He turned around, following the direction of Wanda's finger. A tall, black woman made her way across the parking lot, confidently striding toward the Caddy. She smirked when Moreland caught her eye.

His face fell. He knew Jasmine Miso. Well, that was her name *before* her marriage—the last time he'd seen her. It was now Jasmine Miso-Johnson. They'd run into each other more than a few times back in those days. Jazz didn't fear the wrath of the Council of the Realms. And with good reason.

Back then, she'd bailed them out on numerous occasions—times when she was the only one with the particular talents they needed. As far as Moreland knew, she was the only person in Salem, or for that matter, the New England region, who knew how to apply an entity known as an *egregore*—an energized astral form or a non-physical entity that can perform the will of a group.

No one in Salem with any magical ability knew how to deal with the vampires. The Council hadn't the first inkling about how to deal with them. So, the vampires pretty much did *what* they wanted, *when* they wanted, and *how* they wanted. It had gone overlooked for hundreds of years, because most of what the vampires *did*, until the early 1990s, had taken place in the wee hours of the morning. It was unfortunate, especially for those who didn't particularly *want* to become vampires, but the Council, to keep the peace, had raised little fuss.

That changed one day in 1994. It was Christmas Eve, and the midnight mass at St. Theresa's in Salem remained scheduled, despite warnings of an impending blizzard. As happens, with disturbing regularity in New England, the meteorologist got the forecast completely wrong. No snow of any consequence fell that night, but the parishioners had heeded the warnings. The only occupants in the church that night were the priest presiding over the mass, and a couple who'd flown in from Missouri earlier in the day, hoping to surprise family on Christmas morning with their arrival. That would never happen.

A particularly smart, particularly vicious, and exceedingly cruel and out-of-control vampire named Edmond, had decided the rules of his elders—rules agreed upon over centuries by both the Council of the Realms and the vampires who called Salem home—no longer applied to him.

Edmond was a newly minted vampire. His lack of self-control in his life *before* becoming a child of the night followed him. He'd been a heroin addict in his human life. So, to him, taking the blood from the three souls in the church wasn't much different from breaking into someone's home and taking what he needed to get a fix. It was actually, he'd realized, much easier and more convenient. There was no pain-in-the-ass second step of selling what he'd stolen. The 'heroin' flowed directly from their necks.

The police discovered the mess the next morning when the church elders requested a wellness check on Father Moreno. Three bodies were laid out at the front of the church. Two sets of bloody streaks led up the center aisle, ending with two bodies placed side by side at the bottom of three carpeted steps leading up to the narthex. They'd been drained white. The priest was slumped over the altar, face down, his hand still clutching a large, gold crucifix.

Lieutenant Byron Miller was the officer on duty that day. He'd been on the force for just five short years and had seen nothing as brutal as the scene at the front of the church. The *last* thing in the world he would've attributed the bloody mess to was a vampire.

He called the scene in to dispatch over his two-way radio —a frequency monitored daily by the Council. The Council of the Realms sent no one, however. They knew right away what had happened. *And* who was responsible. Edmond had quite the reputation in his short and bloody career. The vampire problem, after this incident, needed to be dealt with.

Earlier that year, Armand Moreland took over leadership

of the Council of the Realms. One thing they'd installed him to oversee was the relationship with the vampires. Much like those before him, he didn't have a clue how to handle them without starting all out war within the city. But he had a problem; he knew someone with the powers to handle the situation, but she was someone the Council hadn't had the best relationship with. They'd threatened her, much as they would Wanda and the League of the Moon years later, with consequences for her actions.

The gypsy had conjured an egregore to keep the vampires away from herself, her fiancé, and the interiors of her home and shop. She'd done this with the help of other shop owners in Salem who also had magical ability, but she was the catalyst for their action and the only one with knowledge of the vampires, so she withstood the Council's disapproval. The Council, chickenshits that they were, had only written the letter to *her* about the situation so they could continue to keep the vampires a secret.

Moreland swallowed his pride, showed up at her shop, told her who he represented, and had the door promptly slammed in his face. But he couldn't leave empty-handed. The situation was dire, and he had to leave with some kind of resolution. After knocking on her door repeatedly, Jazz finally had enough and cracked it open. "What?!"

"I just need a moment of your time, Miss Miso. I represent—"

"I know who you are, pal. What do you *want*?"

Moreland removed the bowler from his head. "I'd rather talk inside, if it's not too much trouble."

Jazz stared him down for what, to Moreland, seemed an eternity. Finally, she rolled her eyes, unchained the door, and let him in.

"Okay, Jeeves, what do you want?" she asked.

He overlooked the jab. "We have a problem. Well, Salem has a problem. One of the vampires has finally crossed the line."

She tilted her head. "The thing at the church?"

Moreland nodded.

"So? What's that got to do with me?" Jazz asked.

He kneaded the hat in his hand, finding it almost impossible to look her in the eye. "We need your help. We need you to conjure an egregore to protect the city. And we need it as soon as possible."

Jazz had turned and continued tidying up the shop as he spoke. With that question from Moreland, she froze, placed the items in her hands on the counter, and slowly turned toward him.

"Let me get this straight," she said as she crossed her arms. "You want me to do *the exact same thing* for you that I did to protect myself? The very thing you and your buddies at the Council gave me a ration of *shit* for? Do I have that right?"

Moreland nodded at the floor.

Jazz stayed silent—waiting him out until he finally faced her. She said, "What's in it for me, Jeeves?"

"What do you want?" Moreland asked.

Jazz smiled.

~

"Jeeves! Long time no see." Jazz turned in her seat. "Hi Wanda! How you been, honey?"

Wanda was grinning from ear to ear. "I'm good, Jazz. It's been way too long, sweetie."

"And who's this pretty young thing with you?" asked Jazz.

"Jazz, meet Mercy. She works for me at the shop and she's the newest member of the League."

"Wow! You must have it goin' on!" said Jazz.

Mercy reached over from the back seat to shake Jazz's hand. When Jazz took it into hers, she felt a mild jolt of energy. And then, briefly, an image flashed in her mind. Shards of colored glass surrounded a body as blood spread slowly across the floor. As quick as the image came, it was gone. Mercy never noticed the tiny change in Jazz's expression, but Wanda had. She would wait until they were alone and ask her about it.

"It's a pleasure to meet you, Mercy." said Jazz.

"Likewise, Mrs. Johnson."

"Oh, no no no. To you, it's Jazz. If you're a friend of Wanda's, you're a friend of mine."

Mercy smiled, "Thank you."

Jazz turned back to Moreland. "So. Where we headed tonight, Jeeves?"

"West."

CHAPTER 14
FUTURE PRESENT

Archie stood in front of a set of large, broad-planked doors, their finish worn away by years of neglect. He reached for the rusty iron handle, shocked and surprised when his hand passed through it. It took a moment to register he was an astral being attempting to manipulate an object in the three-dimensional world. Though Henry warned him about this adjustment of the mind, everyday instinct would probably rule the roost for a while until he got used to things 'over here.'

When the idea finally took hold, he simply walked through the doors and into the front area of the church. He took in his surroundings. Marble bowls hung on either side of the entrance. Spider webs danced lazily above the dust and dirt that caked the bottom of the bowls. Mummified insect shrouds dotted the webs, making Archie shiver and pray they weren't a foreshadowing of things to come.

He moved into the main part of the church. Its layout was unconventional. Pews ringed a hexagonal room, leaving the middle of the floor bare—an intentional canvas for the light passing through the stained glass dome high above. The altar sat directly across from the entrance he'd just passed through, mirroring the width of the entranceway.

Shouting exploded from above, almost ejecting him from his astral body. Though he'd lived this scene a few times before in his dreams, the onset of it still rattled him. He waited until the shouting stopped and the crash came. On cue, colored shards of glass rained down from above, chased by the thud of a body landing flat on its back. The dark mass on the floor in front of him seemed larger than it should. Whoever it was, their breathing stopped instantly.

The first time he'd witnessed this exact scene, he'd assumed the poor soul had died on impact. It was a miracle he, or she, hadn't. A fall from that height would kill almost anyone. The victim was in terrible shape, and lucky to have survived. The mystery person sucked in a great gasp of air, followed by a heart-wrenching moan of agony. So much blood!

Frustrated, Archie returned to the room in the in-between. He needed to get to the point before all this happened. How could he save—*whoever*—from this fate if he couldn't uncover the cause?

He walked further along the length of the room. The doors were to his right as he searched for one leading further back in time. Most of the scrollwork on the doors dealt *only* with events pertaining to his personal life, and he was ready to give up when he came upon a plain wooden door. It had neither scrollwork nor markings of any kind. What it *had* was a feeling—an aura of dread leaked around its frame like heat from a house fire. Despite the feeling, it drew Archie. A moth to the flame. He reached for the doorknob, praying not to be too badly burned.

Byron pulled the Explorer to the side of the road and put it in park. His cell phone hovered above the dashboard on a magnetic stand, seeming to float in midair. He pulled it from the stand, spread his fingers across the screen to widen the area displayed by his GPS, and studied it. His eyes widened.

"What is it, Chief?" asked Henry.

"You said you got a picture from Wanda, right?"

"Yeah," said Henry. "The one from Archie's whiteboard." He found it and held his own phone up so Byron could see it.

Byron smiled. "What do you think the chances are the first two letters stand for this place?" He handed his phone to Henry.

"I'd say pretty fucking good. I never knew this place existed." Henry was amazed—both at the name of the place, and that Byron had put it together so quickly with Archie's message.

"I can't see what you're looking at, but I'd bet a million dollars it's Satan's Kingdom. Am I right?" asked Marla.

Henry and Byron turned to look at her. Henry said, "You've *heard* of this place?"

Marla nodded. "Yes. I know it's history too. Some guy walked out of church in Northfield—I don't remember what year or if there was even a year *attached* to the story—but it was after a sermon on the fires of hell. It just so happened there was a huge fire across the Connecticut River that day and he proclaimed Satan's Kingdom was burning. That's the version I heard, anyway."

"How in the hell do you know something like that?" asked Byron.

Marla shrugged. "I paid attention in geography class, maybe?"

Byron smiled, shook his head, and turned to Henry. "I think the rest of Archie's message is pretty self-explanatory. The 2 and the W are for Route 2 west. The NFLD is for Northfield. I think whatever Archie is up to, he made it vague, but not *so* vague it couldn't be figured out. Pretty sure he knew we'd put it together once we got rolling."

"That sounds a lot like what Joanne and Penny did to us," said Henry. "I still don't get it."

"That makes two of us," said Byron.

Everyone in the Explorer was quiet for a time, mulling over the facts. Without word or warning, Byron put the SUV in drive and crawled it along the shoulder of the road.

"What are you looking for, Chief?" asked Marla.

"I'm not sure, exactly. But I got a feeling I'll know it when I see it."

It didn't take long. About the length of a football field passed when Byron stopped the truck. His galactically bright driver's side spotlight illuminated a fresh-looking set of tire tracks trailing across the dirt and into the woods. He said, "Those look wide enough to be from Jo's Jeep. Whaddaya think, Henry?"

Henry got out and rounded the front of the Explorer, knelt down, and examined the tracks. He knew exactly what the tread on Jo's tires looked like because he'd taken the Jeep to the shop to have them installed less than three weeks ago. He gave Byron a thumbs up without looking back and stayed where he was, studying something on the ground.

"What is it?" asked Byron.

Henry went to pick it up, then thought better of it. "I don't want to touch it, in case it could be evidence."

Byron was smiling on the inside, appreciative and thankful Henry considered the legal implications of potential evidence in an investigation. The chief stepped out of the Explorer, pulled latex gloves from his back pocket, snapped them on, and strode over to the spot next to Henry.

The item was square, about an inch long on each side. It had intricate gold scrollwork as its frame. Within the frame was a ruby red, perfectly flat stone piece with a silver emblem submerged in it.

Byron picked it up and examined it in the SUV's spotlight.

"Either of you ever see anything like this?" asked Byron. '

Henry shook his head. "Nope."

Marla bent for a closer look. "I want to say no, but I can't. There's something familiar about it." She pulled her cell phone from her pocket and snapped a picture. "I'll take a look at it online while we're driving. Maybe something will jog my memory."

"There's a set of footprints here too, Chief," said Henry, pointing.

The prints trailed off into the woods. Byron pulled the flashlight from his belt, turned it on, and made his way into the woods—followed closely by Henry and Marla.

"You two stay to the side of them. Marla, could you snap a few shots of the prints? I want a record of them in case the weather turns to shit tonight."

Marla did as asked. She was right behind Byron, snapping away, when the chief pulled up short. Marla had the phone at chest level, face down, and was staring at the screen trying to get the best shots, when her phone was pushed backward into her hands by the chief's backside.

"I said pictures of the footprints, Marla, not the inside of my ass!"

She let out a sharp laugh. "Sorry. I didn't expect you to slam on the brakes!"

"What is it, Chief?" asked Henry.

"See for yourself."

Henry hopped over the line of footprints and stood next to Byron, not yet understanding what he was supposed to be seeing. He drew in a sharp breath when he finally figured it out. "They just stop."

"Okay, now that's some weird shit," said Marla.

No one argued.

HE WATCHED them from high above. They'd found the medallion and seen the footprints. It would probably be enough for them, later on, to figure out who'd left them—and why. It was all he could do for now. Anything more would only confuse them, and he needed them to stay on schedule. He needed *all three* groups to stay on schedule. Their varied arrival times had been staggered for a reason; someone's life depended on it. The dreams the Red Witch had fed them were doing most of the work for him, but it never hurt to keep a watchful eye. Satisfied, he went to check on the others.

CHAPTER 15
A CHILL WIND

Penny had been walking for what seemed a very long time. Long enough that she turned her cell phone back on and checked it. She saw it had only been fifteen minutes since she and Joanne decided the best way to handle the situation was to split up. Any doubts she had about their plan had only gotten worse in the short time the two had been apart. Still, the pull of the simple potion she'd made from the pineal gland must not be ignored. She sighed, turned her phone back off, and shoved it in her pocket, then waited until her eyes readjusted to the dim moonlight.

Once her night vision returned, she continued to follow the gentle tug of the potion. With every step, the subtle swoosh of pine needles sliding over a carpet of fallen leaves filled in the gaps between cricket chirps and the occasional hoot of an owl. It was hypnotic and threatened to dull her senses at a time she needed them most.

Then, she noticed something. Another sound wiggled its way into the tapestry of night music. It came from above. Penny listened. A momentary burst of wind whooshed, like a breeze strafing the treetops, yet there'd been hardly *any* wind tonight. She looked up. The treetops remained still against bright pinpricks of starlight. Whatever was flying around up there sounded much larger than an owl. Penny tried to push the other sounds into the background and waited silently—her eyes straining to catch the slightest movement. She saw nothing, and only heard the sound one more time, further away now.

JOANNE COULDN'T REMEMBER the last time she'd been this nervous. Almost her entire adult life revolved around the city. Being shuffled from one foster home to the next, she hadn't had the same good fortune as did the few steady friends she'd grown up with. They would talk about how their parents had taken them camping over their summer vacations, while others complained of being deposited at summer camps, learning to cope with both the woods and the same cliquish bullshit they'd encountered in school.

She hadn't envied them that, though she felt the sting of not being in a stable family. And she sure as shit didn't envy those stuck in summer camps. Right now however, she longed for the skills they'd learned about survival in the forest. It took everything she had to concentrate on the direction the potion led her. Jumping at every sound helped little.

Despite everything the pull got stronger, but something felt different. It was *quieter* now. She stopped to listen. The new sound was faint, like the briefest breeze passing through the branches high above. It stopped abruptly—not ebbing gently down to nothing again, as one would expect.

Jo stood completely still, tracking the whoosh and stop of the sound from above. Whatever it was, it *sounded* big. *Too big to be surfing the treetops*, she thought. When the forest went silent, it reminded her of how the jungle in Jurassic Park had gone still as the T-Rex approached. When it finally moved on, it seemed headed in the direction the pineal potion was pushing her, and she had the feeling it was one more thing she'd have to deal with.

Jo walked on. To her great relief, the sound vanished, and she settled into a comfortable but cautious groove.

After some time she stopped once again, remembering she'd promised to call Penny. She reached into the pocket of her hoodie and was about to switch on her iPhone when she heard it. Someone moaned. She froze, not daring to take a breath. It came again, louder this time. It wasn't a moan now.

"Joooooo. Help me."

"Henry?" she whispered. Loud enough for only her ears, as if pondering the impossibility of her husband being out here at all. She was positive he and Byron were on their way, but she was also certain they couldn't be here yet.

"Joooooo. I'm hurt."

The plea was irresistible. Out of an abundance of caution, she didn't answer. But she moved with quiet purpose in the voice's direction, stepping in spots that minimized the sounds of her footfalls.

"Over here."

She was close now. His voice sounded no further than mere feet away. Jo scanned the forest, looking for anything not brown, green, or black. And then she saw it. A patch of red surfaced out of the gloom on either side of a narrow birch. The shoulders and arms of Henry's red Patriots hoodie were a stark contrast to the white of the birch tree. He sat on the forest floor, his back to her, not moving.

Jo gave him a wide berth, circling around his left shoulder. Her iPhone was still in her hand and she powered it up, turning on the flashlight app, and shining it in the man's face. When she saw it was her husband, her jaw dropped.

"Henry? How the hell did you get out here so fast?"

"I just got here. Came in from the other side of the forest," he said.

"You came alone?" she asked.

He nodded.

His being alone struck Joanne as odd. "You didn't bring Wanda or Byron with you?"

He shook his head.

As he stood, Jo saw him wince and clutch the left side of his rib cage with his right hand.

"How did you hurt yourself?"

"Tripped over a pile of branches. Landed on my side on a log. Hurts like hell."

The more he talked, the weirder she felt. It *sounded* like him, but not totally. There was something... off. *Maybe it's the pain?* she thought.

He moved toward her. "Can you look at it? I wanna make sure it's not a broken rib or something worse."

When she heard the question, she knew it wasn't Henry. He'd know right away what his injury was. It was his fucking *job* to know stuff like that. But she realized it too late.

The man in the red hoodie sprang forward. The arm he'd tucked to his body came free with lightning speed, and the thick tree branch he'd concealed connected with the right side of Joanne's head. She'd moved fast, turning her head enough to avoid most of the blow, but it still caught her behind the right ear, knocking her to the forest floor.

Red hoodie wasted no time. As Jo hit the ground, he pounced—straddling her chest and pinning her arms with his knees. He leaned in and clamped a hand over her mouth. It was an icy hand. He used the other to pinch her nostrils closed. She struggled fiercely. Her green eyes glowed with the magic imbued her by Mercy, but it was too little, too late. The green fire of her irises dulled. As she lost consciousness, the last thing she saw was the face of her husband morph into that of Aaron Hendricks as a form dark, terrifying, and all too familiar eased out of his body.

Penny turned her cell phone back on, tapped the messaging app, and selected Jo from her contacts list.

She texted: All is well? Then hit send.

Penny watched the screen, waiting for the message to show as 'Read.' She gave it a few minutes. The status never changed. Out of an abundance of caution, she shut her phone back off. She would try again in a bit, reasoning that her timing with Jo might be a bit off.

When the phone's screen faded to black, Penny held her position, waiting for her eyes to adjust to the pale, almost non-existent moonlight before she allowed herself to move forward. Once confident, she took a deep breath and reached out—trying to reconnect with the feeling she'd had when she'd first drunk the pineal concoction. It was there, but not nearly as strong as it had been earlier, and the urge to quicken her pace had to be weighed against making a careless mistake. If she went too fast, she might not find Archie at all. And worse, she could end up lost in the woods. Just another reason to keep the cell phone off. If the signal held out, she could use the GPS to find her way back to the main road. Not likely with a dead phone.

Penny pushed the negative thoughts away, cleared her mind, and inched hopefully along toward a reunion with her brother. For the next twenty minutes, or what she guessed was twenty minutes, she made steady progress, rewarded with a set of tire tracks that could only be Archie's; it wasn't like there was a lot of traffic out here.

The tracks were hard to see in the sparse light, but it made little difference—she only had to follow the open spaces between trees large enough to allow a vehicle passage.

If she'd walked any faster, she would have slammed head-first into Archie's trailer, now only a few feet in front of her, and seeming to appear out of thin air. She walked around the side, to the back, and banged on the door.

THE SOUND WAS FAR AWAY, seeming to come from outside the walls of the church. Three loud bangs that sounded like someone hammering the side of a metal can. Archie ignored it as he viewed the scene in front of him. This was the third time tonight he'd been in the church, seen someone flying down from above, and slamming, back-first, to the floor. No matter how many times he tried, he couldn't force the sequence of events further back in time.

The knocking outside the church persisted and was now paired with a voice. At first, the words eluded him. They were far away and muffled. But there was something familiar about their tone.

The scene before him faded as the knocking drew him from the depths of meditation and the peace of the astral plane. Archie snapped awake as the banging continued, punctuated by the desperate sounding voice of his sister. He rolled to one side of the rope hammock, too fast as it turned out, and it swung him face first to the trailer's floor.

He moaned in pain. This only increased the urgency of the banging on the outside of the trailer. The thump of Archie's body and the subsequent moaning had sent Penny into a panic.

"I'm coming. Relax, Penny. I'm okay."

Instantly, the banging ceased, replaced by a faint ringing in Archie's ears. *She must have been at it for a while*, he thought as he withdrew the key from his jeans pocket and unlocked the interior padlock. He tossed it to the floor and pulled the middle handles apart, causing the doors to swing open from the middle out.

Penny thought he looked like P.T. Barnum on opening night at the circus. "All you need now is the hat and the cane, you goof."

"Huh?" was Archie's clueless reply.

"Nevermind. What the hell are you doing all the way out here by yourself?" Penny demanded.

"It's a long story. But I suspect you've figured out at least part of it, or you wouldn't be out here now."

"We know you came out here, obviously, to look for them, but that can't be the only reason. It wouldn't make sense to come out here without Wanda... or at the very least Byron, for some kind of protection. The question still stands. Why are you all the way out here by yourself?"

Archie seemed to toss it around in his head for a bit. He trusted his sister with his life, and he didn't want to lie or keep secrets from her if he could help it. But he had to be careful now. The whole point of coming out here before everyone else was to figure out why he kept having visions of someone dying a painful death, and to prevent it from happening.

He was *so close!* If he confessed the true nature of all that he'd seen, it could set in motion events leading up to the very thing he was trying to prevent. Or, maybe, Penny's arrival ended up *saving* someone? He had to consider this now. It wasn't like he was getting anywhere on his own. The possibilities were endless... and maddening.

He took a deep breath, then said, "There's something I need to tell you, Penny."

CHAPTER 16
I WAS BLIND, NOW I SEE

Wanda sat quietly in the back seat of Moreland's SUV, watching the monotonous flow of trees flying by outside her window. They'd just passed the exit for Athol, the western Massachusetts town where the Red Witch, Inanis, and Aaron Hendricks had dumped Raul's cruiser and stolen a car.

Wanda thought about the news clip of the car's owner. She was standing in her driveway with her upstairs neighbor, twirling a bat and inviting whoever had stolen her car back to the house for some coffee.

The news anchor looked puzzled. "Why would you offer them coffee?"

The blonde woman held the bat up to the camera. The petite brunette neighbor cracked a knowing smile. Stenciled on its side was 'Coffee.'

Wanda smiled and thought of Harley Quinn from the 'Suicide Squad' movie. And when she thought about Mondra and Inanis, she smiled and thought about her own version of 'Coffee' resting in the bag at her feet. At that moment, something occurred to her. "Where is your friend Xavier, Mr. Moreland? I was under the impression he would be joining us"

"I couldn't tell you, Miss Heinze."

"Couldn't? Or Won't?" asked Wanda. The suspicion in her voice was plain for all to hear.

"In spite of the impression I've given you, and I don't blame you for being suspicious, I'm not hiding anything about Xavier from you. He does as he pleases. And, now that you know about the vampires, you'll come to find that they *all* do as they please. They're quite an independent lot."

"How did he know to come to the statue of Samantha?" Wanda asked.

"When I put the wand in Samantha's hand, it was like a beacon. He sensed it the moment I put it there. He's uncannily perceptive," said Moreland.

"I never saw him coming," said Wanda. "Did you see him, Mercy?"

"Nope. Didn't see him. Didn't get so much as a hint of his presence," said Mercy.

Moreland looked into Wanda's eyes from the rear-view mirror. "There's a good reason for that. You can't see the vampires of Salem during the day."

"It was dark when we were at the statue," Wanda reminded him.

Moreland nodded. "Yes. But it was still too close to twilight. And the moon, at the present moment, is in a weak phase. In order for a vampire like Xavier to become visible, his cells must be charged by moonlight. If there had been a full moon tonight, he would have been readily visible. I *did* notice him, but I know what to look for."

"What about during the day?" asked Mercy. "Can we see

them at all during the day? Or do they burst into flames or something?"

Moreland smiled at Mercy in the mirror. "That's an old wive's tale, Miss Glass. The vampires of Salem are out in the middle of the day all the time. They're invisible, mostly, though they can make themselves visible under the right circumstances and if the situation calls for it, but those are few and far between. Their bodies automatically take on a visible form in moonlight. Hence the 'Children of the Night' moniker. It seems they've evolved to fit the modern world."

"How, exactly, does that fit the modern world?" asked Wanda.

Jazz took over for Moreland, "They like their privacy. Some of them are hundreds or even a couple of thousand years old. So, with cameras around every corner, the chances of their image being captured and compared to photos from other times have gone through the roof. A camera isn't a mirror. So, it's just safer and makes more sense to stay anonymous and undetected. Saves a lot of time explaining things."

"Why didn't you ever tell me about them, sweetie?" asked Wanda.

Jazz hooked a thumb at Moreland while shooting Wanda an apologetic look. "Jeeves here made it a condition of our deal. I couldn't say anything about them, and in return—" she stopped, looking to Moreland for the rest of her explanation.

Moreland's lips pressed together in a straight line, and then he shook his head in frustration. "Fine. We agreed to pay the entire mortgage on the property her shop resides on."

"And?" Jazz pressed him.

"And also the mortgage on her residence," he said, bordering on disgust.

"And?"

"There's really no need to go into this any further, is there?" Moreland pleaded.

Jazz said, "You might as well go all the way, Jeevesy. In for a penny..."

He sighed in resignation, "Oh, what the hell. One of the conditions Miss Miso put on her helping us with the vampires was that not only were they to keep out of her shop and her residence, they were to protect the witches, wizards, and any other magical beings within the borders of Salem."

Jazz raised her eyebrows, squeezing the last bit out of him.

"And that protection was to extend beyond the borders of Salem when circumstances required. Are you satisfied now?" said Moreland.

"Well done, Jeevesy!" Jazz clapped him on the shoulder and he flinched in surprise.

"I knew there had to be a good reason I didn't know about any of this," said Wanda. "Well done, sweetie! And I'm so happy you got all your shit paid for, too!" Wanda was grinning from ear to ear.

Moreland shook his head and mumbled something under his breath.

"I'm curious, Mr. Moreland," said Wanda. "Where were your vampires on the night Delilah was kidnapped? We could have used your help that night. You were obviously aware of what was going on. The nasty letter you sent to me proves that. So, where were you?"

"We were monitoring the situation, Miss Heinze, and

more than willing to step in. But a higher authority was in control that night, as you may or may not be aware."

Mercy said, "It was Hecate, wasn't it?"

Moreland nodded at Mercy's reflection. "Indeed. We considered you and your coven to be in excellent hands. The best. There was no reason to interfere. Well, other than the warning in the letter. But that was after the fact, and perfectly within our rights—as poorly worded as it was."

This made Wanda wonder why he was so intent on helping them now. And she said so.

Moreland took his time answering, then said, "We've stepped in because we believe Dr. Archibald Love is not only interfering on a level he is ill-equipped to handle, but that he may cause the death of someone in your coven."

"How could you possibly know that?" asked Wanda.

Moreland caught Wanda's eyes. "There is no way to know for sure, of course. I told you earlier, we've been watching your friend. He's been astral traveling to the in-between. We can follow him there, but no further. It is forbidden for anyone but the traveler himself—or herself, as the case may be—to pass through the instances, or doorways, in that realm. We've tasked Xavier with this."

"What did he see?" asked Wanda.

"Well, remember, he couldn't proceed beyond the door. So he *saw* nothing. But it's not what he saw. It's what he smelled," said Moreland.

"Which was?"

He shot her a surprised look when she didn't come up with the answer. "Blood, Miss Heinze."

Blood. Chesrule smelled it as it leaked from behind Joanne's ear. As he carried her through the forest and toward the church, he resisted the urge to taste it. Blood did not have the same attraction for the demon as it did for the vampire. For them, it was sustenance. For the demon, it was the path *to* sustenance. Not the only one. It was merely one of the side effects of inflicting pain: mental, physical, or spiritual. These, to him, were sustenance. The taste of blood was merely a bonus—he *liked* it.

It served another purpose, too. It would confuse the vampire. They knew he was coming. They'd assumed all of them would be coming. Better to fight them one or two at a time—pick them off when they were apart. It was a much better plan than the one that had gotten him annihilated by the wizard Henry. Chesrule's master had been arrogant, and he'd underestimated the white witch and her coven. Most of what they'd tried, the witch had expected.

Things were different now. The Red Witch had seen to that. Inanis was still powerful, but *she'd* orchestrated the ceremony that bound them together, not his master. And she'd made certain, at the moment she'd claimed him from the child, that Inanis would follow her lead—whether he knew it, or not. The spell binding his master to her was plain to see, if you knew what to look for.

Witches were more powerful than demons, and the times Inanis thought he was in control now were the times she controlled him the most. When she'd pulled him forth, the love spell on both the professor and Zachary Villitz had still been active. The witch had merely applied it to Inanis, modifying it slightly. There was no need for the love component, it wouldn't work on him anyway. Demons knew nothing of love. Obedience was the component retained and applied. And it was working.

Chesrule was hers now, too. She'd brought light to the void. Brought duality!

The true nature of all existence was duality. The light can't exist without the dark. Evil cannot thrive without good. Joy is formless without sorrow. Pleasure is hollow without the existence of pain. And the void cannot exist without the everything—but they *can* be separated. Light is visible where darkness is not. You can watch evil happen—absent of good. You can experience joy apart from sorrow. And he knew, all too well, pleasure can be reveled in without pain—though he enjoyed mixing them.

Freed from the void, he knew another timeless secret. Light *equals* existence. The void was a prison, apart from light. Souls or entities caught within it were stilled—sealed off from the light. The humans spoke of Heaven and Hell. But there were worse things than those. There was nothingness.

Somehow, the Red Witch had broken the seal. A barrier existing through oceans of time. He didn't know the how of it, but he understood the why. Power. The witch wanted to rule the three realms. What better way than having an army of the forgotten at your side?

The witch's plaything walked ahead of him. Another fool believing she was in love with him. Oblivious to the knowledge that within the witch there was only enough room for love of self. He waited as Hendricks pulled the door open for him, then stood aside as he carried the green witch over the threshold and into the church.

CHAPTER 17

ILLUMINATION

They were on foot now. Byron had spotted Joanne's Jeep out of the corner of his eye. He would have missed it completely if he hadn't swung the spotlight in its direction at just the right moment.

Henry was frantic with worry. He was first out of the Explorer, leaping from the door before the vehicle had fully stopped. Byron and Marla were close on his heels, and all three of them combed over the Jeep, looking for any clues to where Jo and Penny had taken off to.

"Both of the flashlights and the rain gear are gone," said Henry.

"There's two sets of footprints here. They head off in opposite directions," said Byron. "My guess is Penny went looking for Archie and Jo went looking for them."

Marla picked up an empty water bottle, holding it high in front of her and shining her flashlight at its bottom. "Guys. Look at this."

They made their way over to Marla, who kept the bottle suspended above her flashlight. When they got close enough, she swirled what remained in the bottle. A grainy mixture sloshed around in less than half an inch of water. Pulling the bottle down, she uncapped it and stuck her nose over the top, and then gagged. It smelled disgusting.

Byron motioned for her to hand him the bottle and smelled it. "They drank the pineal gland. Goddamn it!"

"The one Penny had in the Ziploc at the Cracked Cauldron?" asked Henry.

Byron looked at Henry, his head tilted in confusion. "You know of any other pineal glands in Ziploc baggies I'm not aware of?"

Henry looked chastened. "Sorry. Dumb question. Why wouldn't they wait for us before drinking it down?"

"Henry," Marla began, "didn't you mention something about a dream this morning?"

"Yeah. I dreamed of someone falling from someplace high, and then I heard screaming. It *sounded* like Jo, but I can't be sure of that. The last thing I remember was a hazy outline of someone lying on the floor, surrounded by colored glass."

"Colored glass? You mean, like, stained-glass windows?" asked Marla.

"I don't know. Maybe. Why?"

"Just thinking back on the history of the place. There's a church out here. Probably the same one where the guy came out and saw the fire and named this place." She stopped for a moment, then said, "I'm wondering if Jo had a similar dream. Maybe something having to do with you? It would explain why she felt she needed to do this without you. Or at least leave for this place before *you* did."

Henry shook his head. "When I woke her up this morning, the only thing I know for sure—she was dreaming about Barney."

"That dinosaur thing the kids love?" asked Byron.

Henry nodded, "Yeah. She threatened to shove a banana up his ass if she had to hear that song he sings one more time."

Byron smiled. "That sounds like Jo. And I don't blame her. But I think Marla has a point. It's no accident they left before us. Didn't the *Order* mess around with your dreams, Henry?"

Henry thought it over. "Yeah. It was different. They were watching to see what I knew, but they could adapt it any way they please, I would imagine."

"I think that's *exactly* what they did," said Byron. "But don't forget, Mondra pulls the demon's strings now. Knowing that *could* be to our advantage."

"Then we should probably meet up with Wanda and Mercy before we move ahead. Like you said, they want us arriving two or three at a time. We'd be harder to handle together. Now that I think of it, she pulled the same shit at Wanda's place last time," said Henry.

"Okay, let's head back out to the main road. Henry, call Wanda and tell her what we've figured out."

"Okay, sweetie. We'll see you there really soon. Jeeves just pulled off of Route 2 now."

"Who the hell is Jeeves?" asked Henry.

"It's Jazz's name for the guy that wrote that nasty letter."

"You're with that asshole?" asked Henry.

Moreland shifted uncomfortably in his seat as Jazz, Mercy, and Wanda burst out laughing.

"I'm on speaker, aren't I?" asked Henry.

"Yes, honey," said Wanda through a sprinkle of giggles.

There was a brief silence, then Henry said, "Oh well. Fuck that guy. We'll see you soon."

Wanda hung up. Moreland drove on in silence. Sporadic giggling peppered the rest of the ride to the rendezvous point.

CHESRULE LAID Joanne behind the filthy altar. He looked at Hendricks and snarled, guarding his prize like the alpha in a wolf pack.

"Leave us."

Hendricks, still in a daze from being possessed by the demon for the second time in the last twenty-four hours, nodded absently and loped out of the room.

The demon ran his eyes over his prize. When he'd first come across her in the library, back in 2018, he'd imagined doing all kinds of things with the raven-haired beauty. He'd tasted her blood that night at the library, and it made him hungry. Made him want more. There was something about this one that appealed to him like none before. Maybe it was the taste of witch blood? Oddly enough, given how long he'd been in the earth realm, she had been his first.

Now she lay before him. Eyes gleamed orange-red with excitement in the sockets of a featureless, dark mass no one in their right mind would call a face. He drew a knife from his cloak and caressed the line of her chin, poking it just enough to draw blood, watching with fascination as the drop traveled the length of the blade.

He flipped the knife on its dull side, dragging it down her neck and to the opening at the top of her hooded sweatshirt. Chesrule flipped the knife in his hand so that the sharp side rested against the inside of the hoodie and pulled slowly upward, holding the garment with one hand while he sliced it open down the middle. It came apart without a sound and flopped to either side of Joanne. The sleeves were next, and the rest of the hoodie fell away from Joanne, exposing the black tank top she wore underneath.

She stirred, moving her head from side to side. Chesrule remained still—the knife held at the ready in case she woke, but she remained unconscious. When she settled, he reached for the bottom of the tank top tucked into her tight black jeans, pulling gently until the top was freed, exposing a flat, muscular midsection. He gasped. She was a work of art, and he felt the want rise within. Now he *needed* to take in all of her before he played. He placed the knife on the dirty floor—both hands would be required to undo the tight snap and the zipper. As he reached for the top of her jeans, the knife glowed a curious shade of green.

HE WATCHED FROM HIGH ABOVE. Three of them huddled around the crashed orange Jeep, studying the scene. When they were done, one of them pulled a cell phone from his pocket.

He slid down as far as he dared, listening in on the conversation. They intended to rendezvous with the others —this wouldn't do. They needed to be kept apart or the consequences could be disastrous. And the one he swore to destroy might escape yet again.

As the man talked on the phone, he used the cover of his voice to drop silently from the trees. They were far enough away from the police vehicle that the sound of air fleeing the tires as he gashed each of them went unnoticed. Once the big vehicle rested on four flat tires, he crept up into the canopy of cover the trees provided, and disappeared back into the night. The last group—the one with the white witch—were no longer a concern. They would arrive at the time and place he needed them most.

There were a lot of moving pieces to this dance. Archibald Love had only complicated matters by meddling on the astral plane. It had turned out to be both favor... and disservice.

The favor was, by going where he didn't belong, Dr. Love had exposed both the hiding place of the Red Witch and the demon, something that, until then, had been a well-hidden secret. This was good. It had allowed him to prepare the way. If Love had stopped *there* and sought the advice of Wanda, things could have been different.

There was no doubt—now that Wanda was aware of the Council's existence—she might have seen them as a viable option and sought their help. Moreland's inept handling of the situation made it less likely. That stupid fucking letter! But he had faith in the wisdom of the white witch and believed she would have seen the situation for what it was—a problem beyond the powers of her coven alone.

But the good doctor *hadn't* stopped there.

The disservice was he'd kept going back, trying to alter the future. Intending to save one mystery person, but *instead* multiplying the potential outcomes. Every time he went back to the in-between, he altered timelines, setting things slightly off-kilter in each one of them, and growing the possible outcomes exponentially. He'd become the living embodiment of the double-slit experiment. That was bad enough.

The unintended consequence: he'd provided the Red Witch the opening she needed to unseal the void. To make matters worse, Archie was the witless gateway for the Red Witch to plant dreams in the minds of the League of the Moon.

Even though the League of the Moon had defeated the Red Witch, the connections forged during the failed spell at Wanda's shop still existed. This tied the Professor and Mercy, by the thinnest of strands, to Mondra's power. Xavier doubted the League knew this. What he suspected was Mondra Tibbets was *well* aware of this.

All she'd needed was a once-removed link to the power that lay within Mercy—a connection to the light from Mercy's near-death experience. And who better to provide that link than Archie, her former lover? So, she watched and waited for it.

It didn't take long. On the night Archie had driven Mercy home, and after they'd hugged, the connection happened. After that, it was a matter of time.

When Archie had begun astral traveling, she'd known right away. All she had to do was drop a few bread crumbs in his dreams—hinting at their location in the remote area of Satan's Kingdom. Given her relationship with Archie, and her knowledge of his 'boy scout' ethics, she knew it would force him to act alone—to shield his loved ones.

On the night he'd first astral traveled into the church, Mondra was ready with Inanis—her connection to the void

—at her side. Though Inanis never ended up in the void, he'd glimpsed it. Hanging by a spiritual thread over its black and depthless jaws just before he'd found a life preserver in the passing of Delilah Davis.

Inanis had simply guided the Red Witch in her meditations to the level of vibration at which the hellish nothingness of the void resonated. Mondra did the rest, steering Archie toward a door in the in-between he was all too willing to walk through. The doorway led to a happy memory from childhood—his thirteenth birthday party. It was something he dreamed about often. Mondra wondered if it was a crucial point in his life. Then realized she didn't really care.

In the end, it was enough. Hiding just beneath that memory from Archie's past was the Red Witch's consciousness. Mercy's hug with Archie had been all she needed, and she used that residual spark to ignite the children of the void.

Fortunately, the Council understood her plans. The Red Witch *believed* she controlled the situation. That was good. It worked to their advantage.

Mondra believed, by using their love for each other, she could force them to arrive separately. Their protective instincts would cause them to rush out alone and confront her. Joanne, the green witch, was the fiercest. She would have to be the first to die. Xavier smiled as he wondered about the wisdom of that choice.

CHAPTER 18
VAMPIRES?

A thick fog had settled upon the woods of Satan's Kingdom. It seemed to spring up quickly, blanketing the forest in a silver soup of mist. Byron was the first to arrive at the Explorer and could tell something was wrong just by standing next to it. His head was at least six inches higher over the roof than normal.

"Fuck!"

Henry and Marla pulled up short behind the chief. "What's the matter?" Henry asked.

Byron pulled the flashlight from his belt and shone it at the front tire.

"That!"

The long gash along the bottom of the driver's side tire was all the explanation needed.

"Who the hell would slash our tires in the middle of nowhere?" asked Henry.

"Someone who needs to slow us down," said Byron. "Or keep us apart."

"What do we do now?" asked Marla.

Byron didn't answer. He didn't trust his own mouth, angry as he was. Instead, he stormed around the truck and flung open the rear door. It rose slowly on its pneumatic hinge—too slowly for Byron—and he shoved it skyward. He kept spare flashlights in the back and handed one each to Henry and Marla.

Byron said, "Well, now that we don't have a fucking ride, we head back to Jo's Jeep and follow their tracks as best we can. This fog isn't gonna be much help, that's for sure."

Without another word, Byron stormed off toward Jo's Jeep. Henry and Marla followed.

In less than a minute, they were back at the orange Jeep. It looked like a metallic beast felled by a hunting expedition, guts strewn across the forest floor. Clean (thank God) diapers had exploded from the box kept in the back seat. Cheerios fanned out in an ever-widening arc across the forest floor. Papers from the glove box had flown out from the passenger's side. When the truck had landed, it pinned some of them to the ground beneath. Henry shone his flashlight on them and noticed one with strange writing on it. It looked similar, but not identical, to the message he'd seen in his mirror just this morning.

He handed it to Marla and asked, "Do you think you can translate this one?"

Marla took the small, square piece of paper from Henry, "The Theban letters translate to 'M O R O I I.' But it's another word I've never seen before."

"Bet it's Romanian," said Byron.

Marla whipped out her phone and found the Google translation page again, but the signal this far out in the forest and away from any major cities or towns was spotty at best. She had one bar. It took almost three minutes for the little spinning time circle on her phone to stop. When it did, her eyes went wide.

"It translates into vampire."

Byron held out his hand. "Can I see that paper, Marla?"

Marla handed it to him. He studied it for less than a second before he declared it written by Penny.

"How can you tell she wrote it?" asked Marla. "It's in the Theban alphabet."

"I've been married to Penny almost as long as Henry's been alive. She could have written this in Russian and I'd know it was from her."

"So what does that mean, exactly?" asked Henry.

Byron stayed silent and thought about it. He said, "I think it means Penny may have had her own dreams about what's going on tonight."

"She mentioned nothing to you about it?" asked Marla.

Byron shook his head. "No. But this kind of stuff isn't anything she'd discuss with me, anyway."

"Why not?" asked Marla.

"Well, until the shit happened with that redheaded psycho, I wasn't exactly what you'd call 'open-minded' about stuff like that," said Byron.

"But she knows you've changed your tune, right?" asked Henry.

"Yeah," he conceded. "But it's kinda like someone who's just gotten sober in AA. You only give them what you think they can handle. You wouldn't send someone who's been sober for a month into a bar to preach the 'AA way.' He'd either end up drunk or getting the shit kicked out of him."

"Good point," said Henry.

"So," Byron continued, "now we have to figure out what

in the world vampires have to do with this whole clusterfuck. And the way we start that is splitting up."

Byron pointed the flashlight at the ground, illuminating the footprints Penny and Jo had left. "I'm going to follow Penny's tracks to wherever the hell she's gone—and I'm pretty damned sure she's on her way to Archie. You two follow Jo's tracks."

Byron reached into his back pocket and pulled a small, portable Motorola two-way radio out and handed it to Henry. "These have a range of about five miles. They're fully charged. Keep it on, but keep the volume low. We don't know exactly what we're dealing with yet. When you get a chance, Henry, call Wanda and let her know what we've found and why we can't meet up with her and the others."

"Okay."

Byron turned and started off.

Henry and Marla watched as he walked away, laughing as he threw his hands in the air and raged against the heavens.

"Fucking vampires, now! What else?" asked Byron.

"So ALL THIS time you've been having visions of someone dying?" asked a stunned Penny.

Archie tilted his hand back and forth in front of her. "Maybe, but not definitely."

"I'm not sure how to process that, Arch."

He frowned and considered how to continue. "I've seen *someone* fall from above and land bleeding on that floor several times now. But the beginning and the end of that vision remain unclear. I can't force it any further forward or backward. So, I don't know what causes the fall, and I don't know if the end result is death. But I think, given the height of the fall and the amount of blood on the floor, it's a pretty good guess it doesn't end well."

Penny nodded. She understood now why Archie had wasted no time coming out here. But she still didn't know what had prompted him to come out here all alone. And she told him so.

"Well," he said, "I have a small confession to make. I've been having dreams about this place. Someone in the League dies, I can feel it."

"All the more reason you should have told us!" she yelled.

Archie hung his head. He knew she was right, but something in him wouldn't allow the ones he loved to be put in harm's way. If he could handle it himself, he would. It was prideful and stupid—he knew that—but it was the same instinct that had driven him to flee the vehicle in the parking lot at Wanda's Wicca'd Emporium to save Delilah. He felt responsible for what was going on because of his relationship with Mondra. It hadn't changed.

Penny shook her head. "One of these days, you're gonna realize anyone can make a mistake, Archie. You aren't responsible for your ex-psycho girlfriend's actions. For fuck's sake Arch, she had you under a spell! As much as I detest that bitch, she's one of the most powerful witches I've ever met. And it wouldn't surprise me if she's the one responsible for our dreams."

Archie tilted his head, confused. "What do you mean 'our dreams?' Have you dreamt of this place, too?"

Now it was Penny's turn to look confused. "Um, yeah. Joanne too. And she told me Henry did, but she didn't want to get him involved. She saw him ending up dead in hers. That's why we took off without telling Byron or Henry. The same rationale you used."

She neglected to tell him about the *message* in her own dream. She didn't tell Jo about it, either. Wanda was the only one who would understand, and she trusted her friend was smart enough to bring what was needed. Neither witch spoke aloud about the Christmas Eve event—or what they'd done afterward. Penny put it out of her mind for now.

Archie said, "That probably means Wanda has had her own version of this dream. What in the world is going on here?"

"I don't know," said Penny. "The dreams we've all been having seem designed to bring us here, but they're of a nature that exploits the protective instinct in each of us. That, to me, seems intentional. Like whoever is behind them knows we'll try to shelter each other from harm. My money is on Mondra, but the only thing I can't figure out is why she would take the risk. Wanda alone is more than enough trouble for her. Add you, me, Henry, Joanne, and Mercy to the mix. She doesn't stand a chance."

"What if it's not Mondra?" asked Archie. "What if someone or something else is behind the dreams?"

"Who?" asked Penny. MOROII—*Vampire*—flashed through her mind once more. She quickly banished the thought.

"I can't say. But it's curious. I can only see what happens within a very specific time frame. Like someone is blocking the visions at both ends."

"Do you think Mondra is capable of something like that?" asked Penny.

"I honestly don't know," said Archie. "Like you said

before, and I agree, she *is* a powerful witch. But nothing I ever saw in my time with her gave me any indication she could alter time or affect real life outcomes."

"That doesn't mean she can't. It just means you've never seen her do it," said Penny. "I wouldn't put anything past her. And don't forget, she made you see what you wanted to see. You were never *actually* in love with her. Remember?"

Archie nodded. "True enough."

They were silent for a long time. It was a lot to consider. Nothing about this made sense. And it had only gotten more complicated as the night wore on.

Penny turned her cell phone back on to see if Joanne had responded to her text. Nothing. Now she knew something was up. Missing the first text was something she could understand; their timing could have been a few minutes off. But it had been well over an hour now, and there was no way Jo would have forgotten to check in. It was time to get moving.

"Let's go Arch."

He snapped his head up. "What? Where are we going?"

"To the place in your visions, doofus. You can astral travel out here until the cows come home; it won't accomplish a damned thing. And Joanne isn't answering my texts, which means she's in some kind of trouble."

He turned around and walked into the trailer.

"What are you doing?" asked Penny.

When he returned, he held up the GoPro camera, attached earbuds to the device, and inserted one of them into his right ear. "I'm going to listen to this along the way. I recorded the sessions. It might help."

CHAPTER 19
SPELLS AND DREAMS

"Pull over here!" said Wanda.

"Why here?" asked Moreland.

"I think I saw something," she said, looking left and pointing. "Right there."

Moreland swung the big SUV onto the right shoulder and brought it back around, cruising slowly on the opposite shoulder now.

"There!" Wanda said.

He brought the Escalade to a stop, and they piled out.

Moreland looked at Wanda, surprised, and asked, "How did you know he was there?"

Xavier Saulis stepped from the shadows. "Impressive, Miss Heinze."

Wanda winked at him. "Not really. I figured we'd run into you again tonight."

"You put a spell on me. When we were holding hands in the seeing room at the Council would be my guess. Yes?"

"Very good," said Wanda. "Now, would you like to

explain why you're dividing us, or should I just tell everyone myself?"

Wanda watched the briefest glimmer of shock cross his face and disappear just as quickly. *He'd be a decent poker player*, she thought, *but even the best give something away now and then*.

Xavier tilted his head. "Excuse me?"

Wanda went all-in, laying her cards on the table and calling him. "Flattening tires. Causing deer to overturn Jeeps. Watching a demon capture a witch and not lifting a finger. Sound familiar?" asked Wanda.

Xavier and Moreland stood side-by-side at the front of the Escalade, bathed in its headlights. Wanda and Jazz sat on the front bumper. If the situation were not so dire, the simultaneous dropping of their jaws would have been hilarious. Later, Wanda would discover they were both surprised for very different reasons.

Xavier recovered quickly. He was nodding as a smile crossed his face. "It's Mercy Glass. She's helped to give you this ability. Yes?"

Wanda shrugged and smiled. "Who knows? The magical world is a mysterious place, Mr. Saulis."

"Indeed," he said. "And it appears Miss Glass has learned how to disappear now, too."

CHESRULE STARED at the glowing green knife, understanding instantly the source of the color. He knew better than to make a grab for it. The witch she'd been when he'd attacked her at the library was a distant memory. *This* version of the green-eyed witch was a threat who could send him back from where he came, and he wasn't about to risk *that*. Without so much as a glimpse backward in her direction, he leapt from his crouch over Jo's midsection and fled for the stairs leading up and away from the altar.

Jo reached for him but missed, her nails skimming along his body's surface as he eluded her grasp. His footfalls pounded up the creaky wooden staircase and echoed back at her until they faded to nothing. He'd felt ice cold, and the texture of whatever material comprised his skin reminded her of the cold, slimy skin of an eel. *Apparently with the brains to match*, she thought.

Still sitting on the dusty floor behind the altar, Jo looked down at the tattered hoodie and contemplated her next move. He obviously wanted her to follow him upstairs and into the loving arms of his companions. So that was out. But it made her wonder why he hadn't just taken her directly to Mondra. It seemed awful risky for the smelly bastard to interrogate her on his own, given the powers she now possessed.

She looked down at the undone snap of her jeans, the tattered hoodie, and the wrinkled bottom of her tank top, which was still hiked up on her right side, exposing her belly.

"That fucking perv!" she hissed.

When she realized exactly the type of 'interrogation' he'd had in mind—the kind where questions weren't the aim—she seethed. Jo yanked the bottom of her black tank top down, tucked it into her jeans, and buttoned back up. When she leaned down to pick up the knife the idiot had left behind, the entire room spun, and the lump on the side of her head throbbed. As she steadied herself and waited for the room to stop spinning, the attack from earlier flashed in her memory. Jumbled images of Henry injured, then attacking her, bubbled to the surface. She knew, obviously, her husband hadn't attacked her. *So what the hell happened?*

Jo closed her eyes, trying to fish the memories out of a sea of confusion. They wouldn't come. Frustrated, she grabbed a handful of hair on either side of her head and pulled them toward the back of her neck, tying them together in a haphazard ponytail. Next, she slowly knelt and picked up the huge hunting knife Chesrule had left behind. There was no place on her body she could safely carry the knife without impaling herself, but an ominous feeling of need swept over her. She *had* to keep it with her. There was more to it than self defense. Intuition was as much a part of her life as breathing now, and she heeded its call.

Jo scanned the room, looking for anything she could use to carry the knife with her. When she looked down, the answer came in the form of her shredded hoodie. She grabbed it up from the floor and shook the dirt from it, then cut the sleeves off from the main body, tying them together to form a belt, running it around and through the belt loops of her jeans. Next, she cut another strip, slid it through the loop on her left side, and tied it tight under the hilt—making sure the fabric didn't contact any part of the sharp edge. With that done, she stepped out from behind the altar, strode across the hexagonal room, and into the misty forest. The hefty weight of the knife slapped against the side of her left thigh, calming her with each stride she took. Echoes of David.

Jo focused. She slipped into the cover of the forest to watch and wait.

Mercy thought about the dream as she ran through the forest. She hadn't told a soul. It happened the night following the escape of her mother, Mondra the Red Witch. A sense of déjà vu overwhelmed her. *This was how the dream started,* she thought.

How she'd *gotten* here had been the only missing part of the dream. The ride out here explained that. It had always puzzled her how she could end up in the middle of nowhere, running through the woods, looking for a dilapidated church. Each stride brought her closer, and each turn felt familiar.

Scenes from the dream flashed through her mind as the church emerged like a ghost through the fog. She'd been running flat out since slipping away from the others, and rested against the huge trunk of a black oak tree. It hid her from the church.

Mercy lowered herself to the cool, slightly damp ground —closing her eyes, catching her breath, and calming her mind. Images from the dream surfaced on the dark side of her eyelids. She saw herself at the rotted double doors of the church, feeling the slippery coating of moss on the black iron handles as she inched the doors apart. The oil-starved hinges creaked. Her footsteps crunched filth and debris.

A faint shaft of moonlight lit the altar at the far end of the room. A silent invitation. She accepted, stepping into the hexagonal room with the curious arrangement of pews along its sides, wondering what kind of church this must have been, then realizing she didn't care. Survival was all that mattered now. She was on foreign ground. Enemy territory. Her focus sharpened. All six senses probed the night.

Though less than twenty feet ahead of her, the unprotected space between herself and the altar seemed vast. Each step she took felt bloated with danger, and every little sound felt like a sonic magnet poised to draw malicious attention. She felt the phantom weight of eyes pressing down from above. Mercy stopped in the middle of the floor, chancing a look. Beautiful and broken stained-glass windows, pocked by open sores of moonlit fog, returned her gaze. Eerie. But malice-free.

When she leveled her eyes at the altar once more, it had changed. Buttery yellow light glowed from behind it, stopping her in her tracks. Someone *had* been watching. Mercy threw caution to the wind and rushed the altar, hoping to glimpse whoever or whatever was its source. No one was there. Off to her right, a single white candle stood flickering atop a brass candleholder with a finger ring on its edge. It sat at the bottom step of a staircase leading up and away from the main area of the church.

Mercy stared at it, wondering what came next, when the smells of the church hit her full force. This seemed strange to her. In all the nights she'd dreamed of this place, not once had she actually *smelled* its rotting interior. She realized this wasn't a dream anymore. Somehow, in the time between the sprint to the tree, then resting, and then slipping into the all-too-familiar dream, she'd awoken in the middle of it. Mercy bit down on her lip, hard enough to draw blood. *Yep. Real.*

To further convince herself this was no longer a dream, Mercy walked over to the foot of the staircase, bent, and ran her palm slowly over the candle's flame.

"Ouch!" she hissed.

She stood at the foot of the stairs, staring at the flickering flame. *Up the stairs or back into the night?*

Mercy looked around the dark and barren room. Maybe a clue to what came next lay hidden somewhere within this forgotten space. Something on the filthy walls? Or the pews pushed to its sides? Maybe the answer hid somewhere on the altar itself?

She was stalling, and she knew it. The candle at the bottom of the staircase had been in her dreams. Every time. Its heat nuzzling cobwebs up and away from her face as she held it out in front of her, climbing slowly, up and up, each step bringing light to the darkness ahead. The next step had *always* been clear. Fear had merely clouded the answer from her mind.

Mercy turned, bent, and picked up the candle by the finger ring, then placed her left foot on the first step. With a loud creak, she began the climb. Bringing light to dark, and dream to reality.

CHAPTER 20
TIME FOR CHURCH

Archie and Penny made their way slowly through the misty forest. Penny was in the lead, stopping to check her iPhone every few minutes for a return text from Joanne. Nothing. With every passing minute, Penny's concern grew. Her imagination tortured her with increasingly gruesome fates for Jo with every step she took.

Archie was, of course, oblivious to Penny's state of mind. He kept a casual eye on his sister as they made their way through the forest, but his attention was solely on the GoPro audio he'd captured. The video part he considered mostly useless, but reminded himself to check it later. Just in case.

Most of what he heard was gibberish in the form of his own voice. He rewound and fast-forwarded several times, trying—and failing—to understand things he'd said while under. Frustrated by his failure to harvest anything tangible from these sessions, he was about to rip the bud from his ear when something he heard made him freeze in his tracks—heart hammering in his chest.

Penny walked on for a few moments until she noticed

her own footsteps were the only sound. She stopped and turned around. Archie was about twenty feet behind her and standing still, his head bent and twisted to one side. Joanne was out there alone and Archie was fiddle-fucking around with his headphones! As she stomped toward him, ready to unload, he held up a hand. This only served to piss her off even more.

"What the fuck do you think—"

"Shh!" Archie hissed at her—shooting an angry glare in her direction.

Penny pulled up short. Archie was a gentle soul not given to anger easily, and never with herself. Her anger melted, supplanted by an intense and immediate curiosity. She watched as her brother experimented with the controls on the GoPro. When he finished, he yanked the earbud from his ear, then offered the buds and the GoPro to Penny.

"I couldn't hear it at first. My voice drowned it out a little. But it's there. Faint. Concentrate on the silence between the two things I'm mumbling in the foreground. It's hard to hear, but it's there!"

Penny shot him a questioning look. Archie returned the favor, gesturing impatiently with both hands for Penny to get on with it already.

"Just put the buds in your ears and press play. It's all set up," said Archie.

Penny did as her brother instructed. She was unfamiliar with a GoPro or how it worked, but the play button was pretty much a universal thing on just about every electronic device created by man. She put the white earbuds in both ears and tapped the button.

The first thing she heard was Archie mumbling in the lazy chatter of sleep talk. Little of it made sense, and the only words she recognized were Mercy and Mondra. After that, a brief silence. Then... something very faint. Another voice. Far away, as if the words were being spoken several rooms away but within the same structure. Penny knew right away the words were distinct and clear, but the volume was just low enough that she had trouble hearing them. She checked the counter on the screen, ran it back, cranked the volume, and hit play.

"No, mama. Don't go there. I forgive you—," said Mercy.

Penny heard the pleading in Mercy's voice. It brought her close to tears. The love and forgiveness of a daughter for her mother, regardless of her mother's faults, (and in this case, there were some seriously fucked up faults), Penny thought, bled through Mercy's voice. It broke her heart.

"—are going to kill you." Penny heard a gasp. "All of you. I can't stop—" said Mondra.

Then Mondra said to someone else, "Do it!"

A third voice screamed, "No!" It was Joanne.

In the next moment, Penny heard a scream, then the sound of shattering glass, then nothing for several seconds until Archie started dream-mumbling again. The last thing she heard was the sound of pounding, and she realized it was the sound of her own fists on the outside of Archie's trailer. She pressed stop on the GoPro.

"Mondra is going to kill Mercy!" whispered Penny.

Archie nodded—a grave expression on his face. "No surprise there."

"Let's get moving," said Penny. "I'm sorry I ever doubted you. You did the right thing coming out here as quickly as you did, Arch."

He took the GoPro and the buds from Penny and shoved them into his coat pocket. "You two weren't far behind. And judging by what I just heard, there's a chance Joanne can stop it."

"At least, going by this, we know Jo is safe."

Archie tilted his head from side to side. "Maybe. This is only one potential outcome. But I think it's the most likely, given there are actual voices attached to this one. None of the others I've recorded have anything like what we just heard."

They talked as they walked. Archie followed Penny as she let the fading remnants of the pineal potion guide her toward their ultimate destination—praying they would arrive in time to alter events that, in this world, would only have one outcome.

Jo WALKED the perimeter of the church, staying hidden in the thick forest but never letting the building out of her sight for too long. It was a slow process. The mist in the forest had thickened considerably, and she walked to its edge several times. She couldn't dart back and forth, as she would have liked—the thick mat of leaves on the forest floor would announce her presence to anyone within earshot. And Jo was pretty damned sure someone was listening.

After an eternal slog through the forest, she spotted the part of the church she'd been looking for—the bell tower. It was the place she'd seen in her dream. Every instinct in her body screamed at her to make a mad dash for the tower. To scale its walls. To get to the top and take action. Some action. Any action! She fought it off, choosing to stick to what had gotten her this far.

Melting back into the woods, she continued as before.

One careful, excruciating step at a time, she made it to a point roughly twenty yards from the very back of the bell tower, staring up at a scene that only a few nights ago had happened in a dream inside her head, in the safety of her bedroom. *Mama always said follow your dreams.*

The impulse to act—to do something—was almost overwhelming. Her nerves jangled, and her breathing was shallow and rapid. Jo forced her arms to drop to her sides, took a deep breath, and let it out. She repeated this several times until she felt the muscles in her body relax and the knot in her stomach loosen. The time to act was fast approaching, but something inside made her stand down. Her left hand brushed against the hilt of the knife. It comforted her.

Byron had only been walking for a few minutes when he heard voices. He stopped and listened. Whoever was talking was either keeping it low and quiet, or they were further away than they sounded. He crept forward, stopping every few seconds to listen. The talking had stopped, and the only sounds he heard now were footsteps crunching leaves. The chief stood pat and let them come to him.

They were closer now. He heard someone say, "I don't think it's too much farther, Arch."

"How can you tell?" asked Archie. "It's like walking through soup. I can't see a goddamned—"

Byron was standing about three feet in front of them when he put the flashlight under his chin, turned it on, and said, in his best imitation of Dracula, "Good eve-ah-ning."

Both Archie and Penny jumped out of their skin, taking the Lord's name in vain as a family.

"By! That was not funny," said Penny with an angry grin.

He was smiling, "Oh really? The look on your face says otherwise. Besides," he said as he shoved his right hand in his pocket and produced a small piece of paper and handed it to Penny, "it seemed completely appropriate, given this."

Penny didn't bother opening the small square of paper. "How did you get that?" she asked.

"It was pinned under Jo's Jeep. Why didn't you tell me about it?" asked Byron.

Penny tilted her head down. "I didn't think you'd believe me."

Byron sighed.

Penny held up a hand. "You didn't let me finish."

Byron nodded and rolled his hand.

"As I was about to say—I didn't think you'd believe me, at least not right away. And time was not on our side. The last thing I wanted to do was get into a debate about what's written on that piece of paper. When Jo called me this morning, it was shit or get off the pot. I had to decide."

Byron nodded. "Okay. Fair enough."

His reaction surprised Penny. "So you're okay with it?"

"Yep," said Byron.

Archie stood between both of them, a confused look on his face. "Okay with what? And what's on that piece of paper?"

Penny said, "Okay that we came looking for your sorry ass without telling Byron or Henry." She gave him a playful elbow.

Byron asked, "And the word?"

Penny nodded and handed the piece of paper to Archie, asking, "Do you know what this means?"

He answered without hesitation, "It's written in Theban. The word it spells is Romanian. It means vampire."

She was relieved her interpretation was correct.

"That's the message I received in my mirror when I got out of the shower this morning. After my dream. Everything going on tonight seems like a slightly different version of the same dream. So, on top of having a demon, a dark witch, a possessed cop, and whatever the hell else... whoever is running this shit-show we call the universe has decided that wasn't quite enough, and added a vampire to the mix. How ya like them apples?"

Archie hung his head, shaking it from side to side. "Now the vampires are involved. Not good."

Penny and Byron both stared at Archie, stunned.

"You already knew about the fucking vampires, Arch?" asked a stupefied Byron.

"I'm afraid so. Yes."

CHAPTER 21
THE DRAGON AND THE WOLF

Henry and Marla stood at the edge of the forest, staring at the front of the church. Its rotted, moss-covered doors stood open inside the framework of two hexagonal spires stretching several feet into the misty night air. Defiled crucifixes sat atop each tower. The horizontal beams of the crosses on both sides were snapped off, and the tops of the vertical beams were filed into sharp tips. With the bell tower at the far end, Henry thought it looked like a dragon lying low, mouth open, ready to strike—or consume them in fire.

"Should we go in?" asked Marla.

As if the dragon heard, the front doors slammed closed.

"Well, that answers that question," Henry said as he pulled the Motorola Byron had given him from his pocket. He turned the volume down as low as it could go while still able to hear it and depressed the transmit button. "Byron, it's Henry. The church doors just shut in front of us. I think they know we're here."

The radio in Henry's hand crackled with an answer, but

it was only a static-filled imitation of Byron's voice. Neither Henry nor Marla could make out a word he was saying.

"Range of five miles, my ass," said Henry.

He tried it again, getting the same result. Frustrated, he turned the dial and shut off the radio, then pulled his cell phone out. Henry tapped the screen and was about to dial Byron when he noticed the reception icon on the phone had zero bars, and to its right were the words "No reception."

"That's weird. My phone has zero bars. How 'bout yours?"

Marla took out her phone, tapped the screen, and held it out for Henry to see.

"Shit!" said Henry. "What the fuck is going on?"

Wanda held the phone to her ear with her right hand and chewed the thumbnail on her left. Moreland, Xavier, and Jazz watched and waited. They could all hear the phone ringing in her ear and then the annoyingly efficient voicemail lady came on the line, imploring Wanda to leave a message at the tone. Wanda yanked the phone away from her ear and stabbed at the screen.

"I can't get a hold of them!" she said.

"They must be close, then. Yes?" asked Xavier.

"Why do you ask that?" Jazz pegged him with a stare—a suspicious look on her face. She'd dealt with vampires more than anyone else in Salem who *wasn't* a vampire—she didn't trust them as far as she could throw them. This one seemed particularly manipulative.

Xavier understood the look on the gypsy's face. "I assure you, Miss Johnson, I am not responsible for the drop in communications. But I know we are in a weak cell area, and thickening fog will only make matters worse."

"You're telling me *fog* can kill a cell phone signal? ... Fog?" demanded Jazz.

Moreland stepped in. "It's true. We're already in a weak area, and the fog cover bounces those frequencies around, interfering with cellular and radio transmissions."

"It seems awful strange this fog just came out of nowhere. And at this exact point in time," said Jazz. "Wanda, can she do something like this?"

Wanda had been staring at the ground, deep in thought. Her head snapped up at the sound of her name. "Mondra? I don't know for sure, honey, but at this point, nothing would surprise me. The only thing I know for sure is the weather is supposed to be clear for the next few days. So, there's that."

Moreland turned to ask Xavier a question. When he didn't see him to his left, he turned in a circle, looking for him. "Where is Xavier?"

Both Wanda and Jazz imitated Moreland, spinning and searching for the vampire. He was nowhere to be found.

Moreland swore under his breath, then headed for the SUV. Jazz hopped in the front, Wanda jumped in the back and scooted to the middle so she could be between the two front seats.

"Where are we going, Jeeves?" asked Jazz.

"Church, Miss Johnson."

"I CAN'T GET Henry on this piece of shit," said Byron. "And my cell has nothing."

"It's not the radio, Byron," said Archie.

"How do you know that?" asked Penny.

Byron answered for him. "It's the fog. Especially shit as thick as this stuff. This far out from any tower..." Byron trailed off, raising both hands palms up in a 'what are ya gonna do,' gesture.

"That's interesting," said Archie. "The fog and the reception thing. I didn't know that. And that's not what I was driving at, either. Mondra is doing this."

"You think she can control the weather?" asked Byron. The look on his face said he thought that was utter bullshit.

"Oh no. I don't think it. I know it," said Archie. "It may or may not be intentional. It's probably got more to do with whatever spell casting she's doing—or has already done. Witches draw their power from nature, Byron. The elements. Earth. Air. Fire. Water. When a dark witch like Mondra does this, she does as she pleases—consequences be damned. The natural balance of the elements in the general area can be affected. We are seeing vast amounts of fog at the moment. Which, to me, means that whatever spell work she's been doing probably has a large fire element to it. That's why the air is saturated with moisture."

Archie swept his right arm across his body, asking Byron to observe. "Fire spells draw the dryness right out of the air, leaving the opposite in its wake. She's literally playing with fire. What she intends to do—who knows? The fog *itself* might be the point. It's cut us all off from each other pretty effectively."

Byron listened intently as Archie spoke. What his brother-in-law had said, under the light of current events, made sense. If this conversation took place six months ago, he would have listened politely, then wondered how to approach Penny about getting Archie a date in the rubber room. Not now. Byron had witnessed way too much in the last few months. He considered it both a blessing and a curse. Right now, this fell under the curse category.

One thing Byron was great at, and the reason he was Chief of Police, was his ability to take random pieces of information and slap them down next to each other—putting the puzzle together, if you will. But what made him exceptional was his ability to see the complete picture before all the pieces were in place. He saw it now. It blazed in his mind's eye.

"You still getting something from that potion, Penny?" asked Byron.

"Yes. It's faint, but it's there."

Byron fixed his wife of over thirty years with a stare. "We gotta move. Now!"

CHESRULE ENTERED the room at the top of the bell tower.

"Where is the green witch?" Inanis asked his servant.

The demon knew he couldn't confess the truth to his master. And he knew he couldn't allow him to use touch and meld with his consciousness or his master would see what he'd tried to do with her. So, he lied.

"The one she seeks," he said, pointing to Mondra, "came in to rescue the green witch, releasing her into the forest."

"Mercy is here?" asked a surprised Mondra. "Already?"

"Yes." said Chesrule. "She has just entered the grounds."

"See to it she finds her way up here," said Mondra.

Aaron Hendricks spoke from a corner of the room. "I set a candle on the bottom step. She won't miss it—or its intent."

Xavier flew high above, leaping from treetop to treetop. He moved with the grace and stealth only possessed by a vampire of his age. When he found the spot he was looking for, he settled in and waited, closing his eyes and thinking about the long and timeless journey that had brought him to this moment. It also kept the white witch from watching through his eyes.

He thought about that night, over nine hundred years ago, as he lay bleeding and on the verge of death following the Battle of Artah. As his spirit hung in the chasm between life and death, figures darted and dashed in the periphery of his vision. Stars twinkled. The landscape glowed with the sparse light of a fingernail moon. The grass became a luminous silver carpet, splotched with puddles of blood that appeared black in the dim light. Dashing between the broken bodies and black pools, demons and vampires raced to claim their prizes.

Xavier's brother clung to life not more than twenty feet away. Xander was closer to death than he was. Xavier saw the astral body of his younger brother struggling to escape its shattered shell. But the will to live is strong, no matter the condition of the earthly body.

Xavier saw the massive demon approaching, helpless to do anything about it. It carried something—a bottle or urn of some kind. The hideous beast knelt down, straddling Xander, a knee on either side of his brother's chest. With one taloned hand, he held the bottle above the forehead of Xander, and Xavier watched in horror as the astral essence of his brother disappeared into the container, which was then sealed by the demon. With the last of his brother's soul captured, the demon faded from sight. When the seal was complete, the pewter flask clattered against Xander's chest piece, then tumbled to the grass with a soft thud.

All was quiet, and Xavier mourned the motionless corpse of his brother. Until it moved.

Xander sat up, the breastplate of his pierced armor scratching against the heavy wool beneath. To Xavier, it was the loudest sound in the world. His brother turned his head, then tilted it from side to side, seeming to stretch out the stiff muscles of his neck. Whoever was within his brother took stock of his surroundings and tested the fit of its new body, as if trying on a new suit of armor.

The alien presence living in his brother turned to face him, and Xavier's blood ran cold. Glowing red eyes and snakelike pupils mesmerized him, and Xander understood what a rabbit sees when the wolf bears down on it. It smiled. Though it was his brother's face into which he stared, he did not recognize him.

What was once Xander rose, never taking its gaze from Xavier as it pulled a dagger from the sheath at its left side. The demon started toward Xavier at a slow walk, its malicious smile widening. And then it stopped. The smile vanished. It raised its nose in the air, sniffed twice, and fled. Xavier let out a ragged breath, realizing he would die now, but at least it wouldn't be at the hands of his possessed brother. He could let go if he wanted. Something made him hang on.

Xavier didn't *see* anyone so much as feel a presence. Next came the smell—earthy, like fallen and decaying leaves—but something more. Flowers. The smell of red roses filled the air. It made him wonder if he was dead, and perhaps this was something the departed sensed at the moment of crossing.

"You are not dead yet, Xavier."

If he'd had enough strength left to be startled, he might have jumped out of his skin. Instead, he rolled his eyes around inside his immobile skull, seeking the source of the gentle voice. When he finally found it, he wasn't sure what he was looking at. It was a dark form, fathomless black at its core. Its body was outlined in a shimmer of sparkling silver and gold. As it bent forward, the features resolved. Before him stood a raven-haired beauty. Deep brown eyes regarded him with sympathy—and something more. Hunger. Just underneath the beautiful face and its facade of sympathy swam a predator. For Xavier, the recognition was as simple as looking in a mirror. A kindred spirit stood before him.

"Who are you?" Xavier asked.

"Opportunity."

"For what?"

"Whatever you desire, Xavier," she said. The hint of a smile was there and gone.

"At what price?" he asked.

"Your soul, of course."

Xavier laughed but drew up short as pain rocketed through his chest and fresh blood leaked from the corner of his mouth.

"You laugh. But I offer you a chance to save your brother's soul. The demon has captured it, and now uses the body of your brother as its own—his soul trapped in a vessel, sealed until the demon sees fit to release him. And he will *never* see it as fit."

Visions of the lifetime they'd shared rose unbidden in Xavier's mind; Xander looking up at him as a toddler, following him around like a loyal puppy, thankful just to be in the presence of his older brother. Returning home from new battles as a young soldier, his adolescent brother crying with joy at his safe return, and then begging him for stories from the battlefield; Xavier obliging—talking far into the night.

When he'd come of age, Xavier trained his younger brother in the art of war, and had burst with pride when they'd fought, side-by-side, their first battle together, both returning alive and unhurt. They'd been through many battles together, and the result had always been the same—until tonight. He'd failed Xander. It was almost more than he could bear.

"You can set it right, Xavier. You can save Xander."

The woman appeared wavy in his vision, and he feared it was already too late. Was this the last stage before he left this world? When she reached for his face and placed her thumbs on his eyes and swiped, he realized he'd been crying.

She leaned in close. "Say yes, and it all goes away, Xavier. Say yes to saving your brother's soul. Say yes, and taste eternity."

Xavier drew in his next-to-last breath, and said, "Yes."

She smiled. The last thing Xavier saw before night became day, before he looked on the world with new eyes, and before he became an immortal child of the night, were the gleaming tips of white canines resting on the bottom lip of a beautiful and deadly smile—dripping crimson life into the wounds of his ravaged body.

CHAPTER 22
MOTH MEET FLAME

Joanne couldn't believe her eyes. If she hadn't had her own experience with unexpected magical power, the shock of what she was seeing might have made her pass out. A very well-dressed man landed high above in the tree beneath which she stood.

You don't see that every day, she thought.

He'd have gone unnoticed by her if he hadn't snapped a tiny branch, causing it to graze her left shoulder as it tumbled toward earth. Now the whooshing sounds she'd heard right before Chesrule had attacked her made more sense. For obvious reasons, she'd assumed it was Chesrule making them.

Jo considered her next move. The feeling of time running out was now omnipresent. What it was running out *on*? That was the question. The effects of the pineal potion remained —barely—and she threw caution to the wind. Tightening the knot around the knife in the makeshift sheath, she leapt for the nearest low-hanging branch sturdy enough to support her weight, pulled herself up, and began a stealthy climb toward the top of the tree. She focused on him, reaching ahead for branches using peripheral vision and only looking elsewhere when no other choice presented itself.

He was only a few feet away now, and Jo noticed he sat with his eyes closed. *Is he meditating at the top of a tree?*

In the instant she thought this, his eyes popped open. Jo froze. He looked down at her and smiled.

Damn! That is one sexy man.

"Hello, Joanne," he said, and patted the branch beside him. "Join me. Yes?"

She hesitated. "Momma always told me not to talk to strangers at the tops of trees."

"Well, my name is Xavier. See, now we are not strangers anymore. Yes?"

"I don't think that's how it works," she said.

"No, I suppose you're right," Xavier replied. The corners of his mouth pulled up in a smile. "Would it help if I told you I just left your friend Wanda at the side of the road?"

Green light flared at the edges of Jo's irises as she pictured Wanda bleeding or hurt—or worse, dead. "What do you mean 'left her at the side of the road?'"

He held up both hands. "My apologies, that was poorly worded. I left her, quite alive and well, with her friend, Jasmine, and Armand Moreland."

"That asshole from the Council of the Realms?" Jo asked.

Again, Xavier smiled. "That seems to be the prevailing opinion on him. Yes?"

Jo decided he wasn't a threat and heaved herself onto a branch directly across from him. "Yes. You know about the letter, I'm guessing?"

He nodded and frowned. "Poorly written and completely

unnecessary. Armand is a good man, but seriously lacking in tact."

"That's putting it mildly," said Jo. Then, "Why are you up here?"

"To make sure that you came up here."

Jo wrapped her right arm around the vertical bulk of the tree, placing her left hand on the hilt of the knife. Bright emerald flared once again on the rims of her irises.

"Again, I am no threat to you. And I am almost ready to take my leave of you. I've merely drawn you here to put you in position."

Jo kept her hand on the knife hilt. "Position for what?"

He stood, backing away from Joanne. Again, both palms faced up. Jo noticed he never reached for a branch or a limb to balance himself. "I must leave you now. When the time comes to act, you will know."

Almost faster than her eyes could follow, he leapt from the branch he was on to another several feet away, and then another until he was out of sight. Jo shook her head and whispered, "Now that's some Twilight shit right there." Unaware of how close to the mark she was.

When she was sure he was gone, Jo hopped onto the branch Xavier had vacated, turning herself so she sat exactly where he'd been. She wanted to see the reason he'd picked this spot. Twenty feet away, dim orange light pulsed through a rectangular hole in the fog. As her eyes focused, Jo realized she was within leaping distance of an opening at the top of the bell tower.

∽

"There's that sound again," said Henry.

"What sound?" asked Marla.

"I heard it earlier, right before someone slashed the tires on Byron's truck. Listen."

Marla strained to hear it. Nothing happened for a few moments, then she heard. "An owl, maybe?"

Henry shook his head. "Sounds kinda big to be an owl. But I'm not exactly Mr. Outdoors, so who knows?" He nudged Marla. "Get it? Who knows?"

She stared at him. "Are you for real? Dad jokes?"

Henry shrugged and smiled. "I'm nervous. Just tryna cut the tension. And I have a kid now, so I'm qualified for dad jokes."

"I'm nervous too," Marla conceded.

Despite his misgivings, Henry decided the time to act was now. "Someone closed those doors for a reason. I don't know about you, but I wanna know why. You game?"

Marla swallowed, then nodded. "Let's go. Beats the shit outta waiting for something to happen."

She reached out and took his hand. Henry thought briefly about giving her shit for it, but wisely decided now was not the time. Together, they took their first careful steps toward the mouth of the dragon.

Xavier watched from above.

THE SUV, ironically, wasn't made for this kind of terrain. All three passenger's heads lolled back and forth in time with the dips and rises of the forest.

"We look like three bobble heads just out for a pleasant drive in the forest from hell," said Jazz.

"It's not ideal, that's for sure," said Moreland.

"Can you still see the tire tracks, Armand?" asked Wanda.

In the dark, Wanda couldn't see how pleased he was by her use of his first name. He hoped maybe he'd passed some test and earned her forgiveness.

"Yes. Barely. I hope we're following the right ones," said Moreland.

"Well, do the best you can. There's no need to rush, and we'd probably end up lost if we did," said Wanda.

"There's been three sets of tire tracks, that we know of, coming through here tonight," said Jazz. "What do we do when they split? How do we know which ones to follow? Or if the ones we do follow lead to the church?"

Wanda reached from the back seat and put a hand on Jazz's shoulder. "When the time is right, we'll know, sweetie."

Jazz looked back. A sly smile crossed her face. "You know something we don't?"

Wanda shrugged, "Just a feeling. It always seems—"

Before she could finish, orange light erupted to their right, silhouetting the trees through the mist, making them appear as angry guardians of a forbidden land. Moreland stopped the truck, and they watched as the orange corona first grew in size, then shrunk and glowed steadily.

"Armand? I think you can forget about the tire tracks," said Wanda.

Moreland nodded. Without a word, he turned the SUV toward the fire.

∼

Penny, at Byron's impatient insistence, had been following the fading guidance of the pineal potion for a while when she realized it was no longer working. Archie and Byron trailed behind her and kept silent, fearful of breaking her concentration. When she stopped to look around, they knew it might mean trouble.

"What's the matter, Pen?" asked Archie.

Penny held up her hand, turned around a few more times, then shook her head. "I'm not feeling it anymore."

"You sure, baby?" asked Byron.

She closed her eyes, took a deep breath, and swiveled her head around. When she'd finished, her shoulders slumped in defeat. "It's gone."

"Maybe we should head back to my trailer. One of us could astral travel to the place. It might be the only way—"

Archie never finished his sentence as orange light lit the mist like the colored lights of a rock concert. Byron broke into a run, Penny on his heels. Archie stared at the orange light for several seconds, mesmerized. When he realized he was alone, he took off after them.

Even in the mist coating the forest floor, there was enough light to see Henry approaching. He had someone with him. Excitement lit her up when she saw the height, build, and even the hair color. It was Wanda. It had to be. Who else would be with Henry, out in this forest, coming for her and the others in this place?

Mondra watched them from the opening at the top of the bell tower, smiling as she performed the spell, setting the grass surrounding the entire perimeter of the church ablaze. She'd been waiting for the next wave to show up. After the disappointment of Joanne's escape, and with Mercy safely within the walls of the church, the rest of the League of the Moon were a threat. The moment was close! She wouldn't risk another episode like the one in Wanda's shop. They needed to die. They deserved to die. Two would die right now.

Closing her eyes, she smiled as the last image of Henry and Wanda played on a loop in her mind; The shocked look. The hands flying up instinctively to protect their faces, and then both of them swallowed by the wall of flame. It thrilled her to the point of ecstasy. If she hadn't had so much to do, she would have thrown Aaron to the ground and screwed him until he broke.

CHAPTER 23
TRIAL BY FIRE

This is how I die, Henry thought, as his hands flew up to protect his face from the flames. He'd always heard people say your life flashes before your eyes in the moments before your own death. But that didn't happen. Instead, he saw flashes of all the good times he'd had with Joanne. Though their time together in this lifetime had been short, the moments had been deep. Flashes of laughter, lovemaking, tears, joy, happiness, sorrow—too many to count—marched by in an odd and impossible mix of rapid slowness. Henry bore witness to something most never experience on this side of life; time does not actually exist. There is *only* the present.

You *can't* change the past, though you can relive it. You *can* change the future, but only by creating something different in the here and now. The only *true* existence is in the moment. Every moment of life is full of potential outcomes; choices made in the present are history in the making. And as those choices and experiences stack one atop the other, the illusion of time takes hold. Even when he'd travelled the astral plane to the in—between and then back to the year 1692, it happened in *his* present. And though in astral form when he'd been there, the things needed to kill the demon remained where they'd always been—the present day.

All of this ran through his mind in an instant; which was exactly how long it took to realize, though he stood amid the flames, neither he nor Marla burned. Flames never touched them, though steam rose in tired puffs at their feet. Henry lowered his hands from his face and saw why.

A man stood before him. He was tall, a couple of inches taller than himself, with long dark hair that disappeared in a shiny black flood down his back. The guy was in good shape, Henry thought, and then wondered why in the world he was thinking about the man's appearance as he stood in the middle of an inferno.

Without taking his eyes from the black irises staring back at him, Henry reached for Marla. She was still covering her face, trying to protect it from the flames. With his left hand, he gently pushed down on her arms. Marla instinctively fought him, but came to realize quickly that if Henry could push her arms down, the danger, *somehow*, must have passed.

She blinked her eyes several times until she trusted opening them fully wouldn't boil them in their sockets. She turned to face Henry. When she did, she saw he wasn't looking at her at all, only straight ahead. Marla followed Henry's gaze, and her mouth fell open in surprise.

"Eddie?"

Byron was the first to break through the ring of shrubs surrounding the courtyard at the front of the church. Though the flames burned bright enough to hurt his eyes, he couldn't look away. Two figures; a tall man that looked a lot like Henry, and a short woman he knew could only be Marla, stood in the middle of the raging inferno. What he expected to see—both of them writhing in pain as the fire cooked them alive. And what he was witnessing instead—both of them standing alive and well in the middle of a bright-blue, sparkling orb—rendered him speechless.

There was nothing he could do for them. So he stood and watched in awe, waiting for Penny and Archie to catch up and assure him he wasn't losing his mind.

Penny ran as fast as she could but was still a good twenty yards behind him, holding her side from the stitch of pain her overtaxed lungs doled out. Archie had given up running after the first few minutes and settled for power walking the rest of the way. Astral travel was one thing. Running on the earth plane was not his jam.

When Penny reached the shrubs, she turned to look for Archie. After a few seconds, he materialized from the mist, and she waved him forward impatiently. Together, they made their way to Byron's side.

Penny put her hand on Byron's shoulder and leaned over to catch her breath, then looked up at him. Byron barely acknowledged her. She was about to say something when he held up his left hand like he was directing traffic. He lowered it and pointed at the spot where Henry and Marla stood, talking to a man in the middle of an inferno. Penny and Archie were speechless.

After a time, the trio in the bubble of sparkling blue light finished talking, and the tall man with the long black hair beckoned them forward. Byron, Penny, and Archie watched as Henry and Marla followed the man to the front doors of the church and walked inside. When the doors closed, the protective blue barrier winked out. The fire raged on, with no signs of slowing.

WANDA'S EYES WERE CLOSED. Her head bounced from side to side as the SUV made progress through the forest. Though it was a four-wheel-drive vehicle, it was made for city driving and snowy conditions. Moreland had all he could do to keep the steering wheel from snapping his arms off as he battled the uneven terrain and steered around tree after tree. But the orange inferno got steadily closer, and Wanda's connection with the vampire improved by the second.

Using this power was something she never imagined herself doing. She'd wrestled with her conscience, almost daily, about even *allowing* herself use of this power. On more than one occasion, she'd considered using a spell to remove it. To make sure she was never tempted to recover the power, she called Jazz and told her what she was thinking of doing. Wanda knew Jazz could come up with something to make her forget she'd ever had it. Jazz had talked her out of it...

"—but I don't know if I can trust myself with it, honey," she'd said.

Jazz rolled her eyes. "If there's anyone in the world who can handle that kind of power, it's you."

Wanda bit her thumbnail. "I don't know. I don't think this is something anyone should be able to do."

"Weren't you the one who told me to trust your intuition? No matter what?" Jazz asked.

"Yeah, but—"

"Well, I'm telling you now, I have a feeling you're gonna need to use it. And I got a feeling that time is in the not-too-distant future."

That surprised Wanda. "What makes you say that?"

"You know the answer to that already."

With her eyes still closed, Wanda smiled. She *had* known the answer. For Wanda to have called Jazz, after not seeing or talking to her for longer than she cared to admit, was *the* sign. They'd been good friends for longer than Henry had been alive. For some reason, they were only drawn together when they needed each other the most. Like now. And like the time when Henry was just a boy, and Jazz had shown up and helped her defeat Inanis and Chesrule. So when Wanda had called her, asked her advice, and then gotten the answer she *didn't* want to hear, it was all the confirmation she'd needed.

Through Xavier's eyes, she saw the attempt on Henry's and Marla's lives, and how he'd saved them. Jazz had made it all possible by the way she'd handled the vampires. It was further proof trusting in Jazz had been a good idea.

When Wanda finally opened her eyes, Jazz was looking back at her, smiling. "I told you."

Wanda tilted her head down, an appreciative smile of concession crossed her face. Orange firelight lit tears of gratitude in her bright blue eyes. "You did, sweetie."

Moreland stopped the SUV at the back of the church, behind the bell tower and roughly twenty yards from the fire's edge.

"What now?" he asked.

Jazz pulled two identical disk-shaped items from her satchel. The gypsy held them up for Moreland to see. The silver etchings gleamed bright orange in the firelight's reflection. Moreland saw the names of angels etched along the outer rings of each disk. Michael. Gabriel. Tzafqiel. Tzadkiel. Samael. Raphael. Haniel. Names he loved and respected.

"What are you going to do with those?" asked Moreland.

"Gonna catch us some demons!" said Jazz.

CHAPTER 24
REUNION AND SACRIFICE

Mercy crept slowly up the bell tower's winding staircase, candleholder in hand. The sparse light was just enough to see a foot or two in front of her—nothing more. The darkness had an unnatural quality to it. It was thicker somehow—more dense. As she conquered each step in front of her, cobwebs moved up and away from the heat of the candle's flame. Each one like the drawing of a curtain in a TV game show from hell where the prize behind it was black nothingness every time.

After what seemed like forever, she reached the top of the staircase. A smaller version of the rotted wooden doors at the church's entrance stood cracked open. The smell of burning wood tickled her nose, and a stronger smell—something akin to sulfur and rotting eggs—wriggled like a snake just underneath. When she gently nudged the door forward, the rotting smell enveloped her, permeating the darkness surrounding the candle's impotent glow. A frigid hand clamped around the arm holding the candle, and the holder tumbled from her hand. By some perverse miracle, it landed flat on the floor below, between Mercy and Chesrule. In the cone of light cast upward from the floor, Mercy looked into eyes that were part of a dark mass she couldn't really call a face.

Instinct kicked in, and Mercy struggled to escape. The demon hissed laughter, pulling her forward and wrapping itself around her in a reverse bear hug. "Mercy the lightbringer," it whispered into her left ear. "We've been waiting for you."

Numbing cold radiated from the being, and the smell of rot and decay sank into every pore of Mercy's skin. Her head spun with fear, and her body felt heavy and weak. Something cold, wet, and barbed dragged across her left cheek. When she realized the demon had licked her, was *tasting* her, it was more than her mind could handle. Mercy fainted.

∼

"You recognize me. Yes?" asked Xavier.

"Of course I do, Eddie. But what are you doing here?"

"Don't you mean 'Stinky Eddie?'" the vampire asked.

Marla shuffled her feet. "Yeah. Sorry about that. It was mean, but we were kids then..."

Xavier waved it off. "This is something I know. It helped to be seen that way in those times. I believe the police call it 'being undercover?' Yes?"

Marla nodded. "But what are you doing here now? And how did you do what you did?" Marla pointed to the entrance. "Out there?"

"I protect the creatures of Salem. Witches, warlocks, gypsies, and others. The night you saw me from your bedroom window, I was there to protect you, Marla. The dog was simply in the alley that night, starving and close to death. I revived him."

"Protect me from what?" asked Marla.

Xavier looked back toward the double doors. Steam puffed in uneven spurts from underneath their ragged edges.

Marla followed his gaze. "The fire?"

"Yes."

Marla tilted her head in confusion. "I don't get it. You said you were there to protect me that night which, if I had to guess, was thirty-five to forty years ago. What's that got to do with tonight?"

"Everything," said Henry. He thought about the visions from the fire. "He can see the future. That's how you saved us, isn't it? You knew that fire was going to happen."

Xavier raised a hand and tilted it back and forth. "It's not as simple as that. But you are close, Henry. If Marla were a normal person instead of one with magical power, I would have seen nothing. But she *has* magic. Powerful magic. When I saw her that night, flames engulfed her. They leaked from the edges of her body. When I see a thing like that, it is a warning from the future. But when and where it will happen is not, at the time of the vision, entirely known."

Marla's eyebrows raised. "That's an awful long time to follow someone around, waiting for that one day."

"Again, there is much more to it than that. Perhaps there will be a time when I can explain it to you more fully. But for now, you must remain in this room. The fire will rage until the witch meets her destiny."

With that, the vampire disappeared. Henry and Marla twirled around, looking in all directions at once. Marla caught the movement of one door at the front of the church just before it closed on the fire outside.

"Where'd he go?" asked Henry.

"I can't be sure, but I think he went out the front door."

"*Fast* moving fucker, ain't he?"

"Yeah," said Marla, lost in thought.

"What is it, boss lady?"

"He said the fire will end when 'the witch meets her destiny.' I was just wondering who he meant."

"My guess would be Mondra, since she's the one who started the fire," he said and shrugged.

"True. But if that's the case, why doesn't he just kill her? I'm pretty sure he could if he wanted to."

It was a good point, and one Henry had no answer for. It made him nervous all over again. This place was now crawling with witches, both inside and out. If the vampire *hadn't* meant the Red Witch, then someone he loved was in danger. No matter what the vampire wanted, he wasn't about to sit on his hands and wait for shit to happen.

He took a deep breath, relaxing his mind so he could think straight. Panic was the enemy now. Though his revelation about the nature of time had affected him profoundly, he knew it only applied to existence as a whole. Time was running out on his options in the physical world and the here and now.

Orange light filtered through the filthy windows on either side of the hexagonal room. Had there not been a fire glowing through them, he would have missed the fragment of black cloth peeking out from one side of the altar.

Henry gave Marla's shirtsleeve a tug and beckoned her to follow. They climbed the two steps at the altar's front and circled around its left side. On the floor before him, Henry saw the tattered remains of the hoodie he'd given Jo last Christmas. He picked it up and held the pieces out in front of him. The hoodie was split down the middle and the arms had been sliced off.

"Marla. Could you put your phone's light on this?"

Marla did as asked. It was hard to tell if the dampness on the black cloth was blood in the sparse light, but Henry removed doubt when he swiped the hood with his fingers, then held them up to the light. Dark red, partially coagulated blood smeared them. Dazed, he lowered his hands and wiped them on his jeans.

"I'm sure she's alright, Henry. Jo's tough."

Henry didn't answer. He looked around the room, his eyes falling on the door leading up to the bell tower. Without a word, he strode to the door, seized the knob, and flung it open. The rotted door smashed the corner of a marble shelf running along the back of the altar and splintered along its left side. Henry took one step up and walked into the darkness.

IN A SCENE eerily similar to the one that happened less than thirty minutes earlier, Xavier and Moreland stood at the front of the SUV. Wanda and Jazz sat on the front bumper. This time, the lights were off and the engine silent. Fire roared, low and steady, behind them.

"What are you up to, Xavier?" asked Wanda.

"What do you mean?"

"Just what I asked. I want to know why you're moving us around like chess pieces. I'm not the sharpest tool in the shed, but I can see what's happening. And since everyone in my life that matters is involved, I have a right to know. So, spill it!"

Moreland gave him a warning look. He ignored it completely.

"When I say I'm sworn to protect the magical ones of Salem, do you believe that, Miss Heinze?" asked Xavier.

"I don't know whether or not to believe it. I saw you save Henry and Marla, so you've got a sliver of credibility with me as of now. But I know there's something you're not telling us, obviously. The thing I don't understand is—why?"

"I simply cannot do that yet. If I told you all I know, you'd try to stop me. You would be perfectly within your right, and it would *seem* you are doing the right thing. If I were in your shoes, I would feel the same. But if I allow you to do as you please, you will regret it. And you will never forgive me—or yourself—for interfering. I beg you trust me. And that is all I can ask. Remember, I trusted you enough to show you what happened on my voyage to this land. Which, I now realize, could have been a mistake on my part."

"Then why show what happened on the boat at all?" asked Wanda.

"To prove to you I have a stake in events here tonight. I'm not merely manipulating things."

Wanda said nothing and waited with an expectant look on her face.

"If you close your eyes and think about my visions in the tree, you'll understand," said Xavier. He saw her surprise and smiled. "I know you were watching. Now that I'm aware, I can feel it."

Wanda did as he asked. In her mind's eye, she saw Inanis poised over the soldier on the battlefield. Without context, she'd assumed it was Xavier. Then she realized that made no sense—because her visions were through *Xavier's* eyes.

"It was your brother he possessed! The man who was trapped in the flask!"

"Yes, Miss Heinze. And the demon must pay."

"How?"

Xavier considered how much he could tell her. It wasn't a lot. But the cost, if they ever knew beforehand, would be unacceptable.

What was about to happen tonight was *going* to happen, whether or not he intervened. Someone had to die. And the unfortunate task of arranging things so the right person died had fallen to him. So he said the only thing he could.

"A sacrifice, Miss Heinze."

CHAPTER 25
SNAKES

Joanne watched the fire as it raged below her. Instinct told her to get the hell out of the tree, and right now! She was about to do just that when something stopped her cold. Where was the smoke? A fire that big couldn't possibly be burning below her and not yield smoke. Yet it didn't. Why?

There was only one explanation; the fire wasn't real. It was real in the sense that if you stuck your hand in it, it would burn. But that was the only *real* thing about it.

The Red Witch was controlling this fire. The flames were meant to keep light magic, and those who wielded it, out of the church. If it were yielding the type of smoke a blaze of its size *should* be, it would drive *all* the inhabitants of the church outside. *That* wouldn't quite fit into Mondra's plans.

Jo was starting to understand the vampire's logic. Having her up here was a strategic move on his part. Though she didn't appreciate being manipulated, she had to give the devil his due. The pale fucker was one step ahead of Mondra at every turn. That was all well and good, but she still couldn't figure out what his end game was.

As she looked back up from the fire and through the opening in the bell tower, she got at least part of her answer.

Chesrule carried Mercy into the room and laid her next to the dying interior fire. Jo almost leapt from the tree and into the room when two more people emerged from the gloom, stopping her mid-leap. Mondra stood over Mercy, and Aaron Hendricks was by her side. Suddenly, Jo didn't like her odds.

She crept as far along the limb as she could, straining to hear what was about to be said. When the thick limb bent under her weight, she slowed and crouched, turning her left ear toward the opening.

The first voice Jo heard was the unmistakable rasp of the demon. "What comes next?"

"We prepare her for the ritual," said Mondra. "My baby is coming home."

Byron, Penny, and Archie couldn't do anything to help Henry and Marla. The fire was too intense, and the tall man who'd led them through it was nowhere to be found. The cop in him put Byron in motion, and he walked the perimeter of the fire, looking for a way in. Penny and Archie silently followed.

The three of them had broken to the right of the church's entrance, walking and observing. Hoping against hope to find a way in. Byron peeled his eyes away for a moment to check the footing ahead of him when he noticed a glint of something through the trees.

For the second time that night, someone walked into his backside. It was Penny.

"What is it By?" she asked.

Byron pointed toward the woods. "You see that there?"

Penny followed the line of his finger. "Yes. What is it?"

"It looks like glass. But it's up off the ground."

"It's a headlight," said Archie.

"Who the hell *else* is out here tonight?" Byron wondered aloud.

Penny started for the line of trees. "Only one way to find out."

The mystery was short-lived. As she drew closer, Penny heard the familiar voice of Wanda Heinze. As she broke through the last of the trees, she said, "You know, we end up meeting in the weirdest places, witch."

Wanda's eyes bugged in surprise, then grew warm with recognition. "Penny! Thank God you're alright!"

"No thanks to my wandering brother," said Penny.

Byron appeared behind Penny, followed by Archie. Wanda got up from the SUV's bumper, ran over to him, and gave him a fierce hug. "I was so worried about you, Arch!"

His friend's loving embrace moved Archie, and he hugged her back just as hard. When they separated, Wanda punched him in the shoulder.

"Ouch! I thought you were happy to see me!"

Wanda smiled. "I am, you big shithead. But you had us all worried half to death when we couldn't reach you by phone."

Archie winced an apology at her. "I'm sorry. Really. But I didn't want anyone following me out here. Mondra has caused enough heartache already. I didn't want anyone else in harm's way. I thought I could handle it on my own."

"So you—Mr. 'Answer on the First Ring'—thought none of us would find that odd and *not* come looking for you?" asked Wanda.

Archie gave her a sheepish grin. "I guess I didn't think it all the way through."

Wanda asked, "So what made you come all the way out here by yourself?"

Archie gave her a quizzical look. "You don't know?"

"I have an idea that it might have come from a dream. Every one of us has dreamed about this place. And it compelled each of us to come here and defend someone we love. Isn't that what brought you here, Arch?"

"Yes, but it's much more than that."

Archie told them what he'd seen in his visions, from the time they'd started and right up to the one he'd been having when Penny had pounded on the trailer's wall.

"So you don't know who ends up bleeding on the floor at the end of these visions?" asked Wanda.

Archie shook his head. "No. If I had to guess, I think it's Mercy. It makes sense, given Mondra's obsession with capturing her soul."

Byron broke in. "Well, as of now, there are four possibilities: Mercy, Joanne, Henry, and Marla."

"Henry and Marla? You've seen them?" asked Wanda.

"Not only did I see them, I watched them walk through that fire with some tall, freaky looking guy. Just a little while ago. They're in the church right now. As to the why of it?" Byron shrugged. "That remains to be seen."

Wanda frowned and pointed at Moreland. "That's this guy's vampire friend. It seems Xavier—that's his friend's name—is up to all kinds of wonderful and devious shit. He's the one who slashed your tires, by the way."

Byron shot Moreland a ball-shriveling look. "That motherfucker!"

Penny saved Moreland's ass by asking, "Has anyone seen Jo? We split up after the Jeep crashed in the forest and I haven't been able to contact her."

The worried silence of all the others was the only answer Penny would get—until her phone chirped. She'd turned it on as they'd left the front of the church, hoping against hope to hear from Jo. She pulled it from her pocket, clicked the side button to illuminate the screen, and saw the text message from Joanne. She read it aloud to everyone. "Look up!"

They all did.

A small square of light shone down from the tree. From high above, Jo waved the phone back and forth a few times.

Wanda smiled and said, "Now how the hell did she get up there?"

Byron said, "Trust me when I tell you, it wasn't a problem."

Immediately, he thought of Jo climbing the telephone pole back in Salem a few short weeks ago. She'd been in a rage, defending her child from a faceless hooded entity, and had scaled a telephone pole and leapt onto the roof of an adjacent building to tear the hoodie a new asshole. He'd gotten away, at least temporarily, but the memory of what Jo had done was scorched in his mind forever.

Looking up at Jo now, Byron felt much more confident things would work out. This gave way to a question in his mind. He put it to the others. "Do you think the vampire put her up there?"

"Is water wet?" asked Wanda. "He's blocking me. I'd been watching him through his own eyes, but now that he knows, it's much harder. I knew Jo was safe, but I couldn't figure out where she was. All the trees kinda look the same, no matter whose eyes you're looking through."

Penny looked down at her phone again as it buzzed in her hand. She relayed another text from Jo. "Mercy at top of tower. Ches, Mon, and AH have her."

Wanda put a hand to her mouth. "Oh my God."

Archie hung his head. "I knew it."

Byron was counting bad guys in his head. Joanne had accounted for three out of four in her text. Someone was missing. "Where is Inanis?"

The answer came from behind him. He knew the voice well. "I'm back here, boss," said the demon through Raul Martinez.

Jazz knew all about the demon and his possession of Raul. While it pointed a gun at Byron, Jazz slowly slipped her hand into the satchel at her left side, feeling around for the seal of Solomon. In her mind, she sent a message to Wanda. When Jazz saw Wanda's head tilt ever so slightly, she knew it was received.

Inanis grinned wickedly through Raul's face, and his dark crimson eyes glowed with malicious glee.

It always amazed Wanda how the possessed, though their outer features remained the same, looked nothing like themselves when a foreign entity controlled everything that made them who they were. Inside, she was terrified. Not for herself; she'd dealt with a multitude of entities forcing their way into the bodies of the innocent, but for the souls trapped inside, hiding to remain safe—and sane. It pissed her off. It was time to be rid of this bastard once and for all.

"What kind of demon has to hold people at gunpoint? Are you really that weak?" chided Wanda.

Inanis flinched at her words, then pointed the gun in her direction. She was relieved the gun was off of Byron.

"I should pull the trigger and silence you forever, old woman."

Wanda gave him an amused smile. "Go ahead. We both know that's a temporary solution. I'll hunt your pathetic ass until the sun burns out."

Raul's face contorted with rage, the eyes inside glowed an even brighter red. The demon went to pull the trigger, not caring about the witch's return in her next incarnation to hunt him down. Nothing happened. Inanis tried again. The gun would not fire. The trigger wouldn't move.

Byron moved quickly, realizing what was happening. He seized the gun by the barrel with his right hand, then chopped down hard on Raul's wrist with his left. The gun came away easily.

Jazz wasted no time. In one fluid and lighting quick motion, she pulled the Seal of Solomon from her bag and tossed it at the demon's feet. Penny knew exactly what was happening and shouted, "Grab him!"

To everyone's surprise, Moreland was the first to react. With shocking speed, Armand Moreland slid behind Inanis and sweep-kicked the demon's legs out from under him. Raul hung briefly in mid-air, then came crashing down on his back—the wind knocked out of him. Moreland pounced on Raul's prone body, flipped him over, and in one savage move slammed the demon's face into the Seal of Solomon. Raul spasmed like he'd grabbed a downed power line, and the form of the demon slipped from his body. When Jazz saw this, she got on both knees next to Moreland and said, "Roll him away! The trap has him!"

Moreland and Jazz pushed with all their might, rolling

Raul across the grass until he was well away from the reach of Inanis. Once they were sure he was free of trouble, they rose and joined their circle of friends to watch as Inanis fought with everything he had to escape the trap.

"I'm going to kill every last fucking one of you!" he screamed.

Half of his essence was already claimed by the seal.

As it slowly consumed him, Wanda, in a calm and amused voice, asked Byron, "Do you remember the snakes?"

Byron looked at her, confused. "Snakes?"

"Yeah," said Wanda. "Those little black cylinder shaped thingies. We used to get them when we were kids. You'd light them on fire and they'd grow and curl out this long snake made of ash. Sometimes we'd light a bunch of them up at the same time. It looked like Medusa's head was growing out of the street right in front of us. So much fun."

Byron was smiling now. He snapped his fingers and said, "I *do* remember those! And we used to do the exact same thing!"

"Doesn't he remind you of those? Only in reverse?" asked Wanda as she pointed at the incredible shrinking demon.

Byron laughed. "He does! He's even the same color!"

"Fuck you, cop! When I return, I'm going to kill you, your wife, your children, and your grandchildren!"

Byron walked toward the demon. Only its head and shoulders remained.

Byron leaned down, getting good and close, and said, "Do you really think I'm scared of a demon who's too fucking stupid to flick the safety off before trying to use his gun?"

Inanis roared in frustration.

And then he was gone.

CHAPTER 26
TEXTING IN THE TREES

Jo watched with amazement the action taking place forty feet below. Raul had them at gunpoint and, from what she barely heard, Wanda was taunting the man with the gun. This didn't surprise Jo; Wanda had balls the size of grapefruits. What *surprised* Jo was when the gun swung in Wanda's direction, it never ended up fired.

Shit got good from there. Byron moved quickly, disarming Raul, and then the chubby guy with the nice clothes moved in a way that shocked her. He pulled some Kung-fu shit and had Raul on his back in seconds. When it was all over, she watched as Jazz calmly walked over and picked something up from the area Raul had been seconds before, wondering what it was. She texted the question to Penny.

Penny felt the buzz of the phone in her pocket, pulled it out, and read Jo's question.

"Jo wants to know what just happened."

As Penny typed her response, an idea struck Byron.

"Penny. Ask Jo if the other demon is still up there in the bell tower."

Penny typed out a brief recap of events, followed by Byron's question. When she hit send, everyone looked up at Joanne.

"What are you thinking, Byron?" asked Wanda.

Byron, his eyes still skyward, said, "Let's see what she says."

The phone buzzed in Penny's hand. "He is."

"Tell her I'm gonna bring her something," said Byron. "Jazz, do you have another one of those demon trap things?"

Jazz reached in her bag, pulling out a second Seal of Solomon, and held it up. "Don't leave home without them."

Byron reached out for it, but Moreland put a hand on his arm. "I can get it to her faster, Chief Miller."

Byron looked Moreland over from head to toe, unimpressed. Regardless of the entire leg sweep business, some underhanded shit had gone down tonight. He didn't trust him. "I think I can handle it."

"I've no doubt you can. But please trust me when I tell you, I'll save us valuable time if you let *me* handle it."

Byron knew Moreland was right about time being precious now. He didn't want to waste it arguing; threats were more effective. "If you fuck us over, I promise you you'll wish your father had pulled out."

Moreland's eyes bugged at the crude threat, and simply nodded because he was at a loss for words.

Jazz quickly wiped the smile holding back the laughter from her face when Moreland turned to her. Though a million hilarious quips ran through her mind, she took the safest route and said nothing. The guy *did* do a good job helping her with the demon. She handed him the medallion.

Armand Moreland turned to the tree holding Jo on a branch forty feet above. He took a deep breath, deposited the Seal of Solomon in the left pocket of his suit coat, and in less than thirty seconds made believers of the people he'd left on the forest floor.

They watched in awe as Moreland leapt from the ground, grabbed hold of the lowest branch, vaulted himself upward, and bounced with effortless grace from one limb to the next. Branches and leaves scarcely shook as his arms and legs moved with machine-like precision, bounding from one point to the next.

"Holy fucking shit!" whispered Byron. "Is he a vampire, too?"

Jazz was in just as much shock as the rest of them, but somehow found her voice. "Old Jeevesy is full of surprises tonight. It looks like he might be," she said as she leveled her eyes at Byron. "But there *are* other options."

Byron shook his head from side to side, "Don't tell me. At least not tonight. Finding out vampires exist is about all I can swallow right now."

He received sympathetic nods from everyone.

Jo watched in awe as the asshole who'd written the letter made quick work of the tree. He settled on the limb across from her.

"You guys from the Council of Assholes sure know how to make an entrance," Jo said.

Moreland extended an arm, handing Jo the Seal of Solomon. The look on his face told Jo he was tiring of all the potshots. "I know what you and your coven think of us, but haven't we all but proven tonight that we are on your side?"

Jo tilted her head from side to side. "More or less, but the night's in diapers. I'm what you'd call a 'hard grader.' I'd give you both a C-plus so far. Keep it up and I'll give you one of the gold stars I give my hubby!"

Moreland shook his head with disapproval, but couldn't keep a slight smile from showing. He liked this witch, and felt worse about the letter than he did at the beginning of the night. She *had* only been trying to protect her child. He promised himself he would formally apologize to her and her coven when all this was over. And maybe he'd go a bit further, but that would have to wait.

The rest of the night would go a long way toward how things would unfold afterward, but telling this witch what he was thinking at the moment would only put his balls in jeopardy—and he liked them just fine where they were, thank you very much.

"So, what am I supposed to do with this thing?" asked Jo.

"It's the Seal of Solomon. A demon trap. You need to get it near enough to the demon to trap him in it."

Jo was shaking her head. "Mercy is my primary concern. I don't give a flying fuck about that pervert from hell."

"I'm just the messenger," said Moreland.

"Not anymore. After what I've seen you do in the last fifteen minutes, consider yourself drafted. You're going to trap the demon. I'm going to save Mercy from Mommy Dearest. You pickin' up what I'm puttin' down, GQ?"

Moreland stared at her, speechless. Jo tilted her head forward, eyebrows raised. An answer was expected.

He closed his eyes and pinched the bridge of his nose. "Fine."

"That's a good little tyrant," Jo cracked. "I need you to lead him away from them. After seeing how fast you got up this tree, that shouldn't be too hard. You ready?" Jo asked, handing the medallion back to him.

Moreland sighed, "As I'll ever be."

Inside, he was regretting volunteering to deliver the Seal of Solomon to Joanne.

As if Jo were reading his mind, she said, "Some things are just meant to be, GQ."

HENRY AND MARLA crept up the last few stairs leading to the top of the bell tower. Muted voices floated toward them in the darkness. At the bottom of the stairs, rage had fueled Henry upon seeing the tattered remains of Jo's hoodie. Now, at the top, he had to fight the urge to just barge in and start kicking ass. Marla sensed the tension, and whispered, "Take a deep breath, Henry. We don't know what's on the other side of that door."

Henry wisely conceded the point. "Okay," he whispered back.

After a few moments, his anger tamped down, he said, "I'm going to open the door just a crack. I need to see the layout of the room. Maybe I can figure something out. They sound far enough away. It should be safe."

"Sounds like a plan. Just be careful. These doors are old and probably creak like a mother."

"Shit. Yeah, good point," said Henry.

He twisted the knob, thankful it made no sound, then flattened his left hand against the door and pushed it slightly forward. It creaked for a fraction of a second, then whispered open the rest of the way. Henry sent silent thanks to his Higher power.

Once there was a large enough opening, Henry slipped his head between the door and its frame and peered into the gloom. He waited a moment for his eyes to adjust. When they did, he was relieved to find the room empty.

It was an entrance hallway. Rusty tools covered in dust and forgotten by time hung on the wall to his left. He assumed the tools were for maintaining the bell. To his right, an empty wooden bench sat beneath a coat rack. Wood pegs jutted out from a board running the length of the room. Dust covered the unused pegs, and two coats hung next to each other at the end closest to the next room; they were the only sign of fresh life in the forgotten space.

The door at the end of the hall stood open. Soft, undulating firelight leaked through the opening and dust from the hallway floated through the shaft of light, twinkling like stars and then disappearing into the surrounding darkness. Henry and Marla inched closer. The voices on the other side of the door grew louder. Jo's was not among them, and an ember of panic formed in Henry's belly.

"I don't hear Jo," Henry whispered to Marla.

Marla heard the worry in his voice and knew it was only a matter of moments before he did something rash. She put a hand on his arm to calm him. "We don't even know if she's in there, Henry. We know nothing about what's behind that door. If you fly in there now, there's no telling what could happen."

"I really don't give a shit. I —"

She held up a hand. "Your phone. Do you still have it?"

Henry tilted his head, then reached for his back pocket. He'd completely forgotten about it, and also forgotten to shut it off before he'd started up the stairs. Thankfully, it had remained silent. Without delay, he turned the sound all the way off and dimmed the screen.

Marla did the same with her phone, then said, "Try sending her a text. It can't hurt. Right?"

He thought about it. But only for a second. If she was in danger, or captured, or worse, the only thing that would happen would be his text going unanswered. The only way he'd receive a reply was if she could safely do so. He tapped out, "Where are you?" To his surprise, the answer came back almost instantly.

Jo: *In a tree. Near top of BT.*

Henry: *WTF? How?*

Jo: *Long story. NIRN.*

Marla asked, "NIRN?"

Henry answered her without looking up from the phone and typing away. "Not important right now."

Marla just shook her head. She was good with a phone and texting, but some of the shorthand still eluded her.

Henry: *What do u c?*

Jo: *Mondra, Mercy, Ches. Aaron.*

Henry: *No Inanis?*

Jo: *Captured. Wanda and gang right below me.*

Henry: *Wow! Nice.*

Jo: *The letr guy is OTW in there. Going 4 ches. Has trap. Where R U?*

Henry: *In BT. Top Fl.*

Jo: *Really? Tell me later. They are moving. B rdy!*

Henry: *K. Love u*

Jo: *Lu2*

Henry pocketed the phone, grabbed Marla's face, and planted a kiss on her cheek.

"What was that for?" asked Marla.

"For thinking of the phone, you fucking genius!" His smile faded. "Now let's be ready."

CHAPTER 27
A VISION REALIZED

Armand Moreland made it into the bell tower undetected. Instead of entering through the opening in front of Joanne, he used his innate agility to maneuver further up the tree, step lightly across the roof, and then drop to the ledge ringing the outside of the tower. All done in almost complete silence.

The opening he found was sealed by shutters. To Moreland, they appeared whitish-grey in the sparse moonlight. Chipped and peeling paint revealed the natural wood beneath. He thought to himself this must have been a beautiful church at one time, and it angered him to know demons freely roamed its grounds—something unthinkable in the not-too-distant past. Faith and light had departed this structure long ago.

He tuned his supernatural hearing to pick up on the words of the demon, the Red Witch, and their accomplice, Hendricks.

"Put her down on the floor, inside the pentacle," said Mondra.

Moreland pictured the room, assuming they would lay Mercy at its center, and the demon would do the witch's bidding. If he could pinpoint the demon's location, things might unfold as he hoped.

He heard Mercy struggle, and then a muffled scream, followed by a loud thump.

"You *must* let me play with her when this is finished," the demon hissed.

"You can do whatever you want with her when this is done," said Mondra. "I don't think she'll be to into it, considering what will take her place. But I'm pretty sure that doesn't matter to you, anyway."

"It does not," said Chesrule.

Another muffled scream from Mercy.

They have her gagged and bound, he thought. He was well aware of the Red Witch's intentions to consume Mercy's soul and incorporate it into herself—it made her a modern day wendigo, or soul-eater, as they were called today. Something he'd dealt with in the past. None of them had been a witch, however. And this witch was powerful. He shuddered at what she'd become if he and the League of the Moon failed tonight.

With that in mind, Armand Moreland inched the weathered shutters open, leapt to the sill, and lowered himself into the bell tower. The Seal of Solomon sat in his suit coat pocket, its weight pulling down one side. It was vibrating. He put his hand in his pocket, closing it around the medallion and feeling comforted by the *aliveness* of the piece; as if it sensed the demon's closeness and was eager to consume it. If all went well, it would get its wish.

"Aaron, I need you to lie down on the floor next to Mercy. Just outside the pentacle, if you please," said Mondra.

"What?!" said Hendricks. To Moreland, he sounded both startled, and terrified.

"It's nothing to worry about, sweetheart. I just need to use you as a bridge, in case things go sideways. We don't need another scene like what happened at Wanda's," said Mondra.

Aaron didn't move. Mondra was getting impatient and angry. "How's your mother doing these days, Aaron?"

Aaron said, "She's fine. Why?"

Mondra shrugged, "Oh, you know... the elderly—fine one minute, the next—" she trailed off.

Mondra had healed Aaron's mom of several infirmities. To look at her now, an outsider would never suspect she was in her late fifties and had overcome Parkinson's disease. Not one iota of a tremor had resurfaced since the time Mondra had done her thing and healed his mother.

Aaron got the message. He knelt on the floor next to Mercy, his back toward Mondra, and mouthed the word 'sorry' to her. Mercy squinted at him and he could tell, even through her mask-covered face, his apology fell short of acceptance.

Chesrule stood a few feet behind the prone forms of Mercy and Aaron, and directly across from Mondra. The Red Witch was about to begin the ceremony when she noticed the demon's head tilt to one side. "What is it?" she asked.

"I heard something. Shall I investigate?"

Mondra rolled her eyes to the ceiling, took a deep breath, and sighed. "Fine. If this wasn't so important, I wouldn't have you bother. But better to be safe with the League of the Moon on the grounds."

Chesrule left the room.

Henry and Marla were close to the door at the end of the hall now, hanging back just far enough to keep the weak firelight from exposing their faces, but close enough to see what was happening in the next room.

Mondra had just issued her passive-aggressive threat to the health of Aaron Hendrick's mother. When he'd lain down in front of her, Henry and Marla were ready to make a move.

Then the demon did something unexpected, leaving the room by another door to check on a noise. It had been loud enough that both Henry and Marla heard it. That's when Henry remembered Jo's text. She'd said the Council of the Realms guy would handle the demon. He'd assumed Jo would make the next move, which would draw Mondra's attention away from the entrance, where he and Marla waited. It put his nerves on edge.

The opening on that side of the bell tower was clearly visible over Mondra's right shoulder. It was almost completely dark, save for the occasional reflection of firelight on leaves clinging to survival before the impending autumn claimed them. But then, out of the darkness, something white surfaced in the night. The last thing Henry and Marla saw before the door in front of them slammed shut in their faces was the white of the ankle between the bottom of Jo's jeans, and the black of her running shoes.

∼

Jo was inside now. The Red Witch was less than six feet in front of her and concentrating on a scroll. Jo drew the knife from the makeshift scabbard at her side and kept it pointed down, the sharp side facing away from her leg.

"Need help with the big words?" asked Joanne.

Mondra whirled around, her eyes growing wide with surprise, then narrowing as her instinct for survival kicked in. Her gazed drifted downward to the large knife at the green witch's side. "I'm not surprised to see you here tonight."

"Really? You should tell that to your eyes."

"Still a know-it-all smartass," said Mondra, her face dripping with contempt.

Jo held up her right hand, index finger pointing skyward, "That's know-it-all smartass with a big scary knife to you—you arrogant twat."

Jo motioned with the knife, pointing to a corner of the room. "Get over there, by the stained glass window. If you move from that spot, I promise you you'll make Heath Ledger's Joker look like a supermodel."

Mondra didn't move, challenging Joanne to make good on her threat.

Though not prone to acts of violence without good cause, Jo considered what this woman had done—or tried to do—to her baby, her husband, her father-in-law, and the rest of the people she loved. She considered it for less than a second, then took two steps forward and jammed the tip of the knife into Mondra's neck. Not deep enough to kill her, but enough to draw blood. Giving Mondra a taste of what she'd done to Byron a couple of months back.

For the second time in five minutes, Mondra's eyes grew wide. This time in fear for her life. She threw up both hands; the scroll flew from them and seesawed through the air and onto the floor.

Joanne withdrew the tip of the blade from Mondra's neck, but held it at face level. A thin river of blood ran along its shiny surface, down the hilt, and curled around Joanne's wrist. "Move!"

Mondra focused her eyes on the blade's tip, then slowly backed herself into the corner next to a large stained-glass window.

Once she had the Red Witch cornered, Joanne backed away from her and toward Mercy and Aaron. When she reached the middle of the room, she glanced quickly down at them to get her bearings, then back toward Mondra. Pointing the knife at her, she said, "If I hear you move an inch, the next one goes through your neck and out the other side."

Mondra glared at Jo, saying nothing.

Joanne knelt down, cutting the wire cuffs from Mercy's arms and legs, then pulling the gag out of her mouth.

"Thank you, Jo."

Jo nodded. "You're welcome, sweetheart. Are you okay? Did Chester the demon molester do anything to you?"

"No. Not yet. But he seemed pretty excited about the after-party," said Mercy.

Jo looked up at Mondra, a disgusted look on her face. "What the fuck is wrong with you? Your own flesh and blood!"

"I didn't ask for her. She was a mistake." Mondra sneered at both of them. "Still, it turns out she's useful after all. What's inside her is valuable. And when I get it, I'm going to use it to kill you first."

The Red Witch's words demeaned her daughter, but they cut Jo even deeper. Joanne's mother was a sober alcoholic. Though she was happy her mother had finally gotten her shit together, the damage had been done. Jo's formative years had been spent bouncing from foster home to foster home. She was twelve when the first foster "dad" made a move on her as she slept. He tried little the first night, just put his hand under her blanket and rubbed her thigh, but Jo knew what was coming next—and prepared accordingly.

When dinner was finished the next night, and "dad" reminded her it was her turn to do the dishes, she slipped a fork into the front pocket of her jeans. Later that night, she pretended to be sleeping. When he came into her room, he was bolder than the night before—slipping under the blanket and putting his hand right where she thought he might. Jo sunk the tines of the fork at least half an inch deep into the back of his hand. The next day, she was sent back to social services by the family, citing Jo's inability to 'get along' with the other members of the house. The cycle repeated for years until she was old enough to be on her own. And she never forgave her mother for the drinking that placed her on that path.

Red hot rage at Mondra's words swallowed her mind. The knife came up as Jo stepped over Mercy, ready to cut Mondra a new asshole. Aaron Hendricks lay forgotten on the floor beside Mercy, and he kicked out with his left leg, tripping Jo and sending the knife flying to the far corner of the room. It tumbled through the air, glinting firelight and blood from its gleaming surface, then clattered to the floor. Mercy and Mondra bolted for it, reaching at the same time. Mondra got her hand on the hilt first, and Mercy seized her mother's wrist. They rose together, struggling against each other for control of the knife, looking like dance partners that didn't quite have their routine worked out.

Jo recovered fast, but not fast enough. Aaron saw the

beginnings of the emerald glow in her irises. It was something he'd seen two months earlier in the parking lot at Wanda's Wicca'd Emporium, and he knew if she got up off the floor and could use her magic, they were all going to pay. He dove on top of her, sat on her chest, and pinned her arms to the ground with his knees, trying to keep her down while watching Mercy and Mondra battle each other for the knife. Praying his lover would overcome the younger woman.

The witches fought fiercely, knocking over rotted antique furniture from one corner of the room to the other. Mondra was, by far, the larger of the two, but Mercy was compact and powerful. They jockeyed for position, slamming each other against the bell tower wall and then rolling on the filthy floor, only to rise once more—screaming, kicking, and punching—all the while joined at the junction of Mondra's wrist and the prized knife. In their fury, neither realized they'd fought their way back to the bell tower opening.

CHAPTER 28
THREADS

Moreland stood in silence in the dark hallway, waiting. The space was identical to the one Henry and Marla were trapped in on the other side of the bell tower. A fact Armand would come to realize in the next few moments.

He knew he'd never hear the demon coming. The bastard was quiet, especially when it was on high alert. But he wasn't worried. Chesrule might be stealthy, but even in his human form he stunk. Not as bad as either his ethereal form, (which was the worst), or his animal form, (a close second). The smell hit his nostrils only seconds after Chesrule had entered the room. Armand withdrew the Seal of Solomon, tossing it on the floor a few feet away, making sure the medallion made enough noise to draw the demon's attention.

Chesrule took the bait, moving toward the sound slowly. He was close now. In the pitch-black, the intensity of the rotting smell grew until Moreland was close to gagging. It took every ounce of control in his being not to retch and give himself away. In the end, it didn't matter.

Chesrule was almost on top of the Seal when the fighting broke out in the main room. The smell receded as Chesrule fled to investigate. Armand pulled his cell phone from his pocket, turned on the flashlight app, and retrieved the medallion. His disappointment at failing to trap the demon evaporated in the mayhem unfolding before him as he followed Chesrule into the main room.

Henry reared back and kicked the door with everything he had. It didn't budge. Old or not, whatever the door was made of, it was solid as steel.

"You're not going to get through it that way, Henry," said Marla.

He was about to give the door another blast with his foot and instead pulled up short at her words. "Why not?"

"Someone doesn't want us in that room. You saw what I saw. No one in there was focused on the door. It either closed on its own—or someone else is in there with them."

"I don't really give a shit! Jo's in there and whatever's going on doesn't sound good," said Henry.

Marla ignored his fear-fueled anger. If they were going to get on the other side of the door, she needed to reach the rational part of Henry's mind. And quick.

"Think about it, Henry. The four people in there wouldn't shut that door for several reasons. When it closed, Jo just came through from outside. Mercy was tied up on the floor, and Aaron was forced to lie next to her. Psycho-witch was dealing with Aaron *and* preparing a ritual. Oh, and the

Council of Assholes guy is dealing with the demon. Everyone else is outside. Who does that leave?"

Her words snapped Henry from his budding panic. "Your buddy. Eddie. But why would *he* lock us out?"

Xavier had been a vampire now for nine hundred and fourteen years. In all the centuries before this, there had never been an opportunity like the one in front of him now. Something made clear to him on the night he'd been changed forever.

When the vampire had approached him as he lay dying in the battle's aftermath, Xavier knew for some time he was different than others. It was a secret he believed he'd kept safe throughout the entirety of his mortal life—even from his beloved brother. And one he'd not shared in the nine hundred and fourteen years since. It made him a great warrior back then, but led to his unlikely death on the battlefield. It was what the demon had *really* come for that night. Inanis had been witness to every battle Xavier had fought and had puzzled out the secret to the man's success.

Inanis always meant to kill and possess Xander. But the demon's true motive, until that night, remained hidden. Xavier, and his secret ability, were always the prize. Incapacitating Xander would draw Xavier's attention from his own battle. It would force a mistake. The dark one might have achieved the same result had he chosen another soldier's body—maybe. But the demon was well aware of Xavier's prowess on the battlefield. The surest way to derail Xavier in battle long enough for an enemy to defeat him would be for the warrior to witness his bother's demise. Inanis made sure it would happen.

Inanis, and demons in general, fed on the violence of war. They smelled it coming long before the first drops of blood ever stained the earth. With regularity, they'd insert themselves before anything had begun. Possessing the souls of leaders whose decisions meant life or death for thousands and then giving them that last nudge. It had happened since Cain slew Abel. And it was about to happen again. The unfortunate part for Inanis; the vampires knew it, too.

Sekhmet, the Egyptian goddess of war, considered by many the first vampire, prowled the battlefield that night. Her gift mirrored Xavier's. One few alive possessed. Throughout time, many claimed to have this power. Nostradamus was one, and he was frequently proven correct—by some interpretations. But in the light of scrutiny and with the passage of time and history, most others were exposed as charlatans.

Sekhmet had watched Xavier for a long while, and observed repeatedly his successful use of this power. In a twist of fate, the power would desert him tonight. Something Sekhmet saw coming—because the power she shared with Xavier was the ability to see the future. It wasn't a precise power, by any stretch, but on that night it had worked flawlessly.

The only power on earth with the strength to blind one with this ability was love. Inanis, though he knew nothing of love, understood this. The demon arrived at the same conclusion Sekhmet had—Xavier could see into time's horizon, but not if his focus was elsewhere. Threat of imminent death for Xander would achieve this. This was something that only a being existing *outside* of linear time could affect.

Vampires and demons were dwellers in that realm. They could outmaneuver someone who could see the future, but was restrained *within* that linear time, as Xavier was then.

Sekhmet moved quickly to intervene, knowing the demon would sense her approach and flee. Her action had achieved two goals simultaneously; she had prevented the demon from acquiring Xavier's ability to see the future, and she affected the outcome of events that would occur several centuries down the line in a land that was yet to exist. A time when metal beasts would soar the skies.

As Xavier hid in the shadows in the main room of the bell tower, the words of Sekhmet came back to him. After she'd made him a vampire, and the shock of the change faded, she said, "You will have your revenge on the demon. Your brother will be set free. But not now, and not by you. Pursue Inanis to the new land when the new land forms. You *will have* opportunities to free your brother, none of them will bear fruit. The ones who can help you are yet to be born, and their alignment must be exact. They will, one day, free Xander."

Xavier was confused. "If they are to free him, why must I follow the demon?"

"His actions will set something far worse in motion. Beware the coming of the Red Witch. She seeks to upset the balance between realms. She seeks power. When the demon aligns with her, the time will be at hand. The Red Witch must never possess all three realms."

"Shouldn't I just destroy him? Or her? Yes?" asked Xavier. "Will it not prevent what will happen?"

"No," said Sekhmet. "If he is destroyed, another will take his place. Kill the next. Another will follow. Every demon with knowledge of the Red Witch will clamor to fill his role."

"I shall kill the witch then," declared Xavier.

Sekhmet shook her head. "Again, it will only set things backward. The cycle will begin anew. There is always someone craving power at the ready. They must die within a day of each other."

Xavier stood in front of Sekhmet, her body as dark as night, her mind as depthless as the universe. He struggled to understand what she wanted from him—feeling like a child learning to read.

"There is one thread that runs through all of it, Xavier. That is the thread you need to pull. It unravels all the Red Witch seeks," said Sekhmet.

Her words echoed in his head. Xavier stood in the dark corner of the bell tower, his hand firmly on the door and holding back Henry and Marla. He watched as the Red Witch and Mercy struggled for the knife, knowing what was about to happen. The thread he'd been pulling at had almost fully unraveled.

Things could still go wrong. Knowing the future didn't guarantee an outcome. The free will of others still played a major role. It was the ultimate paradox contained within the gift he'd been given; one still had to move the pieces on the board into their proper places. Sometimes right up until the final outcome was achieved.

It was then, as he was thinking about how things could still go wrong, Henry and Marla exercised some free will—just as the Red Witch and Mercy were where he wanted them.

CHAPTER 29
LOOK OUT BELOW

Jazz was facing the back of the church when the fire went dark.

"It's out!" she yelled, pointing over their shoulders and hopping up and down. "Let's get in there!"

Everyone turned to look as Jazz took off at a full sprint—her long, dark hair flying out behind her as she picked up steam. Wanda, Byron, Penny, and Archie kept up as best they could, but Jazz could move. When she got to the front of the church, she yanked the doors open, kicked the doorstop down on the left and held the right with her foot because the other doorstop had rotted off. She was bouncing on her feet with impatience when she saw first Byron, and then Penny, round the left side of the church. Archie and Wanda would follow shortly.

"Go!" said Byron. Waving his right hand at Jazz as he ran forward. Jazz let the door go just as Byron reached it. He waved Penny inside and waited for a full minute before Archie and Wanda, winded and waddling, rounded the corner. If the moment wasn't so serious, he would have busted a gut laughing. *They look like penguins on meth,* he thought.

After an endless wait, Byron ushered them through the church's entrance and turned to close both doors. As he drew them shut, he paused. Movement in the circle of shrubs surrounding the scraggly, abandoned lawn of the church caught his eye. Dark shapes emerged from them, advancing on the church. He wasn't sure who or what they were, but he wasn't about to ask them for I.D. either. Byron slammed the doors shut, then turned to look for something to barricade them with. At that moment, Henry and Marla emerged in the main room.

"Henry!" yelled Byron. "I need your help. We got company coming and it ain't the church choir!"

The last thing in the world Henry wanted to do right now was divert course. Jo was in trouble. Mercy was in trouble. But the fear in Byron's voice made him pull up short. He rushed over.

"What do you need me to do, Chief?"

Byron whipped his head back and forth, searching for something to barricade the doors with.

"There! Help me move this thing in front of the doors, Henry!"

Henry followed Byron's eyes. A large and dusty wooden bookcase filled with thick, leather-bound bibles stood against the wall in the church's entranceway. They dashed to the case, each grabbing a side of it, and then heaved it forward, inch by inch.

"This fucker is heavy!" said Byron.

Henry nodded, grunting with the strain. When they got close enough, Byron said, "Now get behind it and let's tip it forward!"

They took two steps back and heaved at the bookcase from the back side. Just as the case was about to tip, the right-side door to the front of the church inched open. A blackened hand with filthy, yellowed fingernails reached through, curling its fingers around the latch on the left-side door. The momentum and the weight of the falling bookcase slammed the door shut, crushing the arm just above the wrist and severing it from its owner. A muted wail of pain floated through the thick wood doors. The hand plopped on the filthy floor of the church entranceway. The fingers flexed, grabbing at the floor and making their way toward a horrified Byron. He pulled out his nine-millimeter Glock and shot the thing twice.

Henry looked at him, stunned.

"What?" asked Byron.

"Nothing," he said, smiling. "Gomez Adams might not like it though."

Byron looked down at the twitching hand. It went still. He shrugged at Henry. "Fuck Gomez Adams."

Henry ran to the window overlooking the front lawn. He said, "Now I get it."

"Get what?"

He waved Byron over. "See all those nasty-looking fuckers out there?"

Byron's eyes went wide. When he'd closed the doors, he'd only glimpsed a few of them. Their numbers had grown. He said nothing. His mouth hung open. His jaw worked, but words failed him.

"I had a visitor earlier today at work. He told me the Red Witch had brought light to the void. I think those happy assholes are the result."

Byron finally found his voice. "Fuck," he whispered. "That crazy bitch is raising her own army."

As if to answer the chief's declaration, the 'army' outside pounded at the barricade.

"Where were you heading when you got down here, Henry?" asked Byron.

Henry pulled his eyes from the approaching throng of reanimated void dwellers and said, "Shit! I was heading to help Jo. We were up at the top of the bell tower, about to go in, but something slammed the door in our faces. We couldn't get through."

Without another word, Henry and Marla took off at a run for the staircase leading to the other side of the tower, passing Wanda, Archie, Penny, and Jazz as they were joining Byron to defend the front of the church.

"Jazz, honey... I need you at the far left end of the entrance. Penny, please go to the far right," said Wanda.

Neither Penny nor Jazz questioned her. They knew what she was going to do and were ready for it. Once they were at the far ends of each side of the entranceway, Wanda pulled a small, black velvet bag from the pocket of her robe. As she walked over to Jazz, she undid the gold-roped knot at its top, reached into the bag, and retrieved a small amount of the mixture within. Wanda sprinkled a little of the salt and brick dust on each of Jazz's shoulders, quietly cast a protection spell on her friend, then tipped the bag forward slightly towards the floor. Without fear, and without undue haste, she calmly drew the barrier across the entranceway, stopping to repeat for Byron what she'd already done for Jazz.

"This some kind of magical Head and Shoulders?" asked Byron.

Wanda smiled. "Not exactly. But it'll keep your head and shoulders where they are. For now, at least."

"Whaddaya mean for now?"

Wanda winked at him, then moved on, tipping the bag toward the floor again and continuing to draw the line until she reached Penny. She closed off the protection by repeating the process she'd performed on Jazz and Byron with Penny and then herself.

"So mote it be," said Wanda. Their protection, for now, was complete. Except, she suddenly remembered, for Archie. She whirled, hand in bag, ready to dust a bit on Archie. He wasn't next to her anymore. Archie was at the side of the hexagonal main room, ripping dusty old cushions from the pews and tossing them into the middle of the room. Three or four of them were scattered haphazardly at the room's center.

"What on earth are you doing?" asked Wanda.

When he looked up, the frantic expression on his face sent a chill down Wanda's spine.

"Help me!" yelled Archie. "It's about to happen!"

Wanda tucked the bag into her robe and rushed over to him. "What's about to happen?"

HE HAD them where he wanted them now—fighting each other and oblivious to his presence in the room. The same went for the green witch. Her struggle with the Hendricks kid kept her distracted. The moment to act closed fast, and Xavier wasted no time. He wasn't about to let nine hundred years of planning go, pardon the pun, out the window. But the two witches needed to do exactly that.

In a blur of motion, he leapt from the shadows and hurled himself at Mercy and The Red Witch. Just as he crossed the middle of the room, the green witch caught sight of him out of the corner of her watchful eyes. Joanne reacted reflexively, jabbing her left foot out and tripping the vampire. He went down, face first, onto the filthy floor—cutting a path through the dirt as he slid across it. He pushed up from the floor, hissing at Joanne, and then continued on with his lethal errand.

Jo kneed Hendricks in the groin and jumped to her feet just as Henry crested the top of the stairs to her left. Their eyes met; no words passed between them. They sprinted as fast as they could to the spot where Mercy, the Red Witch, and Xavier were on the far side of the bell tower—a moment too late. Xavier shoved them over the edge.

Marla did the best she could to keep up with Henry, but fell behind fast. She cursed herself for not sticking to her diet plan because, several steps from the top, she was beyond winded. A stitch of pain hit her just below the ribs, and she struggled up the few remaining steps. She got there just in time to see Henry and Joanne rushing to a spot at the far end of the main tower room. Both of them leaping and desperately trying to grab hold of two pairs of feet as they went tumbling through the bell tower opening and into the night. The man she'd once known as Stinky Eddie ran past her almost too quickly for her to see. But she saw. Someone she'd once thought of as a kind and gentle soul—a supernatural healer, no less—had just sent two women flying into the night and toward the end of their lives. It broke her heart.

∽

Chesrule arrived in the room in time to see the warlock Henry and the green witch running toward the stairs. Hendricks had remained behind, too stunned by events to move from his spot on the floor. The Red Witch and her daughter were gone. The demon's survival instincts were in overdrive. If the Red Witch was about to die, he'd need to preserve himself, and also find a safe way out of here. With this many witches on the church grounds, the task got more dangerous by the moment. The man on the floor before him would fit both needs. Besides, he'd already possessed him twice, so he knew shoving his essence aside and taking over his body wouldn't be a problem. Hendricks was weak willed.

"Oh. I wouldn't do that, dear demon."

The demon whirled. "You!"

"Ah. You remember," said Moreland. "Then you realize trying to run from me is futile. And hiding in this young man will do you no good. Obviously. I can smell your kind from a mile away, regardless of the package or form you hide yourself in. And your recent return from a place you were never meant to leave has only added to your distinct aroma, I'm afraid."

Chesrule didn't hesitate. In the blink of an eye, he dove into the body of Aaron Hendricks. After a confused second, Hendricks's body sprang from the floor and fled toward the opening in the bell tower. There seemed to be a moment of struggle, as if the soul inside had found the courage to fight the will of the demon, and then quickly lost. Chesrule hurled himself and Hendricks through the bell tower opening.

Moreland sighed, shook his head, and strolled to the stairs.

CHAPTER 30
REDEMPTION?

Falling. It seemed to take forever. It seemed to end so quickly. Time; it was a funny thing, she thought. Depending on the circumstance, it was as flexible as rubber. She'd always heard your life flashes before your eyes in the moment before you die. Now she knew it was true.

As the memories flooded her mind, the overarching theme was regret. Not all of it, though. There *had* been good times. They were few and far between, but honesty with herself seemed the best policy right now. She *was* about to die. What did she have to lose? It cut her deep when she realized she had only herself to blame.

True, her father had been no prize. And her mother was weak. She'd always hated both of them for how her life had turned out. Blamed them. She'd always believed she had no say in the matter, that *they'd* caused all of her problems. In the end, she'd made her own bed. Realizing, as her body surrendered to the law of gravity, each of her choices—and there had *always been* a choice—were, more often than not, the wrong ones. Based always out of fear and never in love—except love of herself.

That included Mercy. The beautiful young woman who, moments ago, had fought with her for the knife and now would make her own journey toward death alongside her mother. Shame filled her when she realized if she had won that fight, she would have killed her own daughter. Worse, she would have done it slowly enough to leach the girl's soul from her body before she died. Capturing the powerful magic that made Mercy what she was.

And for what? Power? When she got right down to it, that was the truth. She'd wanted to rival Hecate. To become a witch so powerful, there would be no one who'd dare go against her. To control the gateways between realms was power almost equal to God himself. But even then, with the goal accomplished, what would she really gain? She'd have all the power she'd ever craved. Be able to make anyone do whatever she wanted. But they'd always and forever bend to her will out of *fear*. There would be nothing *real* about it. No one would admire her or be loyal to her out of anything but sheer terror. It would be an empty victory, and she would always crave something more.

In a flash of insight, her dreams of unlimited power were reduced to what they actually were. When she finally saw it, the sadness and loss she felt threatened to kill her before she hit the floor. All this time, it had been about love. She'd just wanted to be loved. Every single decision she'd ever made had its origin in the fear of *not* being loved. And worse, not having that love returned.

Tears filled her eyes when she thought of all the things she'd done to others. Forcing her will upon them. In some cases, using black magic to make men she desired—good men, like Archie—fall for her. Never realizing it for the fool's gold that it was. Never actually trusting they might love her for who she was, and not just what she could give them, or what they could do for her. So much wasted time.

Mercy and Mondra crashed through the skylight of the church. When she hit the glass, Mondra caught a brief glimpse of her daughter. Mercy was looking right at her. *Within her*. They were still holding hands, though the knife was gone.

The thing Mondra noticed most, in that infinite millisecond before they both hit the floor, was the look of love on the face of her daughter. Though it seemed impossible to believe, Mercy had forgiven her. How she knew this was beyond her own understanding, and beyond anything she felt she deserved. It made her feel small and petty. Then, she heard Mercy speak to her inside her own head.

"No mama. Don't go there. I forgive you. Now you need to forgive yourself. Let it go."

The moment before they hit the floor, Mondra swung herself under Mercy, hugging her daughter close. The last act of her mortal life would be a selfless act. She would give her life for Mercy.

WANDA PULLED Archie out of the way just in time. The stained-glass skylight above exploded, and three bodies crashed to the ground. Mercy and Mondra arrived at the same time, landing on some of the cushions Archie and Wanda had tossed into the middle of the room. They softened the blow somewhat, but it wasn't enough.

Aaron Hendricks landed behind them, closer to the front

of the church. Ironically, he'd landed where most of the cushions had bunched up. Everyone watched as he sprang up from them, looking around wildly for a path to escape. Though he'd gained the most benefit from Archie's desperate plan to save Mercy, his body was badly damaged.

Aaron lurched toward the front door, looking like an extra from *The Walking Dead*. Byron was about to stop him, but then froze. He couldn't break the chain of protection. Aaron, or whatever was inside him, sensed this. He sneered at Byron as he limped by. Dead black eyes, devoid of iris, pupil, or white, challenged the chief to stop him.

Byron watched as the demon-possessed man made his way to the front door and forced the bookcase back. Filthy and blackened hands ripped him through the narrow opening, sucking Aaron into the dark embrace of the hungry, soulless mass. Outside, they quieted. Satisfied, for now, with their pound of flesh.

HENRY AND JOANNE burst from the staircase to the left of the altar. They'd heard the crash of glass halfway down and expected the worst.

Moreland calmly exited the staircase on the opposite side of the altar.

Anyone not forming the protective barrier at the front of the church rushed to the center of the room. Mercy had been spared injury, other than cuts sustained from the stained glass roof. Mondra lay gasping and moaning on the floor beside her. A large shard of light-green glass, with a sheep grazing in a field as its backdrop, steepled out from the area just under the left side of her ribcage. Bright red blood streaked the glass, and more of it pooled around either side of her back. The entire room was silent, save for the gurgling wheeze of Mondra's labored breath.

Henry and Joanne were the first to Mercy's side. Each grabbed an arm and helped her to her feet, only to be surprised when she immediately knelt back down and took Mondra's hand.

Archie, Wanda, Joanne, and Henry formed a circle around mother and daughter. They kept their silence. This was Mercy's moment—in more ways than one.

Mercy gently squeezed Mondra's hand. "Can you hear me, mama?"

Mondra nodded. She smiled up at Mercy through half-open eyes. "*Mama,*" she said, testing out the word like someone learning a new language. "I can't," she coughed out a fine spray of blood, took a deep, wheezy breath, and continued, "believe you'd call me that after what I've done to you."

Everyone exchanged puzzled looks in the outer circle, but they remained silent.

"I know you won't believe this when I say it, but you need to hear it. Everything happens for a reason. I know how you feel about trying to kill me at the quarry that day," said Mercy. She was speaking faster now, sensing her mother had little time. "Whether it was you or someone else, or some*thing* else, I believe I was meant to die that day. I *know* I was meant to die that day."

Mondra shook her head back and forth as much as her weakened body would allow.

Mercy nodded through her tears. "It's true. It's something I know in here." She tapped her heart. "If it never happened, I wouldn't have met the League of the Moon. And this night never would have happened. We could never say and feel the things we're feeling right now. I told you, on the way down. I forgive you. Let the guilt go."

Tears pooled in Mondra's eyes, spilling down either side of her face. She was breathing faster now. The end was near. In a miraculous turn, where there'd been hatred and the greenest of envy in all ways towards Mercy, there was now, in the end, only love. The pain she felt in her soul for all the lost moments and wasted time dwarfed the physical pain, somehow muting it. It allowed her to tap whatever reserves of energy she had left. It gave her the strength to say, "I need more time."

"I wish we had more," said Mercy. Her voice was thick with sorrow.

Again, Mondra shook her head from side to side. "They are going to kill you!" she gasped. "All of you. I can't stop them now. I'm so sorry." Mondra sobbed.

As if in answer to her warning, the bookcase crashed to the floor.

CHAPTER 31
WITCH BLOOD

When the next child of the void reached an arm through the front doors, Henry broke from the circle around Mercy and Mondra, leapt over the fallen bookcase, and slammed the door on its arm. The dark entity screamed with rage and pain. It stalled it, but the blackened arm of whatever thing writhed on the other side of the door remained intact. The bookcase outweighed Henry by roughly three hundred pounds, and still the void dweller's arm remained stubbornly attached. Yellowed, mud-caked fingernails reached for him, and in no time at all, the horde on the other side of the door pushed with their brother.

Henry leaned lower, bracing the door with both hands, and pushed back with his legs for all he was worth. It didn't help. His sneakers slid and gritted on the dirty floor until they reached the bottom end of the now horizontal bookcase. When his heels hit its bottom, he flipped his body around quickly, putting his back against the door and the soles of his feet against the bottom end of the bookcase. It slowed them, but not much. Inch by terrifying inch, the door creaked open, moving Henry along with the bookcase.

Jo saw her husband in trouble. She rushed to the side of the door, stood a few feet back, and faced the mob of animate shadows. Her eyes glowed bright green, and much like the night she'd encountered Zachary Villitz, green fire flew from her hands. Her magic connected, but had the opposite effect she'd hoped for. They were now more enraged than before.

"Holy fucknuggets!" whispered Jo.

Several darkened fingers slipped around the door's side, gripping and pushing. The bookcase ground through the grime on the floor, scratching loudly across the dirt as it moved another inch. Jo gave up the magical attacks in favor of physical defense, hopping over the prone bookcase and taking up position next to Henry.

"Nothing works on them!" yelled Jo.

Jo's urgent declaration drew Wanda from the heartbreak in the middle of the room. As she rushed over, she fished around in her robe pocket, withdrawing the black bag with the spell powder. When she opened it and reached in a hand, she frowned. Most of the powder lay on the floor and in between Byron, Jazz, and Penny. What she had left in the bag wouldn't be enough to keep the frenzied void dwellers out of the room for long, but it might make them think twice. That would have to be enough.

She tipped the bag over, dumping the contents into her left palm. The mound it made was pitifully small—less than a half inch in height. Wanda closed her fingers around the pile, walked as close to the gap in the door as she dared, opened her palm, and then blew the dust into the opening. It had the desired effect. Several of the creatures screamed in agony and frustration and retreated from the breach. Henry and Jo, their backs still planted firmly against the door and their legs still straining to keep it closed, stumbled backwards as the door slammed shut with a thunderous boom.

With the whirlwind of events happening at the front of the church, the only ones to notice Xavier's arrival were Archie and Armand Moreland. They stood on either side of Mercy and Mondra, keeping vigil over them, when a sound from above drew their eyes.

Xavier's silhouette barely stood out in the dimly lit main room. Archie pulled his cell phone from his pocket, tapped the flashlight app, and aimed it at the shadowy figure. The vampire perched on a crossbeam a few feet above. His face was painted red by an unbroken section of the stained glass ceiling, and his eyes twinkled like diamonds in the LED light of Archies phone. The diamonds from Archie's visions were now real.

Xavier paid Archie and Moreland no mind, but fixed hungrily on Mondra. Archie watched him closely. He knew little about him, only the few morsels Wanda had fed him right before they'd entered this building moments ago. It seemed, according to Wanda, the vampire's intentions were clear—he wanted Inanis.

The visions of the ship back in the seeing room at the Council of the Realms told some of the story, but not all. They would sort it out later. But, she'd told him, an enemy of the demon was a friend of the League of the Moon. Judging by the look on the vampire's face, Archie wondered if Xavier's agenda had anything *at all* to do with Inanis. If it did, it seemed largely a side note.

Archie looked down at the pool of blood spreading from underneath Mondra's back, then up at the vampire again. He felt like giving himself a dope slap. All that pooling blood on the floor was the vampire equivalent of a tub full of Ben and Jerry's Chunky Monkey. Now that he thought about it, the creature was actually showing a remarkable amount of restraint. He wondered why that was.

Mondra pointed a shaky finger up at Xavier, "He can help us."

Xavier smiled down from above, but didn't move.

Mercy asked, "What do you mean, mama?"

"He's a vampire. He can bring me back."

Mercy tilted her head, still unsure what Mondra meant.

Archie spoke up, "Your mother wants him to turn her into a vampire, Mercy. Otherwise she'll die. And soon, I'm afraid."

Mercy's eyes went wide. "What?!"

Xavier spoke for the first time. "It's the only way. Your mother is the one who released the children of the void. If she dies, they remain alive—and all of you will perish tonight. No one else can send them back. The spell is hers and hers alone."

Wanda had made her way back to the middle of the room. "You set this up." She pointed an accusatory finger at Xavier. "You wanted all this to happen from the beginning."

The smile fell from Xavier's face, but he didn't correct Wanda.

"Is what he says true?" asked Mercy. "Can he save her?"

The sympathetic expression on Wanda's face was all the confirmation she needed.

Mondra coughed loudly. Blood sprayed from between her lips, then leaked from her mouth and trailed down the side of her face. "I'm so cold!"

"What do we do?" Mercy asked Wanda.

Wanda answered Mercy as she stared daggers at Xavier. "Your mother must give him permission, Mercy. She's a witch, not an ordinary person. Otherwise, the blood-hungry bastard would already be all over her."

"There's no other way?!" Mercy was beside herself.

Wanda tore her eyes away from Xavier and smiled sadly down at Mercy. "I'm afraid not, sweetie." And then, in an act of true forgiveness, Wanda knelt at the side of her former adversary and leaned next to her ear. She took Mondra's left hand in hers and asked, "Is this what you want, Mondra?"

Even on death's doorstep, the unexpected kindness of the white witch, in what could be her final moments, blindsided the Red Witch. Fresh tears rolled down either side of Mondra's face, and she felt compelled to save them all.

At that moment, the doors at the front of the church splintered and crashed to the floor. Henry and Joanne were sent flying toward the middle of the room. Byron abandoned his post and positioned himself between the angry horde of void dwellers and everyone else. He pulled his nine from its holster and started blasting away.

Mondra locked eyes with Xavier. "Do it!"

The word "it" was barely out of Mondra's mouth before Xavier leapt from his predatory position high above. He floated gracefully down to the church floor and knelt at Mondra's side. His behavior threw everyone for a loop. Moments ago, his face looked crazed with a greedy hunger for the blood of the Red Witch. Now, as he prepared to consume her, he became restrained and respectful.

Xavier gently pulled the blood-matted, auburn hair on Mondra's neck aside, then pulled a linen pocket square from his jacket pocket and wiped the remaining blood from her neck. When this was done, he put one hand behind her neck, and another behind her back, and sat her up slowly. Without warning, he slid the hand on her back over a few inches and ripped the glass shard from it. Mondra screamed in agony.

Armand Moreland looked fit to be tied. "You duplicitous son of a bitch!" He made a move toward Xavier, but Wanda put a hand on his arm to stop him. In that moment, she gained a newfound respect for the leader of the Council, and realized she might have misjudged the man all along.

"I'm sorry for the pain. Yes? There is no other way."

Mondra's eyes fluttered. Consciousness was a struggle. Time was almost up.

"One last chance to change your mind. Yes? Do you want this?" asked Xavier. "There is no going back."

In a slurred voice, Mondra answered, "Yesh. Jus' do it."

Xavier nodded. His left knee already propped Mondra up, his right was against the floor. The vampire slid his left leg forward and out, then gently bunched a fistful of Mondra's hair in his right hand, tilted her head back with his left, and stretched her bare neck out over his left thigh. To Xavier's eyes, the thick line of blood flowing through her jugular glowed like a luminescent river, and he plunged his long, dagger-sharp canines into it and drank at its shores.

The witch's blood tasted better than he'd ever dreamed.

CHAPTER 32
UNLIKELY ALLIANCE

Dying, or becoming undead, wasn't what she was expecting at all. Truth was, it felt wonderful. The only pain had been the damned glass shard being ripped from her back, then the slightest double pinprick of the vampire's teeth on her neck. After that, things went momentarily black.

Then, Mondra glimpsed the light of the afterworld. At least, that's what she believed it was. She felt her soul leaving her body, floating gently upward and toward that all-encompassing, all-forgiving luminescence; she wanted that love more than anything she'd ever wanted in the material world.

It made little sense, at first. Why would she even *get* a glimpse after all the evil shit she'd done in her life? If there was one thing she was sure of, it was that there was *no way* she was deserving of that light—and yet, there it was.

As the life-force of her blood flowed out of her neck and into the vampire, these questions swirled in her mind. The answers came quickly. Her ascension to the light first slowed, then stopped. She hung suspended between dimensions, and felt pulled in both directions at once. Even in death, she was being given a choice; continue on to the light, seek the comfort of what lay beyond, or return to the three-dimensional world with its sorrow, heartache, and tears.

At one time, the choice would have been easy; do what's best for Mondra—others be damned. Now, she'd experienced the forgiveness of those she'd wronged. Felt, for the first time, the love of a mother for her child and realized nothing in the world compared to that transformational power. And in this very moment, though the promise of peace and blissful rest hung just above her soul, just below were people she'd once hated but now inexplicably loved, and wanted to protect. The decision seemed easy. To go on without righting the wrongs she'd committed in this lifetime and carry them into the next life seemed pointless. To become like Xavier meant forgoing whatever lifetimes might lie ahead, but she'd at least be able to save Mercy and her friends. And she owed them that.

"Eternity is eternity," she said. Though no one heard her. "Better to spend it guilt free in one body than tormented by the wrong decision forever."

Mondra allowed herself to be pulled back into her body. In the time she'd been absent, the vampire's bite had worked wonders. When she opened her eyes, the first thing she noticed was how much lighter the room had become. It wasn't exactly like day turning into night, but more like things she knew *should* be in shadows were now clear to her. *Nothing* was in shadow. Everything was clearly defined, like a night vision camera without the irritating shade of green covering everything.

And the smells! Not only was her sense of smell more

acute, but things she'd never noticed before hit her olfactory senses like a freight train: the smell of decaying leaves, sweat, blood, tears, dirt, fear—everything. It all came to her in an overwhelming rush. Compared to this, the vitality of her body in the last life was akin to being almost dead. She'd never felt so alive!

"It is good. Yes?" asked Xavier.

Mondra looked up at the vampire, seeing him with her new eyes. "Yes," she whispered, awestruck.

When she'd been dying a mortal death, the last thing on her mind was how the guy looked. All she wanted was for the pain in her back to end and a chance to redeem herself in the eyes of Mercy and her friends. And that was *still* the most pressing thing on her mind. But it was hard to ignore the staggering beauty of the vampire.

Mondra was a sexual dynamo in her mortal life, and the drive remained. In fact, just looking at the man was making her horny beyond anything she'd ever felt. And in that last life, she would have acted on the impulse instantly. That she *didn't* was all the proof she needed that the roots of her soul drank from fresh soil. And in the moment, she completely believed it.

Xavier helped her to her feet. He saw the lust in her eyes. A sign he was on the right track.

Mondra held out a hand to Wanda. "I can't do this alone. Will you help me?"

Wanda took the hand of the Red Witch. Together, they reached Byron just as his gun clicked empty. Wanda put a hand on his shoulder and he whirled around, a look of terror-fueled anger on his face. His eyes widened when he saw Mondra next to Wanda, and the memory of the almost lethal embrace of the redhead in the front room of

Wanda's Wicca'd Emporium played on the screen in his mind.

Wanda read the look on his face, realizing he probably couldn't hear her after firing over forty rounds at the children of the void. "It's okay Byron. She won't hurt you now," she shouted.

Byron didn't buy it at first, but there was little he could do about it. His gun was empty, and three spent clips lay on the floor at his feet. Wanda's words *did* reach him, but they sounded like she was talking through a foam barrier. He'd gotten used to trusting the pint-sized witch with this new world of magic he barely understood. So he reluctantly stood aside and let the magical people take care of magical things. He would never admit it out loud because he was proud of his role as protector, but he was relieved. The gun had only slowed the scary bastards down.

Jo and Henry followed Wanda's lead, taking position on either side of the Mondra and Wanda. The urge to throttle the woman who'd kidnapped their child was overwhelming. Why Wanda was now holding hands with her was beyond understanding. They'd been on the other side of the room and recovering from the door knocking both of them for a loop as the vampire had brought Mondra back. And with Byron blasting away, they'd heard nothing said in the middle of the room. But the situation was dire and they could sort the details out later.

Penny and Jazz abandoned their spots on either side of the church entrance. Penny stood to Henry's right and Jazz lined up to Jo's left. Six witches were a good number. Seven would have been better. Moments later, though not a witch, they had their seventh. Armand Moreland split the middle of the line of six, taking position at its center.

"What the hell do you think you're doing, Mr. Moreland?" asked Wanda.

"You need a seventh magic wielder. I'm your seventh," he said, shrugging.

"But you're not a witch," said Mondra.

"I beg to differ, Mondra. I am both witch and vampire—just like you."

"You sly son of a bitch!" said Wanda. She was grinning from ear to ear.

Moreland grinned back. "Well, what did you think I was?"

"I wasn't sure. Mostly just a pain in the ass. But after seeing you climb that tree, I had you pegged for your run-of-the-mill vampire. You keep surprising me."

"Hold on to your hat," said Moreland.

Seven witches from Salem joined hands, ready to battle the children of the void in Satan's Kingdom, Massachusetts.

CHAPTER 33
HOLY FIRE

The first of the children of the void stepped over the fallen ones in the church entranceway. They'd served their purpose, sacrificing themselves on the barrier of brick dust and salt. They'd paved the way.

Considering the ferocity of the first wave of attackers, its first steps into the church were curiously cautious. As if it wasn't sure it could safely enter this holy place without bursting into flame.

Towering over the others, Henry guessed it was at least seven feet tall. Its skin was charcoal-black. All of them were varying shades of that color, but the one in the front was clearly their leader. "Ho-ly shit," he whispered.

Once beyond the protective line Wanda had set down, the thing grinned at them. Large, grey-stained yellow teeth emerged between blackened lips. Its canines were long and sharp and dimpled the beast's bottom lip. Its eyes were dull-white orbs without iris or pupil and rested beneath brow bones that could have doubled for awnings. It had no nose. The rest of its body was a mismatched, slapped together mess. Its right arm was huge, muscular, and short. The left was longer than the right, lean and sinewy, and in place of a hand with fingers were six gleaming black talons. It raised them toward the witches, then clacked them together several times. Castanets from hell.

When it spoke, it did so in multiple voices at once. "We are legion," it hissed, flicking multiple tongues from its enormous mouth.

All seven witches realized instantly that this was not one creature, but several entities combined into one hideously mismatched and tortured body. From behind them, Byron whispered in terrified awe, "No wonder it's so fucked up!"

"The children of the void have found the light again. We have answered the call of the Red Witch. We will take what is ours."

It trudged toward the line of witches, flexing its talons. Ready to devour souls.

Mondra spoke first. "The Red Witch is gone. You have no power here."

The beast stopped and tilted its head. It recognized her voice, but knew something was—different. "And who are you to speak to us in this way?"

"I am the Red Witch," said Mondra.

The warped entity took a tentative step closer, straightened its head, and raised its non-nose, seeming to sniff the truth out of thin air. "You are not her. The light surrounds you, and darkness is nowhere to be found. Your heart beats, but not in the right way. Where is the Red Witch? Where is the tamer of the light?"

"She has passed," said Mondra. "What made her what she was is gone now. I am what remains. You must return to the void. There is no place for you among the living."

Mondra, buoyed by the powerful witches surrounding her, began the incantation reversing the spell she'd used to open the void to the light.

"Called by darkness. Fed by light. Return to the void. Depart from our sight."

After the first recitation of her incantation, everyone joined in. The effect was immediate—halting the gathering horde in their tracks. When the incantation had achieved its desired result, and to everyone's surprise, Armand Moreland prayed.

Between the line of witches and the hellish entities, a brilliant ball of light appeared out of thin air. As the light grew in intensity, sparks of silver and gold raced around it—slowly at first, and then picking up speed. The witches chanted Mondra's incantation, and the orb pulsed in rhythm with them.

The void leader backed away from it slowly, raising its mismatched arms to ward off something that, to the naked eyes of a non-magical being like Byron, seemed invisible. But to the witches surrounding Mondra, the ball of light took form. It grew larger, unfolding from the middle. A dazzling flash of purple light shot from either side of the orb, and majestic silver wings tipped in gold spread several feet to the left and right. Another flash of purple shot from the top and bottom of the orb. Muscular legs draped in gold armor formed a few inches above the dirt floor, while broad shoulders, a barrel chest, and powerful arms supported a head flowing with a long mane of regal blond hair.

In one hand, the man held a gleaming sword, its blade sporting angelic script. In the other, a shield appeared with identical inscriptions. When the being of light had fully formed, the witches stood in awe at the presence of the Archangel Michael. His back was to them, and he stretched his wings across the length of the room—a barrier protecting them, which none of the children of the void dared to cross.

Legion stepped back, wide-eyed with fear at first, but then ceased retreating. Contemplating, it seemed, whether it would allow the angel to force him and the others back into the void, or fight to remain in the earth realm. It, and its followers, had nothing to lose. Without a word of command, they moved as one—as if possessing a hive mind with Legion as their queen.

They advanced. Michael raised his sword. As he did, Armand Moreland separated himself from the group. Wanda reached out to stop him, but was too late. Moreland took his place beside Michael, his prayer gaining in volume and intensity. Wanda noticed Michael paid little attention to him. Like he expected Moreland's help.

The mystery surrounding Armand Moreland only deepened for Wanda now. When the night had begun, she'd thought him a witless bureaucrat. A magical one, maybe. Until he'd scaled the tree outside like it was nothing, she'd still thought little of him. Now, she didn't know *what* to think.

Mondra followed right behind Moreland and stood to his right. Her eyes glowed brightly, but there wasn't a trace of the malevolence from her mortal days. Now, as a vampire, her eyes were a brilliant version of the hazel eyes she'd been born with.

Henry was next to break ranks, quickly followed by Joanne. They joined hands and took position to the right of

Moreland and Mondra, who hung close but slightly behind Michael. There was no confusion as to the leader of this battle.

Penny, Jazz and Wanda took up the left flank. Joining hands to increase their strength.

With no thought about what they were saying, and following Moreland's lead, all seven witches said aloud,

"Saint Michael the Archangel, defend us in battle. Be our protection against the wickedness and snares of the devil; May God rebuke him, we humbly pray; And do thou, O Prince of the Heavenly Host, by the power of God, thrust into hell Satan and all evil spirits who wander through the world for the ruin of souls. So mote it be!"

From the line of witches, energy flowed. A distinct color and form of magical energy sprung from their auras, channeled directly at Michael. Red from Mondra. Green from Joanne. Blue from Henry. Violet from Jazz. Yellow from Penny. Orange from Moreland. And Indigo from Wanda.

When the burst reached Michael, he flew into a righteous rage. He brought his sword up high and lunged at the leader, bringing it down in a blinding golden flash. One moment, the entity was a mismatched whole, the next, it separated into its individual parts. Michael gave no quarter. Another brutal slash sideways sliced the resulting entities in half. They crumpled to the floor in a heap of ash. Disembodied screams flew about the church, echoing from its walls. They faded slowly and then were gone. Returned to the nothingness once more.

Still bristling with augmented power from the witches, Michael advanced on the minions who only moments earlier were spoiling for a fight behind their demented leader. One by one, they flew in the opposite direction toward the entrance of the church. Several were cut down before they ever got close, but there were thousands of them still on the outside where they'd waited, hoping to taste the souls within the church. The souls the Red Witch had promised them in return for their help in killing the members of the League of the Moon.

Michael chased them from the church and into the courtyard. The witches remained behind, watching as Michael's blade swung brightly through the darkness, lighting the night with holy fire. They listened to the anguished howls of the void dwellers as they were banished back to the nothingness from which they came.

It was then, during the spectacle of Michael's righteous wrath, the scream of agony—a very human sounding scream—tore through them from behind. It was Mercy.

CHAPTER 34
DOUBLE CROSS

When the seven witches and Byron turned toward the scream, the shock of what they saw took a moment to register. Mercy stood rigidly still. Her arms hung at her sides. Her chin tilted toward the shattered, stained-glass ceiling, and her legs wobbled. Blood bloomed on the front of her bright-orange Salem University hoodie—a hint of polished steel poked through its middle like the stigma of a crimson flower.

From behind her, Chesrule hissed in triumph. "She's yours now, Red Witch. Take her!"

Mondra was still standing next to and slightly in front of Armand Moreland when she smiled at the demon and said, "Well done, my servant. Release her, and I will complete the ceremony."

Chesrule did as he was told. He wrenched the knife from Mercy's back—the one he'd lost to the green witch earlier—swept an arm under Mercy's legs, then the other behind her back, and gently laid her on the stained-glass shards. They rattled softly.

As Chesrule followed the orders of his mistress, Armand Moreland withdrew the Seal of Solomon from his suit coat pocket. Quietly, he said, "Put your left hand behind you, palm open," into Mondra's left ear. Mondra did so and received the medallion. When it was firmly in her palm, she tucked her right hand behind her back and joined it with the left. It appeared she was deep in thought as she strode slowly to the spot where the demon hovered over Mercy. If she were to save her daughter's life, she must act fast.

As Mondra drew closer, the demon grew suspicious. "What have you behind your back, witch? And why do not the others try to stop you?"

Mondra lied. "I put a spell on them the moment the angel chased our brothers and sisters into the forest. The witches can do nothing to you or I. Are you prepared to finish the ceremony?"

Chesrule looked from the Red Witch to the others and back again. They weren't moving, and he believed the League of the Moon would not forego a chance to either capture or kill the Red Witch or himself. This relaxed him, and he focused on Mercy. He raised the knife high above his head, readying the killing blow.

It was over quickly for him. He never suspected the Red Witch could move as fast as she did. Before the knife reached its apex, she was on him. Moving with the speed, he realized a moment too late, of a vampire.

As the medallion flashed before his eyes, and the realization of what was about to happen hit him, he smelled it. It was the slight smell of decayed leaves and freshly turned soil. The smell of blood mixed with roses. The smell of predator mixed with prey—something he recognized within himself as he became *both* simultaneously. And in the last instant, a metallic smell that was all too familiar.

He'd spent seven years trapped in the Seal of Solomon. Seven years as a prisoner within it, and locked away in the store of the white witch. As the lights went out on him, he cursed himself for not catching its scent sooner. The last thing he saw in this world were the pointed canines of the Red Witch. They looked huge. After that... nothing.

WITH CHESRULE CAPTURED, everyone rushed to Mercy's side. Her hoodie was mostly crimson now, and her breath was shallow and rapid. She was going to die. What Archie had suspected all along was coming true.

Mondra knelt on the floor next to her, then sat and cradled Mercy in her arms. Mercy's eyelids fluttered rapidly when she looked into her mother's eyes. "Momma?"

Mondra, through a vale of tears, said, "I'm here, baby. I'm finally here for you."

Mercy smiled weakly. It was a radiant smile, and in it was total forgiveness. It filled Mondra with both joy and remorse. In that moment, she realized what it was to *truly* be a mother. To love someone more than you could ever love yourself or anything else in the entire world. And she realized in that moment she would do anything possible to save her daughter's life.

In the next moment, the hammer of despair came down on her. There was nothing she could do now—and this was all her fault.

Mondra looked up at the somber members of the League of the Moon. All but the green witch had tears in their eyes. Joanne stood with her arms folded. Her face was a mask of skepticism. Mondra both feared and loathed her in that moment, but couldn't blame the green witch for doubting after the things she'd done to her family.

Earlier tonight, she'd meant to kill them all, summoning the children of the void to rip them apart and then feast on their souls. After, she would take the soul of the beautiful, sweet woman in her lap and possess it, and its powers, for herself. The shame she displayed for the League seemed genuine.

"Is there anything we can do?" sobbed Mondra.

Wanda took a seat on the floor next to her, leaned her head on Mondra's shoulder, and put an arm around her. "We can just be here for her, sweetie."

"I swear, on all that is holy," said Mondra, "I would do anything to keep my baby alive."

From the altar, a familiar voice sounded. "Anything?"

They turned in unison to see Xavier standing behind them. He stepped around the altar and strode toward the middle of the room. Henry and Joanne parted, and he slipped between them, staring at Mondra.

She looked up, a mother's desperation in her eyes. "Anything!" she whispered through her tears.

"Even the new life I've given you tonight? Yes?" asked Xavier.

"Anything."

Moreland stepped forward then. "This has gone far enough, Xavier."

"I told you, when this began, to stay out of it, Armand. I will not tell you again," warned Xavier.

"When you told me about it, you said it would only be

the Red Witch. There was no mention of the daughter," said Moreland.

"And you would have stopped me if I had mentioned her. Yes?"

Moreland seethed. "You lying bastard."

Xavier shrugged. "It is for the good of our kind, Armand. Yes? You never were skilled at seeing the larger vision. The girl's powers are too much to leave to the guidance of witches. When she is one of us, she will have eternity to grow under *our* guidance. The vampires will command the magical world in Salem and beyond."

Mercy shuddered as the battle for her soul raged around her. The end was close now, and Wanda shot looks toward Henry, Jo, Penny, and Jazz. They all understood what she wanted, and moved to kneel around Mercy. Each put a hand on a different part of her body, and each donated their life force to sustain her in this world. It was the same thing Wanda and Jo had done for Delilah as she lay broken by Inanis on the floor of Wanda's Wicca's Emporium. They were buying time.

When Xavier saw the witches moving in to surround Mercy, he made a move toward her. Moreland stepped in the way.

"This is your last warning, Armand. Do not interfere."

Xavier's eyes flared red as he threatened the leader of the Council of the Realms. Armand Moreland's arm shot out faster than mortal eyes could see, but Xavier dodged it easily. He was older than Moreland, and in most cases, the younger man would almost always best the older, but with vampires, the reverse was true.

Xavier simply stepped back from Armand's attack, ducked, and in the blink of an eye was behind him. The older, more experienced (and treacherous) vampire grabbed his former friend by the hair, wrenched his arm up behind his back, and kicked out, sending Moreland flying until he crashed into and then tumbled over the altar, where he crumpled in a heap.

Xavier knew this bought him a few moments, but that would be all he needed. Once his fangs were in Mercy's neck, he would drain her dry. His fulfillment of the promise made to Sekhmet centuries ago would now be complete. Mercy's powers, and all that came with them, would now belong to the vampires.

Henry rose first from the circle around Mercy to stop him. Xavier tossed him aside like a rag doll. Jo followed next, her eyes green with fury, but she was no match for Xavier. She cast a spell at him. He merely sidestepped the physical manifestation of Jo's spell, then shoved her across the room to join her husband.

Now the reason Xavier had played out the night's events the way he had was plain for all to see. By drinking Mondra's blood, he'd made himself immune to the magic of the other witches. No one could stop him from taking Mercy—the true prize.

Wanda and Jazz joined hands, casting a protection spell wide around Mercy, but it only slowed Xavier for a moment. It caused the vampire some pain, but not enough, and he strolled across the barrier.

Mondra huddled over her daughter, trying to shield her from the very being who had brought her back from the dead.

"This is how you repay me? Yes?" Xavier demanded.

Mercy shook uncontrollably in Mondra's arms. The life support system of witches keeping Mercy alive was scattered across the room. Mondra was her last line of defense. At least, that seemed to be the case. As Xavier crouched to take Mercy from Mondra, Marla Branch appeared out of nowhere. She'd been biding her time, watching from the stairwell she and Henry had come down earlier. When she held out her hand, Xavier stopped cold.

"Where did you get that?" asked Xavier.

It was a brooch identical to the one he'd left in the forest. With one exception; he could see the drop of his own blood glowing from within it.

"You left it behind. Twice now. The first time was a mistake."

Xavier—Eddie—looked at her doubtfully.

"Don't give me that look, choppers," said Marla. "Even a vampire can fuck up now and then. When you healed the dog, you dropped this in the snow. I know all about you. You're one of Sekhmet's puppets."

The doubt on Xavier's face had transformed into outright shock and terror.

"It's been a long time. It took me a while to place it, once Byron showed it to me. But I've always kept the information in the back of my mind. And in a file on my phone." She shrugged. "You never know."

Marla inched toward him. Her right hand was behind her back, and the brooch was in her left.

"When I was fifteen, I went to Italy for a year as an exchange student. I took this with me." She held the brooch out in front of her, sandwiched between her thumb and forefinger. "My roommate saw it on the dresser and asked me what it was. I told her I wasn't sure. She said it looked real old, and that since we were near Vatican City, maybe we should see if we could find out something about it."

Marla took another step forward, Xavier met hers with another backwards.

"Imagine my surprise when Father Antonio Moreno—"

Marla paused as Xavier's mouth formed a surprised O.

"Ahh, I see you two have met! Well, I'll make this short, since Mercy is bleeding out all over the floor. He knew full well about the *Order of Sekhmet*. And the precise way to kill her followers. Guess who he told?"

Marla pulled the wooden stakes from behind her back. She'd wondered, as she and Henry had drawn closer to the church, why the crosses at the top of the church's spires were defiled. It seemed an odd thing to do. Even for Mondra. So, she figured, Mondra might not be responsible for it. If not her, then who?

It had to be Moreland. He was the first to know about this place. Well, other than Archie. He'd been spying on Archie. It wasn't much of a leap to think he might have been out here ahead of time. Preparing things just in case.

That explained one very huge occurrence, or coincidence, or lucky twist of fate; The appearance of Michael the Archangel. Only she now knew it hadn't been coincidence *or* luck.

When the children of the void had taken form, *Moreland* was the one who'd invoked the angel. The prayer of Saint Michael *is used* occasionally by witches, but it is *not* a witch's prayer or spell. *Hecate* is who witches call on first. Moreland must have suspected Xavier was up to some kind of underhanded shit all along.

Moreland's insistence on taking the Seal of Solomon to Joanne had served a dual purpose. The crafty bastard knew what was coming. All this time, he'd been watching Archie's visions. The moment Mondra had baited Archie, Moreland must have made a mad dash out here, removed the arms of the crucifixes on both spires, blessed them, and hid them in the bell tower.

It was confirmed for her when Xavier had kicked the man into the altar a few short moments ago. As Moreland struck the altar and tumbled over it, the stakes had flown out from his suit coat, landing on the floor behind the altar. Marla had watched the entire scenario unfold before her from the safety of the staircase, and pieced the rest together as she bided her time.

With everyone's attention on Mercy, she'd crouched and scrambled to where Moreland lay unconscious, snatching up the stakes and tucking them into the waistband at the back of her scrubs.

Marla pulled a sharpened stake from behind her back with her left hand, raised it high, and smashed its point into the face of the brooch. The sharp, crunching sound of the glass, to Xavier, was the loudest sound in the world.

"Time to put the lights out. *Eddie*."

CHAPTER 35
THE PRIEST AND THE VAMPIRE

Wanda had brought along two boxes of items from her shop out of an abundance of caution. She'd filled her pockets from those boxes with things she thought she might need, imagining all kinds of scenarios. Mostly, they were items used to combat dark magic. Items she knew were useful in a battle with the Red Witch. The thought of an entanglement with a vampire seemed a remote possibility, but not out of the question.

Up until this night, she'd only heard rumors about vampires within Salem. Open-minded about most everything, she'd allowed for the possibility the rumors might even be true. When Xavier had shown her the scene on the blood-soaked deck of the boat, her doubts about the rumors all but vanished. Though he'd never actually admitted to being a vampire, it didn't take a rocket scientist to figure it out. The carnage on the deck of the ship was a pretty big clue.

Xavier, Wanda figured, intended for her to draw certain conclusions from what he'd shown her. And, given their mutual foe—the demon Inanis—had used that voyage back in time as a way of bonding with her. The way he'd been on their side against Moreland from the start was just more butter on the bread.

It was too much, she'd thought. Xavier had overplayed his hand. On the ride out to Satan's Kingdom, as the others engaged in idle chit-chat, she'd closed her eyes and run the scene on the ship through her mind several times. Something about it didn't sit right with her. She realized she'd been focusing on the wrong event.

And then, as she continued to dwell on the entire encounter, the answer had hit her. It wasn't the scene on the boat. It was his smile just before she took his hand. That smirk. And what had he said? *"Please. I won't bite you."*

Always trust intuition.

It was why, thank Hecate, she'd taken the item in her pocket out of the boxes at the back of the truck, and put it in her robe. It was holy water. But not just *any* holy water. When Marla Branch had mentioned a priest she'd talked to in Vatican City, the name rang a faint bell. It didn't take long for the bell to form a picture in her mind.

Christmas morning, as Byron slept, Penny made a quick trip to Wanda's apartment on Derby Street. She'd been a silent member of the League of the Moon, back then. Penny told Wanda that when Byron had come home from the church in the early morning hours, he'd brought a box of evidence home with him. He told her he was exhausted, and he'd drop it at the station's evidence room in the morning. This was a breach in protocol. They could fire him. But he was so tired, and traumatized by the scene, that he was willing to take the risk.

"Besides," he'd said, "the staff on hand between

Christmas and New Year's is barebones at best. Nobody'll know, much less care."

When her husband had gone upstairs to sleep, she'd opened the box. Inside, she recognized the items he'd secured from the scene right away. There was a small, flat crystal container and something that looked like a wand with a stainless steel ball on the end. She later found out, from Wanda, that the wand looking thingy was called an aspergillum.

"That's kind of a funny name for it," Penny had said.

Wanda had only given her a helpless shrug. "I don't recall where the name comes from, but it's used to sprinkle the faithful with holy water."

"If he ever finds out, Wanda, he'll kill me."

"Well, lets get this done quickly then, sweetie."

The items were smeared with the blood of the priest who'd been attacked. Careful not to smear too much from the evidence, Wanda dabbed a cotton swab in the blood, poured a small amount of the holy water from the flask into her own crystal decanter, and then mixed the contents together.

At the time, it was purely an intuitive move. Spurred by a feeling Penny had gotten from the items.

"The energy from them feels all wrong," she'd told Wanda.

Wanda raised a questioning eyebrow.

"Aside from the fact that three people were murdered in a church, I mean." Penny blushed. "There's an odd feeling. That's the priest's blood on those items. I'm sure of it."

"That's the same vibe I'm getting from it," said Wanda. "It feels... very old, though."

No more words needed to be spoken. Penny left with the

items. Wanda dropped the decanter with the holy water and blood mixture in her robe pocket. The next day, she hid them beneath the floorboards in her shop.

Wanda heard the news about the murders on the next business day when commerce in Salem had resumed.

Three bodies went to the morgue after the Christmas Eve incident. One had disappeared from the morgue in the wee hours of the morning—Father Antonio Moreno's body.

Now, all these years later, Father Antonio Moreno was in another church, at another altar, and bleeding once again—as Armand Moreland.

WANDA USED the vampire's fear to her advantage. As Marla advanced on Xavier, Wanda positioned herself behind him. She pulled the flask from her robe pocket and poured out a crude semicircle a few feet from Xavier's back. Then, to be on the safe side, she removed the aspergillum from her robe pocket, doused it with the blood-tinged holy water, and sprinkled it upward toward the beams framing the shattered skylight. It wouldn't be long before the vampire realized he was trapped.

Armand Moreland regained consciousness and was staring at a pair of bloody feet with a nail through them. It took him a moment to realize where he was and what had happened. He tilted his head upward, slowly taking in the life-sized form of the crucified Jesus. From years of unconscious practice, he automatically made the sign of the cross.

Before becoming the leader of the Council of the Realms, it was something he'd done several hundred times per day. He'd never lost his faith in the divine. But he'd come to realize—even now, as a vampire—that there were many representations and facets of that supernatural omnipotent power. And that Jesus was the power that worked for *him*. As Alcoholics Anonymous put it. *'We came to believe that a power greater than ourselves could restore us to sanity.'* No brand names, no denominations. Just a power. *The* power. He called upon that power now to help him set right the wrongs committed by Xavier Saulis.

Armand rose, dusted himself off, and reached behind his back for the stakes he'd fashioned from the arms of the crucifixes. No one had ever known, not even Xavier, that he'd come out here long before the events of this night.

He didn't have any ability to see into the future, like Xavier or some of the other vampires, but for some strange reason, he'd started dreaming about this place. When he'd investigated his own dreams, he discovered that Archibald Love was the one responsible for fueling those dreams.

It came as a complete surprise to Moreland that Love could do what he was doing. He'd shown no aptitude for traveling in the astral realm, much less an ability to see future events. But the man was infinitely skilled in guiding *others* toward the astral realm. There had to be a connection! And there was. Dr. Love had inadvertently received a boost to his ability from Mercy Glass. Pair that with his skills as a hypnotherapist and parapsychologist, and it was no wonder he'd suddenly become capable of the things he was doing now.

The power was so magnified it had sent out signals all over Salem. Most people probably just had weird dreams they couldn't wrap their heads around, but to those who had certain magical gifts—Xavier, himself, the members of the League of the Moon—their dreams were impacted in very personal and private ways. It was the reason they'd all ended up out here. Though Armand doubted anyone, even Wanda, had figured out who was ultimately responsible. Archie had been the conduit and the source for all of their dreams, but Mondra had fashioned the message. Xavier merely had to rearrange events to suit his needs.

When his hands fell on the area of his back where the stakes should have been, he felt nothing. He patted his suit coat. Nothing. Frantic, he looked to the floor of the altar, scanning its surface in all directions. Nothing. When he looked up and toward the middle of the room, he found them. One was raised in the air in the hands of Marla Branch. Armand could see the glittering spot of ruby blood at its tip. Xavier's blood. The woman, he'd find out later, was Henry's boss. How she ended up out here, for now, would remain a mystery. Saving her from the fool's errand she was about to engage in was his only focus.

With a vampire's speed, he shot out from behind the altar, covered the distance between himself and Marla in the blink of an eye, and plucked the blood-tipped stake from her hand.

Marla felt the briefest breeze as Moreland, stake in hand, stepped in front of her, shielding her from Xavier.

At the sight of Moreland brandishing his demise, Xavier turned to run. He whirled, took two steps, and pulled up short. Before him, a see-through crystalline wall formed a semicircle in front of him. On the other side of it, the members of the League of the Moon stood side by side. Wanda Heinze was in the middle. She winked at him. To her surprise, he smiled back.

Xavier never turned around to face Father Antonio Moreno. Instead, he spread his arms wide, tilted his head toward the ceiling, and marveled at the crystalline ceiling matching the wall in front of him. It was beautiful, he thought. Somewhere, deep down in the soul he'd willingly forfeited long ago, he prayed to a power greater than himself for mercy. He'd die hoping to be reunited with his beloved brother Xander. It was a slim hope, but one he chose to face eternity with. There was nothing else left. He uttered one simple sentence.

"Do what you must, priest."

Armand Moreland closed his eyes. He prayed for the soul of Xavier Saulis. And ended him.

CHAPTER 36
EXIT THE WITCH

Once the vampire was gone, the beautiful, ice-blue, crystalline barrier faded from existence. Though what seemed like an eternity had gone by while Mercy lay dying on the church floor, in real-time, it had been less that five minutes. It was almost five minutes too long.

Armand Moreland dropped the stake, turned, and knelt in front of Mercy and Mondra. In a voice full of tenderness, he said, "Give her over to me, Red Witch."

Mondra's head snapped up, and she pulled Mercy closer to her. "What are you going to do?"

"Save her," was his simple reply.

They were the only words Mondra needed to hear. As Armand put his arms beneath Mercy, Mondra slid out from under her. The vampire stood with Mercy draped over his arms. As he turned, Mercy's lifeless limbs swung back and forth, bouncing in rhythm with each stride Moreland made toward the church's entrance. He strode out through the splintered remains of the double doors. The fog had lifted.

Silvery-bright moonlight painted the courtyard. The League of the Moon followed him.

The vampire priest laid Mercy down on the grass and prayed silently over her. Creatures of the night became strangely silent. In a moment, the reason became brilliantly clear.

Through the shrubs ringing the courtyard, another angel appeared. He closed the distance in great, silent strides. Where his feet touched the earth and then left it, golden footprints lit the ground behind him. When they faded, dark patches of lush new grass glowed silver and thick in the moonlight.

Unlike the Archangel Michael, this angel wore no armor. A luminous robe of the most beautiful shade of emerald green hung from broad shoulders. A rugged face rested on a square jawline.. His eyes matched the color of his robes, conveying both strength in their upturn and kindness with a downturn of minor wrinkles at the corners.

"Thank you for coming, Raphael." Moreland bowed deeply.

Raphael said nothing as he touched Moreland on the shoulder, smiled kindly at him, and then knelt next to Mercy. The angel took Mercy's left hand into his own and placed his right on her forehead.

All was quiet, and the angel closed his eyes. Raphael's lips moved in what everyone assumed was prayer. When they stopped, the emerald light of his robes leached into his hands, down along his fingers, and then spread slowly over the entire surface of Mercy's body.

Ten mouths dropped open in awe as they watched the blood covering Mercy's clothes slowly disappear, and then the hole where the knife had ripped through the hoodie, and

Mercy's front and back, dwindled down to nothing and vanished. Though she didn't wake, Mercy's breath became deep and regular. A smile crossed her lips as if she were having the most pleasant of dreams. In an instant, the smile disappeared. Her brows knitted in confusion, and in a sleepy voice, she asked, "But what about Momma?"

The emerald-tinged energy ran its course through Mercy's body and faded. Raphael swept his hands from head to toe a few inches above her body, closing out the healing session in what seemed to everyone like the end of a heavenly Reiki treatment.

The angel stood and turned to face Armand Moreland once again, and they seemed to communicate without words. Moreland bowed his thanks to Raphael, and the angel turned and went back the way he came in. Just beyond the shrubs, there was a bright green flash. Everyone felt the change in the air and knew Raphael had departed this plane of existence. They felt a sense of loss at his departure.

As Mercy continued to sleep deeply, Wanda spoke up. "What did he say to you, Armand?"

When Moreland turned to Wanda, the look on his face made it plain. It wasn't good.

"He didn't exactly speak to me, but the images in my mind were clear enough. The Red Witch has been forgiven for her transgressions against the earth realm. And the divine realm. Her sacrifice of her own natural life for her daughter's is the reason. But it is conditional."

"Conditional?" asked Wanda.

Armand nodded.

Henry stepped forward. "What exactly does that mean?"

Moreland weighed his words before he spoke. "It's twofold, Henry. The dark entities we encountered tonight were but a fraction of the ones released when the Red Witch, quite on purpose, exposed the void to the light. And with the intention of not only killing each of us, but their payment was the absorption of each of your souls; it's the most extreme violation of natural or supernatural laws one can perpetrate. Only the divine may decide the fate of souls—including when and where they reincarnate. By doing what she did, Mondra was interfering on a scale we can't possibly comprehend. And Raphael made clear to me even *he* didn't understand the magnitude of her transgression. But he damned well knew the consequences."

Henry opened his mouth to speak, but Moreland held up a finger. "The second part may answer questions you have, Henry. As I mentioned before, she has given new life to those meant to remain in the void and removed from the three realms of divine, earthly, and underworld. Though Michael was able to, for lack of a better term, clean up her mess *here*, there is much more work to be done. On the night she exorcised the demon from your child, and tried to move Archibald Love's soul into another, was the precise moment the void was exposed. What she's done since has only made it worse.

"Several entities escaped in those moments, and remain free. Most of the ones *here* were returned by Archangel Michael. Most. Not all. As we speak, many of those entities, along with the ones released during the events at Wanda's shop, are roaming the night in Salem. Part of her penance will be returning them from whence they came."

Moreland let that sink in, then continued.

"Mondra the Red Witch is now a vampire. It *seems* she's had a change of heart, otherwise she wouldn't have sacrificed her life to save Mercy's. This happens a lot when faced with death. It also happens to those who survive death and then return. I believe they're called near-death experiences. Mondra experienced both tonight. That is *exceedingly* rare for a vampire."

"Rare in what way?" asked Henry.

"She has glimpsed the divine. She's seen what comes next. Most vampires will never experience that."

The confusion on everyone's faces was plain for Moreland to see.

"Take myself, for example," said Moreland. "I *chose* to be a vampire. I won't bore you with the circumstances now... perhaps someday. But suffice to say, it's almost always a choice. Mondra did not willingly choose to be a vampire."

"What are you talking about?" asked Wanda. "I *heard* her make the choice."

"No. You heard her coerced by Xavier in order to save her child. Xavier knew in order to claim Mercy's power, he'd need to consume the blood of a witch. With that done, none of us could stop him. Your powers would be useless, and that proved true. You could only trap him because you added vampire blood to your magic. Everything tonight was orchestrated by Xavier to get what he wanted, which was Mercy's soul and the power contained within. Ironically, the same goal as her mother."

"Okay," said Joanne. "What has this got to do with anything?"

"There is still a chance for Mondra to save her own soul. There's a chance, someday, for her to die a natural death and reincarnate. To move on to the next life, like most normal mortals. A choice not given to most vampires. *If* she has truly changed her ways."

"That's great," said Jazz. "So why the long face, Jeeves?"

"She might not want to," said Moreland.

"Maybe she does," returned Jazz. "Why don't we ask her now?"

Everyone turned to see what Mondra had to say about her own fate.

She was gone.

CHAPTER 37
BLOOD, MAGIC & MERCY

The sun was just rising when Archie's VW microbus and Moreland's Cadillac Escalade pulled into the parking lot of Wanda's Wicca'd Emporium. They'd had to leave Jo's capsized Jeep, and Byron's four flattened-tire cruiser behind. Byron spent most of the trip cursing the vampires that he now, reluctantly, had to admit were real. Luckily, for Armand Moreland, he was spared Byron's wrath. The chief had ridden with Archie, mumbling colorful and creative four-letter words under his breath as he slammed his door shut for the two-hour trip home.

When they got inside, Henry and Joanne disappeared into a dark corner of the room and dragged out black beanbag chairs, spreading them around the outer circle of the pentacle. Everyone sighed with grateful relief as they sank into the plush chairs.

Wanda had wanted to talk about everything that had gone down in Satan's Kingdom as soon as they'd come through the door. No one bit. They'd all agreed to come here for the protection of her safe room, especially since Mondra had gone AWOL after Raphael had healed Mercy. But no one had the energy or the desire to talk about it. Before Wanda could even sit down, Byron and Archie were snoring away.

Wanda caught Joanne's eye. Jo yawned, looked around the circle of chairs, shrugged, and gave Wanda a 'what-can-ya-do?' look. She followed her husband's lead into la-la land. Wanda smiled, shook her head, and gave in to peer pressure. As she dozed, she recognized the wisdom of the collective once again proved true, and finally gave up the fight against gravity's pull on her eyelids.

ALWAYS AN EARLY RISER, Henry was the first to wake up, amazed he'd slept for as long as he had next to Joanne and the freight-train-roar of her snoring. It tickled him to death that his gorgeous, sensuous, green-eyed bombshell of a wife snored like a sailor and swore like one too. It didn't *surprise* him, given who and what she'd been in their last incarnation together, and that made it all the more amusing. He felt a dopey and grateful grin spread across his face as he tip-toed to the bar at the back of the room.

Wanda kept a large coffee urn inside the bar's storage area for nights when new, wicca-practicing members of her AA group needed to have a get-together without the trappings of a normal Alcoholics Anonymous meeting. They did away with the 'anonymous' part on those nights and began the process of relying on their particular 'power greater than themselves' under Wanda's careful guidance. Jo was a regular attendee at these meetings. And a fair share of 'newbies' had spent a night or two on the Trank's couch.

These were the things running through Henry's mind as

he made sure coffee would be ready when his friends woke up. As the urn quietly bubbled on the bar's top, Henry took a seat on one of the barstools. He took a deep breath, blew it out, and relaxed the muscles in his body from head to toe. It was something he'd been doing more and more lately, as he tried to bring more calmness and peace into his waking life.

He was about to close his eyes when he noticed a triangle of white sticking out from beneath the back door to Wanda's safe room. No one was awake yet, and he crept over to the door, knelt, and quietly worked the envelope the rest of the way through. It stuck almost halfway through, and his finger caught on the edge, sliding along its length and giving him a nasty paper cut. The four-letter word on the tip of his tongue was cut off by the finger he stuck in his mouth, sucking on it until the blood slowed. When the pain and shock wore off, he used his wounded hand to pull it the rest of the way out.

There was nothing remarkable about the envelope, other than Mercy's name scrawled in beautiful cursive letters across its front. Given the events of the day before, he didn't think it wise to wait. Henry approached the sleep circle and gave Mercy's shoulder a gentle squeeze.

Mercy's eyes fluttered open, and she smacked her lips together to work the dryness out of her mouth. "Henry? What's up?" she whispered.

He stood and tilted his head toward the bar. Mercy got the hint, worked her way silently out of the beanbag chair, and stretched the parts of her body that needed stretching as she followed Henry across the room.

"Where did you get this?" asked Mercy.

"Over there," Henry pointed. "It was sticking out from the bottom of the door."

Mercy turned the letter over in her hands. "Why is there blood on it?" asked Mercy.

"I wasn't being careful enough, I guess, when I pulled it from under the door." He showed Mercy his bloody right finger.

"Ouch!" said Mercy. "Papercuts are the worst." Then, "I wonder who this is from."

"My money is on your mother," said Henry.

"Only one way to find out."

Mercy slid her finger along the envelope's edge, prying up a small corner not glued down to the back. Carefully and quietly, she worked it open and pulled the letter out. Despite her cautious approach, Mercy cut her finger on the letter. A drop of blood fell from it and mixed with Henry's on the outside of the envelope, which was now lying on the bar underneath the letter suspended in Mercy's right hand. Just as Henry had done only moments earlier, Mercy stuck the finger in her mouth to slow the flow of blood. And turned her eyes toward Henry.

Henry felt a rush of heat flash through him as Mercy slowly pulled her finger from her mouth, holding his gaze the entire time. When her finger passed from her lips, it dragged down one side of her mouth, leaving a faint trail of blood at the corner of her lips. Henry fought a powerful urge to lick the blood from the corner of her mouth, and then ride his tongue along her lips, plunging it softly through them, and then exploring what lay beyond. He forced himself to turn away, and was stopped by the power of her voice. It sounded different now. Musical. Magical. Desirable.

"Where do you think you're going?" asked Mercy.

"I thought you'd want to read it alone," he tried.

"I'd rather you read it with me... if you don't mind, that is. I'm kinda scared about what it might say."

"You sure?" asked Henry.

Mercy nodded, sat on the barstool, and patted the one next to her. Henry claimed it.

The letter was one piece of paper, folded in thirds. Mercy unfolded it and smoothed it out on the bar's surface so they could read. They leaned closer together. And that was all it took.

It started slowly. Mercy put her injured left hand into Henry's right. The blood on their fingers mixed, and immediately their heartbeats thumped to the same rhythm. She rode her hand up his arm, sliding from the barstool at the same time. Mercy arched her back and slid it along the bar's polished wood railing until she was directly in front of Henry. Then she moved in, parting his legs with her powerful thighs, and sliding her bloody hand back into his. She rested her right hand high up his left thigh, then slid it to where she knew he wanted it to go.

Henry tried with everything he had to fight it. Drawing on memories of Jo and the times they'd had together—trying to guilt himself out of the all-consuming lust he felt for Mercy at this moment. It only seemed to turn her on even more, making her heart rate soar and driving them deeper into the moment as the blood on their hands mixed and their thoughts intertwined.

In his mind, he saw the first night they'd met Mercy in this very room, but from her point of view. He could hear her thoughts and feel how she desired both himself and Joanne. Saying to herself she would never act on it, and then shutting the thoughts from her mind. But it was different now. Something had unleashed Mercy's innermost desires. Henry was powerless to stop it, and Mercy had no intentions of helping. But they couldn't very well go further where they were, not with Jo and the others sleeping in the same room.

Henry rose slowly from the barstool. Mercy's grip with either hand never wavered until she leapt up and wrapped her legs around Henry's waist. She pulled every part of her body tightly against his, then ran her left hand through the hair on the back of his head, pulling his mouth tighter against hers, wanting to feel and taste all she could. And that was how they left Wanda's Wicca'd Emporium. They never saw a word of the letter to Mercy. But then, *they* were never meant to read it.

CHAPTER 38
THE LETTER

Wanda awoke from a terrible dream. In it, she'd dreamed that Mondra had resumed her wicked ways. As the dream faded, she saw two bloody hands joined together. And right before her eyes opened to take in the protective sigils on her ceiling, she saw an image of Henry and Joanne with their backs turned to each other, their mouths were taped shut, and tears streamed from their eyes.

She took a deep breath and blew it out. "Thank God it was just a dream."

The smell of coffee forced her eyes to open wider, and her mouth watered as she thought about that first sip. She loved her chamomile tea at night, but thought there was nothing better in the world to wake up to than a hot cup of coffee.

Wanda rolled from her beanbag, stood, stretched, and made her way over to the corner of the bar where someone had thoughtfully brewed a fresh pot. As she got there, she turned to see who wasn't sleeping in the protective circle in the middle of the room. Henry and Mercy's beanbags were empty. She'd have to thank them later for making the morning brew for everyone.

Through sleep-bleary eyes, Wanda grabbed a Styrofoam cup from the stack next to the urn, put in a teaspoon of sugar, and added some half-and-half. She finished stirring the coffee, and was raising it to her lips when she saw the envelope with "Mercy" scrawled across its front. Her nerves jangled when she saw the drops of blood smeared on its surface and the bar.

"What now?" she asked the sleeping room.

A letter sat next to the envelope. The top of it had folded over the body. Wanda knew better than to touch it with unprotected hands, given the blood on both *it* and the bar. A black, cauldron-shaped mug sat on the bar's top, filled with pens, paperclips, and other debris. Wanda set her coffee down, grabbed two pens from the mug, and used them to carefully fold the letter open, resting the pens in opposite corners to keep it that way. The letter's opening salutation sent her adrenaline into the stratosphere. It was something Mondra had said to her before, in this very room, when Wanda had figured out what the Red Witch had done to Archie against his will.

Dear Sweetie,

I told you, "You can count on it."
Vampires really do believe they're smarter than everybody, don't they? For some reason, they think being "alive" longer than everyone else makes them geniuses. That all those years of accumulated knowledge somehow makes them smarter than us. Well,

as you've probably figured out by now, that's not the case, but I'll come back to them.

I really did have a change of heart at the church. When I died, as I'd planned to, I did see the other side. It changed me. I'd hate for you to think otherwise. I really do want what's best for my daughter. And believe you me, that's progress!

What's best for my daughter is me. But there's one very large obstacle in my way. There are other obstacles, of course. But you, and the League of the Moon... you are that most important and immediate obstacle. That all ends now. Starting with this letter. And, if you're actually reading it, then you haven't touched it. So points to you! But there are other ways to deal with the rest of you. And it's coming. Oh boy, is it coming! And, if everything went down as I suspect, Henry and Mercy are too! Ha! Oh come on now... that was funny!

Wanda pinched the top of her nose between the eyebrows, clamped her eyes shut, and whispered, "You psycho fucking bitch." When she felt ready, she continued reading Mondra's insane manifesto.

So, that was step one. Tell green eyes Karma is, indeed, a bitch. And so is she. I'm going to turn each of you against one another until there's nothing left. I'm letting you know ahead of time. It's only fair. Regardless, you'll never see it coming.

As I mentioned before. I did have a change of heart. I do feel love for Mercy. Maternal love. So what better way to show that love than to bring her home? And by home, I mean literally. She would have lived on... inside of me! Xavier set things back a bit, but he's not a problem anymore now, is he?

I had to do a fair bit of acting to get past her defenses. It wasn't all that tough. Mercy is smart, but far too trusting. Once this is all over, she'll be where she belongs. And I'll have what I want. Everyone wins! Well, except for you and the League.

Now, as for the vampires. I'm a little disappointed Xavier is gone. He was so hot! And when I tell you he was great in bed... that doesn't do it justice. Vampires know how to fuck! It must be in the blood. Get it? My my, I'm on a roll tonight!

What's that you say? How did I know him before tonight? Here's a little secret... I knew what his "special talent" was a long time ago. I know everything that goes on in Salem, sweetie. He can see the future, obviously. So I made myself look a tad different. You know, black magic and all. But guess what? I didn't just screw him for the hell of it. I made sure, when it was hot and heavy, to bite him. He barely even noticed! When you think about it, it's only fair. Why should vampires have all the fun?

Anyway, this was long before you came into the picture. I made damned good and sure I got enough "Essence de Xavier" to make a spell from it. I pulled his strings while he pulled yours. The smug bastard actually thought he was setting all of you up to take me out. And then he had the balls to try to take what's mine?! Like Tony Montana said to the guy who tried to bomb those kids in the car in Scarface, *"Well, look a' you now!" LOL!*

If I'm being honest, there was only one thing that happened I hadn't planned for. The priest. I knew all about him and the Council of the Realms, of course. They've been after me forever. But I never dreamed the man was a vampire. I mean... look at him! You learn something new every day, I guess. I'll be keeping an eye on that one.

Say hi to everyone for me, would you? And give Byron a kiss from me.

Ta Ta for now. See you real soon.

When Wanda read the last word, she let out a long, shuddering breath she hadn't realized she'd been holding.

There was a lot to unpack from the psychotic rantings in the letter. Genuine fear gripped Wanda at her core; something she'd not felt in a long time. What scared her was how they'd all underestimated the Red Witch. But what terrified her, in the deepest part of her soul, was how easily they'd all been fooled, and how readily every one of them was willing to forgive her for the past. It spoke well of the League of the Moon regarding their humanity, but it made her question their collective judgment.

When she'd thought about it some more, fear morphed into a righteous anger. Why the hell was she thinking this reflected badly on the League in any way? Sure, they'd missed some things along the way, but no one was perfect. Wanda quickly dismissed the self-flagellation, realizing the doubts she was having about herself and her friends were the first step in Mondra's plan. The Red Witch had won this battle. It was time to get ready for the war.

Waking up everyone and discussing it was something she knew she had to do, but she cringed realizing that included telling Joanne. How her friend would react scared her almost more than the letter and its threats of retribution. In that moment, an idea struck Wanda out of the blue. Its simplicity was its beauty, but the complexity lay in its execution. And the success of the plan taking shape in her mind rested on a hunch.

With this in mind, Wanda made her way over to the circle and woke her friends up, saving Joanne for last. She knew Jo slept like the dead, and the first part of her plan was to get her alone so they could talk. One by one, they said their goodbyes. No one, to Wanda's relief, asked about the whereabouts of Henry and Mercy.

Moreland was the last, aside from Joanne, to remain.

Wanda walked him to the door, and it wasn't lost on him she was doing her best to get him out of her shop quickly. He stopped and asked, "What are you up to, Wanda?"

She put on her best poker face. "Nothing. I just need some alone time."

He wasn't looking at her when she said it. Instead, his eyes focused like lasers on the bar's top, and she cursed herself for forgetting to stash the letter. To her utter shock, he said, "You've heard from the Red Witch, I see."

Wanda's jaw dropped. How had he figured out the significance of the letter just by observing it from afar?

Moreland smiled at her. "It's more than just the letter, Wanda. After her disappearance yesterday, it was just a matter of time. There was no good reason for her to go. That is, unless there *was* a good reason for her to go."

"The letter is bewitched, Armand. Mercy and Henry both touched it. And now they're gone. Given what's written, they are, at this moment, most likely—"

"Screwing each other's brains out?" asked Joanne.

Wanda jumped at the sound of Jo's voice. She looked at her young friend, and couldn't come up with one word.

Jo gave Wanda a sympathetic smile. "I know it looks bad right now, Wanda. But there's more going on here than meets the eye."

Jo held up a finger, then leaned back and pulled a satchel out from behind the beanbag chair. She stood and walked over to the bar top, placing the satchel right next to the letter.

"Careful, Jo. Mondra bewitched that letter."

"Did she, now?" asked Joanne, sounding anything but surprised.

Jo shot her a crooked grin as she unzipped the satchel

and withdrew a large hunting knife. Wanda recognized it right away as the weapon the demon had used on Mercy.

The green-eyed witch held the knife a few inches above the letter. When she did so, her irises glowed. A fine green mist floated gently from her eyes and settled on the blade, turning it the same color. It pulsed in rhythm with Jo's heartbeat. The green witch closed her eyes then, and said, "They're in the church with Mondra. The place she took Delilah to. It's almost done now."

"What's almost done now?" Wanda asked. A trill of fear tinged her voice.

"Let's go find out," said Jo.

Moreland smiled and clapped his hands together. "Excellent! How did you do it?"

Wanda threw her hands in the air in exasperation. "Do what?"

Jo held the knife up. "Let's just say it's a good thing Mercy didn't die tonight. Or I would have given my blood to that perv demon for nothing."

She lowered the knife to the bar, tapping the letter from Mondra with its tip. The letter and the envelope burst into flame.

CHAPTER 39
KARMA

Mondra watched them from a darkened room as they entered the main one. Henry and Mercy were tightly wound together now as they came through the thick wooden door. So lost in the moment were they, it struck neither as odd there was a fire already ablaze in the fireplace, with a thick bearskin rug and pillows laid out before it.

They crossed the threshold, their lips fused together as Henry kicked the door closed behind him. Mercy leapt up and wrapped her legs around Henry's waist once more, grinding her hips against his. With Mercy clinging fiercely to his body, he knelt on the rug and they tumbled sideways into its middle.

Mercy reluctantly loosened her stranglehold on his body, but only enough to work her hand between them. She groped for the button to Henry's jeans, then tugged at it manically until it slipped through the hole and loosened his beltline. Only a zipper stood between them. Mercy grabbed hold of the tab, ready to rip it down and let instinct take over. And then stopped.

Mondra saw this and grew instantly wary. Something was wrong. They should have been rolling around on the rug and in the throes of ecstasy by now. The enchantment on the letter was one of her most ironclad spells. For some inexplicable reason, it was running out of power. Everything in her being told her to leave the room. To sneak toward the lovers on the rug and reinforce the magic binding them.

Mercy and Henry, a writhing mass of sexual energy and desire only a few short moments ago, shook their heads at the same time. As if they'd awoken from an intense dream, and came to realize it was just that. They stared at each other in disbelief, and the color in their faces burned a brilliant crimson.

Henry opened his mouth to say something, then closed it. Mercy noticed he wasn't looking at her anymore, and tracked his gaze to a dark corner of the room. Armand Moreland held a finger to his lips, and Henry clamped his mouth closed.

The spell had lost its entire effect. Impossible! She was frantic now. In order for her plans to proceed, this first step had to be consummated. Henry and Mercy *must* make love. It was the only way, to her way of thinking, to drive the first wedge of division into the League of the Moon. From there, they would unravel. Never again would she live in fear of them.

It *had been* the entire point of drawing them away from their stronghold and into the church at Satan's Kingdom. Once the vampire had stuck his nose in, things had gone sideways.

Mondra had put on an Academy Award-worthy performance once she'd realized her plans had gone to shit, and that Mercy, not Inanis, was the true target of the vampire. The bastard had come close—she had to give him that. All the mother-daughter lovey-dovey stuff had made her want to puke. They'd bought it hook, line, and sinker. Except for Joanne. The green witch, judging by the look she'd had on her face, didn't believe any of it. That one was smart. And dangerous. It was why Mondra fled before anyone could scrutinize her sudden and miraculous change of heart.

She was now invested heavily in Plan B, and she wasn't about to watch it go up in flames.

Mondra got quickly to her feet and made for the door. A man appeared suddenly in the doorway, silhouetted in gentle hues of orange from the dying fire. She couldn't make out his face at first. But then, slowly, as in a dream, his features emerged from the gloom. His face glowed a dim green at first, and it steadily grew brighter until the face of Armand Moreland took form in blazing emerald. This struck Mondra as odd, at first. But her confusion was short-lived.

Armand Moreland smiled, but there was no victory in it, she noticed. Only sadness. And pity. "I'm so sorry it had to end like this, Mondra. I only wish your conversion had been genuine. You could have done so much good."

He said no more. Armand closed the door in her face, then slid the bolt home. To Mondra, it was the loudest sound in the world. Her fate was sealed.

When the lock slammed home, emerald light still lit the room's interior, growing in intensity. Behind her, someone breathed softly. Fear shot through the core of her being. When the lid on the floor slammed shut—the very lid Delilah Trank had been transported through when the Red

Witch had kidnapped her only a few short weeks ago—she jumped.

Mondra turned slowly now. Delilah's mother stood behind the closed lid. In one hand, she held a large hunting knife. The Red Witch recognized the knife right away as belonging to Chesrule. The idiot demon's perverted obsession with the green witch would be her undoing.

Jo smiled and tossed the knife into the corner. The look on Mondra's face told her all she needed to know. The Red Witch now understood how Joanne had come to be in this room. And how this was to be her last day on earth.

It was the blood. Mercy's blood, Joanne's blood, and her own were on the knife *together*. A knife created by a demon with the power to transmit thought telepathically to its masters. Chesrule had used Jo's blood to track them last year, imprinting part of her onto his being. They were linked. Joanne had simply reversed that power to track Mercy here.

Mondra was terrified. But she wouldn't give the bitch the satisfaction of begging for her life. Much as Xavier had done just a few short hours ago, she spread her arms and offered herself to the green witch without a word.

And as the stake, fashioned from the crucifix at the church in Satan's Kingdom, came down to end her, the last thing she saw was the word the green witch had carved into its side—and wondered if Joanne had used Chesrule's knife to do it.

Karma.

CHAPTER 40
FAMILY AND FALLOUT

It was raining hard the night the League of the Moon met once again with Armand Moreland. Wanda had suggested they have a sit-down to discuss what came next.

Mondra the Red Witch, and Xavier the Duplicitous (as Moreland chose to refer to his once trusted friend) were no more. Inanis and Chesrule still, unfortunately, existed.

Jazz arrived first, and she'd brought the two Seal of Solomon medallions with her. She'd imprisoned them further in a small chest made of Hawthorn Wood (used for banishment of evil, among a myriad of other uses) which was fortified by a thick steel chain she would ask Armand Moreland to bless this very night.

As luck would have it, the leader of the Council of the Realms was next through the door. Jazz waved to him from her beanbag chair and patted the one next to her. Armand smiled, then strode toward the center of the room, plopping down between Jazz and Wanda.

"It's nice to see you, Armand," said Jazz.

He raised an eyebrow. "Not Jeeves?"

She put a hand on his shoulder. "Nope. You earned your way out of that name. But I do have a favor to ask, if you don't mind?"

"And what's that, Miss Johnson?"

"Well, now it's *two* favors. First, you call me Jazz from now on. I consider you a friend. Second, I need these chains blessed. Don't want Stinky the Molester and Captain Chuckles getting loose again. Would you mind?"

He laughed out loud at her new nicknames for the demons. "It would be my pleasure, Jazz."

Jazz handed the chest to him. He rested his hands on the chains, closed his eyes, and prayed silently over them. When he was done, he handed the chest back to Jazz.

"Thank you, Armand," said Jazz.

"What will you do with them now?" asked Armand.

Jazz considered this for a moment. "I was thinking of bringing them to that museum in Connecticut. You know, the one with all the evil artifacts sealed up in the basement?"

"Ah. The Warrens. So sad they've left us. I loved that movie they made about them!" said Moreland. "The title escapes me. What was it called, again?"

Joanne and Henry had entered during Jazz and Moreland's conversation. Jo was shaking herself out of her leather jacket when she called out, "The Conjuring! I loved that fucking movie!"

Henry laughed. Jo was so used to using the "F-bomb," he doubted she even realized it sometimes.

"What's so funny, hot lips?" asked Jo.

The smile faded from Henry's face. Now it was Jo's turn to laugh. "I'm just messin' with you, Band-aid boy. Relax."

Henry knew she was kidding. They'd discussed what had

happened as a result of the bewitched letter from Mondra. On some level, he still felt guilty. It was irrational, he knew, but it lingered.

Jo never once doubted Henry's love for her. But it wasn't easy. The thought of a beautiful woman like Mercy jamming her tongue down her husband's throat took a bit to get over. It bothered Jo for a bit. Intellectually, she knew she shouldn't be jealous—neither of them were in control of their urges while under Mondra's spell—but emotionally; it had scarred her. Not deeply, but enough to remind her how much Henry meant to her.

Jo put a hand on his arm. "I'm sorry, Henry. I love you. No more cracks about what happened. I promise."

"It's okay. Busting my balls makes you, *you*. It's just a little... fresh. I'll get over it. Besides, it wasn't exactly the worst thing that's ever happened to me." He flashed her a wicked grin.

"I am soooo gonna beat your ass when we get home tonight!"

"Promise?" asked Henry.

Jo pulled him close and kissed him deeply. When they separated, she whispered, "I wish we could leave right now."

"Me too," Henry said through half-closed eyes.

Jo smiled, and a faint burst of emerald flashed at the rings of her deep-green irises. "You're in trouble later."

"Get a room!" said Wanda through a grin so wide it almost swallowed her ears.

Henry and Jo colored a little, then took a seat to Jazz's right.

Archie strolled in late, as usual. Wanda couldn't understand how Mr. First Ring *never* showed up on time. Just another quirk in the amusing personality of her best friend.

It made her love him even more. When he plopped down into his beanbag chair, Henry was ready with a steadying arm. Right on cue, Archie almost tumbled over its back. Henry saved him.

"Thanks, Henry."

"No problem, Arch. I kinda knew it was coming."

"One of these days I'm gonna get the hang of these things," said Archie.

"Your granddaughter will probably be one of your students by then," said Jo.

Archie smiled. "You're probably right."

The back door to Wanda's safe room opened, and the room went quiet. Mercy walked in, flashed a quick look toward those seated at the room's center, and then put her head down as she walked to the bar. She slowly removed her coat, folded it, and placed it on the bar top. Everyone could see she'd been crying. Her whole body shook.

Wanda started to get up, then halted when she saw Joanne spring from her seat. Jo walked over to the bar, made her way around it, and stood next to the trembling woman. Mercy tensed at Jo's approach, her shoulders bunching as if expecting Joanne to pummel her.

"Mercy?" Jo's voice was soft.

The young witch tilted her head up slowly, meeting Jo's eyes.

"You did nothing wrong, honey," said Jo. "We're okay. All of us."

Mercy looked doubtful. As if unworthy of forgiveness.

Jo read her like a book. "There's nothing to forgive. For me, or anyone else, to be mad at you or blame you for what happened would be like blaming a cow for what the butcher did to it."

Mercy nodded, sniffed, and said, "I blame myself for believing her. I should have known better."

Archie struggled from his beanbag chair. Henry put a hand on his back to steady him. As he approached the bar, he said, "Mercy. Take it from me. You *didn't* have a choice. You may *think* you did, and you'll want to hold on to that blame. But don't. I warn you now, from experience. That way lies madness."

Archie had reached the bar, holding Mercy's gaze along the way. He leaned over the bar top. Piercing blue eyes rooted Mercy to the spot. Archie pounded lightly on the bar, emphasizing each word with a beat from his fist. "It's. Not. Your. Fault."

Mercy looked from Archie to Jo. Her eyes welled with tears once more. Only, these were tears of relief. *They really don't blame me*, she thought. It was more than she could handle, and she buried her face in her hands.

Jo pulled her in close, hugged her tight, and stroked Mercy's hair until the last tear fell.

When she was all cried out, she pulled back from Jo and said, "Thank you."

Jo smiled through tears of her own. "You're welcome, sweetheart. Let's go sit down."

They held hands as they walked from behind the bar and across to the inner circle. Jo sat down next to Henry, and Mercy sat next to Jo.

Byron, Penny, and Marla walked through the door as Mercy, Jo, and Archie settled in their beanbags.

"Now *this* is what I call a full house," said Wanda. She waited for everyone to relax, then continued. "Well, I don't think it's a stretch to say we've got a lot to talk about. Now that Mondra is out of the picture, and the demons are contained, I think we can breathe easier. At least for a little while. I invited Armand to sit with us and discuss what comes next."

He leaned forward, then rose from his beanbag. He took a deep breath, then let it out. "First. Let me apologize. I, and the Council, were wrong to send that letter. No excuses."

Jo shifted in her seat but held her tongue. It wasn't easy, but the guy *had* come through in the end.

Moreland continued. "The spirits from the void are mostly returned. Mostly. With Mondra's demise, the link between the void and the light was severed. Some still roam Salem, as we speak. And some escaped Michael's blade in the forest around Satan's Kingdom. Those will be hardest to collect and return."

"When you say 'collect and return,' what does that mean, exactly?" asked Henry.

Armand cleared his throat. "We need to hunt them down and send them back."

"Why bother? Why not just forget about them?" asked Jo. "I don't see the point in anyone risking their lives for something like that. I have a daughter to take care of and a business to run. I don't exactly have time to be chasing boogeymen all around Salem and all the way out to west butt-fuck. Besides, isn't that your job?"

"It is. But there's more to it, I'm afraid," said Moreland.

"There's always a catch," said Byron. "Let me guess. This has something to do with the redhead? Right?"

Moreland turned to Byron, "Correct. When she brought them out of the void, she promised your souls as payment for their help. They will try to collect."

Silence fell for a few moments.

"So what happens next?" asked Henry.

"That's why we're all here tonight," said Moreland. "Your day-to-day lives make you vulnerable. Aside from this place, which, magically speaking, is protected like Fort Knox, you are not safe in your homes. The Council will provide around-the-clock protection, but it will only slow them. Not stop them. Until they are dealt with, none of us is truly safe."

"Well, that's just wonderful! How are we supposed to live our lives? Do our jobs? Pay our bills? It's not like we can drop everything and chase down these shitbags," said Jo.

"I sympathize with that. I really do," said Moreland. "But *they* don't. They are coming for all of us. Whether or not we like it."

"What should we do then?" asked Wanda.

"For now, not much. They are fleeing and disorganized. That won't last. Once they realize the danger of Michael's sword has passed, they'll be back."

"Doesn't seem like much of a threat," said Byron. "I didn't exactly see a lotta MENSA candidates running around the church courtyard the other night."

"Underestimate them at your peril, Chief," said Moreland. "What you saw that night was a frenzied pack of newly reanimated souls, hungry for payback. When they begin to remember who they were is when they become dangerous. It won't be long."

"What can we do to be ready?" asked Henry.

"Watch each other's backs. Keep your wits about you. And sharpen your magical skills. It's going to take everything. They can strike at any time. Also, protect your homes and families," he looked Jo directly in the eyes, "by any means necessary."

Jo nodded. "Not a problem."

Moreland walked toward his beanbag chair, then

stopped. He turned, stood before it, and said, "It's been a long time since I've had a family. I turned my back on God when my wife and daughter were executed for witchcraft in Germany in 1567. Inanis was there, and he was responsible. I swore I'd have vengeance on him. No matter the price."

The room was dead-silent. He took a deep breath, met everyone's eyes, and continued.

"Xavier had been following Inanis for a long time. They were both in Germany when my family was murdered, and Xavier knew I'd lost my faith. So, much like the deal he'd offered to Mondra, he proposed one to me.

"At the time, I'd no idea of Inanis's alleged 'immortality.' Xavier hastily filled me in on that score. I came to realize, in short order, that if I wanted vengeance on the demon for the deaths of my wife and daughter, Xavier was my only path. He wouldn't allow me near the demon, though, for he had his own agenda. I'm not sure if you're aware of this, but the soldier's soul trapped in the flask on the night you defeated Inanis, the first time, was Xavier's brother, Xander."

"Oh my God," whispered Jo.

"And since I'd denounced my faith, accepting the offer to become like Xavier was, as they say today, a no-brainer. Especially when I found out Xavier couldn't act against the demon until all of your souls aligned in 2018. And I *still* had to wait a bit longer for the Red Witch to make her move."

"How did you become a priest?" asked Wanda.

Moreland smiled at the memory. "It's funny. The answer is ironic. Or maybe paradoxical. Almost from the moment I became a vampire, I realized the truth of the divine. You see, when you choose to become a vampire, the sense of something—missing—is almost immediate. I gave it little thought at the time because the sensory overload at the moment of transformation was overwhelming. But that sense of loss remained. Once the 'newness' of vampirism wore off, it returned. I realized the spark of the divine—the one always there, but obscured by tragedy, or calamity, or even just everyday life—was missing. I came to understand my soul was no longer connected to a higher power.

"Xavier's plan was still four hundred fifty-one years in the future. I had to do *something*. Despite my feelings about God and faith, I pursued the priesthood. I needed to know if my wife and daughter went on. I needed to know, even though I'd forfeited my own soul, that they still existed. I... hoped God would forgive me someday. And that we might be together again. So, that's how Father Moreno ended up in the Vatican. That's how I came to hold the pendant of Xavier which Marla brought to me. It was a sign he was alive and still pursuing the demon. It brought me here. And I knew then, and still hope now, I might see Katarina and Victoria again."

Wanda rose from her beanbag and turned to face Armand. She reached up with both hands, put her thumbs over his eyes, and wiped away his tears.

"Thank you, Wanda," he whispered. Then he turned to the room. "I want all of you to know, especially you, Joanne, that when I wrote that letter, it didn't come from a place of piety, or high-handed righteousness—though I know it came off that way. I saw a mother and her daughter being attacked. I saw a witch I greatly respect risking exposure to forces she did not know might be watching. I know it's hard to believe, but I felt I was protecting you. I've become rather fond of all of you. I know it may sound odd, since we've known each other a short time, but that is how I feel. Magic binds us. I will protect all of you with my life. You are family to me."

"Okay. That works for me," said Byron. For the first time since he'd laid eyes on him, Byron smiled at the vampire. "But you still owe me four tires!"

Moreland bowed. "Consider it done, constable!"

"Ooooh, constable! That sounds waaay too fancy for him," said Jo.

Byron raised a fist at Jo.

"Bring it, sugar lips!" She gave him a big, shit-eating grin.

They were all laughing when the door at the back of the room opened. They went silent. Everyone supposed to be in Wanda's safe room was already there. The door opened slowly, and the soft candlelight caught only the reflection of a gold crucifix suspended five feet in the air. Then, fingers emerged from the gloom, grasping the polished metal pull handle and pushing it forward slowly. It squeaked. To the League of the Moon, it was the loudest sound in the world. They prepared for the first battle.

From the gloom, a voice called.

"Chief? It's me, Raul. Can I come in?"

The nine souls inside Wanda's safe room breathed a collective sigh of relief.

Byron laughed, then said, "Come on in, Raul. But aren't you on leave for the next two weeks?"

"Yes, sir. I—"

"Raul, I told you never to call me sir, or chief, or any of that formal bullshit when we're off duty. It's Byron."

Raul seemed uncomfortable with that. It reminded Wanda of Mercy's first few days as her new employee. *The apple didn't fall too far from the tree,* she thought.

"Okay... Byron." His face contorted slightly when using the chief's first name—as if tasting some new, exotic dish.

"So what's up, Raul?" asked Byron.

"I came to take my daughter to dinner," said Raul.

Mercy sat still in her beanbag chair, momentarily paralyzed. The man before her was a stranger, and she'd been so long without a father figure in her life, she was at a loss for words.

Joanne knew exactly how she felt and saw the fear and wonder in her eyes. She held out her hand, and Mercy reached for it slowly, as in a dream. Jo pulled her to her feet, and said, "He's here for you, Mercy. Go have dinner with your dad."

Raul walked over to his daughter and crooked an elbow for her to loop her arm through. Mercy did. She asked, "Where are we going?"

"I was thinking Rockafellas. I heard the steak tips are awesome."

"That sounds good."

Mercy caught Wanda's eye, and Wanda mouthed the word, *Daddy*.

"Daddy," said Mercy.

They walked out, arm-in-arm. Mercy leaned her head on Raul's shoulder as they passed through the door. It closed with a soft click.

CHAPTER 41
HENRY CHECKS IN

Well, I'd say that was one pretty interesting year-plus of my life. Scratch that. It was fucking insane!

I promised you I'd check in down the road. Since the day the GoPro changed my life, I haven't had much time to talk to you directly. So, here I am. And man, do we have some shit to talk about!?

I know you probably have a million questions for me, and I'll try to answer most of them here. Because, believe it or not, I have questions of my own. Just because I'm in the middle of all this magical fuckery doesn't mean I have all the answers. I have *some*. Probably a few more than you. But not much. Anyhoo, off the top of my head, here's what I know.

The first thing you'll probably want to know, because it's the first thing *I* thought about after last night, is how did Moreland have the authority to call down angels from heaven? You don't see that every day.

That should be my motto in life now, come to think of it.

I asked him about it when we were in Wanda's parking

lot after Mercy left with Raul. He was a bit cryptic about the whole thing. All he'd tell me was it's part of his penance for willingly abandoning his soul to become a vampire. And then something about protecting the integrity of the realms. It makes sense. He was there to stop both Mondra *and* Xavier from claiming the powerful magic in Mercy for themselves. And if you think about it, Xavier and Mondra would have become almost unstoppable had either claimed what makes Mercy, *Mercy*.

I told Armand I thought he was holding out on me, and that I thought part of it had to do with Mercy. He just smiled and told me when the time was right, the League of the Moon would know the full story. *That* should be interesting!

I hope he gets to reunite with Katarina and Victoria one day. I couldn't imagine what happened to his family happening to Jo and DeeDee. Well, I *can* imagine it, come to think of it. Mondra came close to making it happen. I just don't know if I could handle something like that.

So... sorry, I need a break. The thought of it just hit me in the feels.

Shut up! I'm not crying! You're crying!

You know what we thought of Moreland. Personally, it took all I had not to deck the pompous fuck on sight. When Jo was busy chasing Zachary Villitz to save Delilah, the *last* thing on her mind was who might be watching. Not to mention she had no idea what she was capable of after meeting and touching Mercy. Armand is lucky Jo didn't fry his ass on the spot!

The guy proved himself to all of us, though. I gotta give him that. None of us would probably be here if he hadn't done the things he did. If there's one thing I've come to realize since my life took this bizarre turn, it's that Wanda was one hundred percent right. Your Higher Power, in whatever form you choose to believe, gives you what you need when you need it. To see that *literally* happen in dramatic fashion right before my eyes? You know, with the angels? I've got chills just thinking about it.

Jazz took the box with the demons down to the Warren Museum in Connecticut. Tony Spera, the Warren's son-in-law, received the box-o-shitbags gladly. He put it to the right of Annabelle, the doll that caused all that trouble in *The Conjuring*. Jazz watched him do it. When Tony put the box down, Jazz said she would swear on a stack of Bibles the doll moved. A psychos-from-Hell reunion? Maybe.

I asked her if she caught it on her phone. When her mouth dropped open and she told me it never crossed her mind, I felt bad for her. To make her feel better about it, I told her about the stuff I caught myself doing on a GoPro, way back when, and how I wished I hadn't taken the thing out of the closet. It didn't seem to help.

"I could have gone viral on TikTok!" she'd yelled.

Some things just aren't meant to be.

When I saw the letters on the mirror in my bathroom, I didn't give much thought as to how they might've gotten there. I was blown away just *seeing* them there. Jo wasn't. She had her suspicions. Tie that to the dreams Mondra put in her head, and it's no surprise she was the first one to follow Archie out west.

Xavier put the message in the mirror at my apartment, and also at Wanda's. The creep snuck in to both places while we all worked. A little oil on the finger, then apply it to the mirror, add steam, and *Voila!*, instant mystery!

How do I know that? Armand told me Xavier admitted as much not long after Wanda and Mercy left the Council's seeing room. It was then he suspected Xavier might have an agenda of his own. Why he told Armand about it is beyond me. Maybe he thought the priest would see the wisdom in his plans? Or, maybe he thought Moreland would go along with him out of loyalty for making him a vampire? Who knows? Pride doth indeed goeth before the fall.

In keeping with Xavier's overestimation of his own intelligence, he believed he was controlling Mondra by staggering our arrival times out in Satan's Kingdom. So the pasty fucker slashed Byron's tires for what turned out to be nothing.

But he wasn't all bad. I mean, he *did* save Marla and me from burning to death in a fire. Just saying. Still, Mondra had him pegged from the start. It didn't hurt that she'd slept with him years before, either. She gained enough from that to simply change her tactics on the fly and let him believe it was the other way around. That woman was scary smart. Thank God Jo was smarter.

Armand Moreland walks the streets of Salem during the day. I didn't think vampires could do that. When I asked him about it, he shrugged and said it was nothing but horror movie bullshit. If you've ever read Bram Stoker's *Dracula*, or seen the movie, Dracula has no problem walking the streets in the daytime. That's good enough for me. I mean, it would be really fucking boring, not to mention depressing, if you could only come out of your coffin at night. Right? Ask anyone who works the graveyard shift how much they like it. You'll get a few that do, but not a lot. I know firsthand from when I worked in the Portland E.R.

He also told me, through some quirk of vampire evolution, they've figured out a way to remain unseen during the daytime, if they so choose. It began shortly after the first cameras appeared on the scene. Since that day, some innate sense of danger had crept into the psyche of vampire culture worldwide. If you think about it, it makes sense.

They live pretty much forever once they've changed—aside from an unfortunate stake impalement here and there—so it wouldn't be the greatest thing in the world to be caught in a picture in 1892 and have to explain an uncanny resemblance to that same person in 1992. I'm talking total duplicate stuff, right down to the butterfly shaped mole under your left nostril—or something else that might seem way too coincidental. I mean, you could always *say* it was your grandmother or grandfather, but I think they'd rather just not have to deal with it. Why invite suspicion?

I gave Marla a ride home that night, after talking to Moreland. She was right beside me during my conversation with him, so she heard everything we talked about. I asked her about the trinket with Xavier's blood in it. I thought it was strangely coincidental that she *just happened* to come with me on that day, and that both Moreland and Xavier *just happened* to be at the church, and then Xavier would *just happen* to drop a clue for us identical to the brooch Marla carried with her at all times.

She said father Moreno/Moreland, when he was in Italy, told her to always keep the item close. He said it was very valuable and believed, one day, it could save her life. I asked her if she'd handed it over to him at any point on the day she met him, or if it ever left her sight. Her eyes went wide when she remembered.

"He took it into the vault at the Vatican," she'd said. "But we watched him through the glass. The only thing I remember him doing out of the ordinary was sticking it with a syringe. I asked him why he'd done that, and he told me the solution in the syringe was a fluid they used to try and determine the age of the item. The fluid was red."

So, with that little tidbit of info, we both realized two things right away: Moreland, once he'd handled the brooch, either smelled Xavier all over it—vampiric olfactory senses are the stuff of legend, so no surprise there—or, he knew what it was right away because he'd seen it before. I'd put my money on number two.

Xavier was no dummy. Xavier could see the future. Combine those two things and it leads to one very ominous and self-sacrificing conclusion. Xavier *knew* he might lose control and try to take Mercy's powers for himself. It's the only thing that explains why he'd drop that clue for us in the forest. There were probably a million different things he could have done to lead us to where he wanted us to go, but he left an *identical* brooch in the woods for us to find. Bottom line; he didn't trust himself.

I suspect there's more to it.

Maybe he'd had enough?

Maybe the guy just wanted it all over with?

Maybe he missed his brother, and was willing to risk annihilation of his soul for the chance to see him once again?

I can't help but feel, after what he saw Moreland do with the angels, the thought of possible forgiveness from a Higher Power might have crossed his mind.

There's also another possibility. Maybe he knew what Sekhmet *really* wanted with Mercy, and in the end realized— whatever it was—it was wrong.

Moreland told me how Xavier came to be a vampire in the first place, so all these scenarios are equally possible. One might be correct. All might be. But the last one scares me the most. I hope I never have to find out, but you know the saying; wish in one hand, shit in the other, see which fills up first. I know little about her, but Sekhmet sounds dangerous.

Last, but not least, is the episode in bay seven at MGH. I couldn't understand how, and why, the same message I'd seen earlier in the day in my bathroom mirror came to be on the forehead of the Vin Diesel wannabe. I understand it now though. And the truth scares the living shit out of me.

I asked myself how, out of the millions of people living in the Boston area, I came to be in the same room with a guy that *just happened* to be possessed by Chesrule, and *just happened* to have a message identical to the one in my mirror seared into his forehead.

There are no coincidences.

Okay, that's not entirely true. Jo's birthday and my mother's birthday were the same numbers that opened a certain box holding a certain key. Wanda called it divine intervention. Maybe she's right. Okay, it's Wanda, so she's probably right. But still.

My God, I'm rambling more than Ryan Reynolds.

Anyway, this turned out *not* to be a coincidence. I was curious to know how the guy was doing, so I called the ER to find out. He was *my* patient, after all.

Was.

He died. Not from his injuries, mind you. No, that would have been too much to ask for. Too "normal."

When I called to check up on him, the head nurse filling in for Marla was the one who'd answered. She wouldn't give me any info. When I asked why, she gave me the runaround and told me to call the pathologist at the morgue. So I did.

"Benny? Henry Trank here. Sheila from the ER told me to

call you about my patient. The car crash vic. I wanted to find out how he died."

"The better question would be *when*, Henry," said Benjamin Watts.

"What do you mean, *when*?"

"Just what I said. I'm having the damnedest time figuring out how a guy who presents as having passed through rigor mortis more than a month ago could end up in the ER only a few days ago... and as the victim of a car crash in which he was the sole occupant."

More like *soul* occupant, I thought.

It was then I realized, even though I'd checked the guy's chart, I'd never checked his name. But now, I had my suspicions. And I dreaded asking the question. But ask it, I did.

"What was the guy's name, Benny?"

I heard him riffling through pages. Benny was old school. Close to retirement. He had use of the hospital network and could've looked it up in two seconds, if he'd wanted to. I knew he wouldn't, and it made me smile. In a lot of ways, he was like Archie. I admired him for sticking to his guns when it came to technology. The clipboard clattered over the tinny morgue phone connection, and the receiver scraped across the metal table as he picked it up. I held my breath.

"Henry?"

"Yeah?"

"Last name is Murphy. First is Roger."

For a few moments, I said nothing. I sat in the front seat of my Camry, too stunned for words. What finally snapped me out of it was Benny. He was practically shouting my name at the top of his lungs. I put the phone back to my ear.

"Sorry, Benny."

"Do you know this guy?" asked Benny.

"Yeah, I know him. Not personally, but the name is familiar."

"How do you know him?"

I wasn't about to tell him. So I said, "He's the brother of an acquaintance. I'll tell her. Thanks, Benny."

"Wait a minute, Henry. How do you explain—"

I hung up. The last thing in the world I was about to tell Benny was that a recently deceased narcissist, sociopath, redheaded, dark witch, vampire used her dead brother to send me a message. I didn't think he'd buy it. Would you?

It's late. Or early, depending on your point of view. I'm just pulling up to our apartment. Mrs. G. is in the hallway with her hands visoring her forehead so she can see the street through the glare of the interior lights. She knows I haven't come home yet.

Nothing goes on in that building without her knowledge. But I'm the only one she waits up for. I kinda like that. I didn't like it so much in the beginning, when I first moved here, but I've come to expect it now. It reminds me of when life was normal. I *miss* normal, now and then. But not much. If anything, she keeps me grounded. It reminds me of how life used to be, and how lucky I am now.

I don't know where all of this is going. But I know there's some nasty shit coming our way. For now, all I can do is wish Mrs. G. a good night, and pray to a power greater than myself for peaceful dreams.

Talk to you soon. Blessed be.

Henry.

FROM THE AUTHOR

Hi, Rob here. Just checking in. Kinda like Henry.

Thanks for reading *Blood, Magic, & Mercy*. I hope you liked it.

So, this one went a lot smoother than *The Red Witch*. We've been settled in our new home for some time now, and I was able to work on this one almost without interruption. I've gotta say, this story flowed quickly from wherever that spot in the universe is where stories seem to come from. As I've mentioned, probably ad-nauseam, I'm a discovery writer. I don't outline my books, and I don't plan out plots. I let the characters do their thing and the story goes where it wants. It's much more fun that way!

Henry, Joanne, Wanda, Archie, Mercy, and everyone else you've come to know and love, will be back as soon as they start to do the things they seem to do while I'm not looking.

As I drove around the other day, Wanda popped into my head. She didn't say anything. And yes, I know she's not real, (at least as far as we all know), but I had a hazy vision of her at an AA meeting. She was up front, introducing herself, and

FROM THE AUTHOR

I got a bad feeling about it. Like maybe someone at the back of the meeting was, you know, not supposed to be there. I think Wanda sensed it too. Just sayin'.

Take care. Be safe. And thank you for reading my books.
Rob.

ACKNOWLEDGMENTS

As always, I have to thank my wife, Diana, and my sister, Susan. They are the first to read my books and their input on this one, as always, was invaluable.

I'd like to thank Tony Spera for allowing me to use his name for the last chapter of this book.

I also want to thank T. Melendez. When I was stuck at a certain point, our discussion about a scene in Book 1, *In Your Dreams*, jarred everything loose, and the floodgates opened. I finished this book much quicker thanks to you!

Next in the League of the Moon Series

vinci-books.com/envy

A new merchant arrives in the Witch City.

Jagger Corey seemed to appear from nowhere. He's arrived with a dark wish, and strange things have begun to happen in Salem.

Turn the page for a free preview...

PREVIEW OF BLACK MAGICK AND ENVY

CHAPTER 1 — JO IN THE SNOW

Snow. Already. It was only November ninth, and it had been sixty-five degrees the day before, but leave it to New England to serve up a semi-blizzard the next day.

Joanne closed the Cracked Cauldron coffee shop early. No sense keeping the place open when most everyone was hunkered down at home. In short order, she would regret that decision.

Normally, on a day like this, Henry would wait out front with her orange Jeep. Not tonight. Henry's dad hurt his back, so he'd packed up the Jeep and Delilah and headed for Portland, Maine. Jo insisted he take the four-wheel-drive for the trip. The storm started by the time he left, but once he crossed into New Hampshire it was supposed to pick up steam.

She closed the door, locked it, and pulled the collar of her navy peacoat up around her neck, then stepped into the storm.

"Not much of a storm *here*," she complained to the empty street.

Fat flakes seesawed toward the ground like feathers loosed from a giant Snow Owl. Jo turned her head toward the sky, stuck out her tongue, and caught one of them.

"Mmm," she cooed.

She loved the snow. Ever since she was a little girl, it never failed to enchant her. It didn't matter where she lived, what family she was currently a part of, or how bad the circumstances at the time were; snow equaled refuge.

Anything which helped evade the endless parade of pervert foster dads was a refuge. But there was something about being outside when it snowed that made things seem better.

Maybe it was the quiet peace of it. Snow shaved the rough edges from the harsh city sounds. As if God decided enough was enough, and it was time for some peace and quiet.

She felt cozy being bundled up as it fell all around—her own private little snow globe. Just her, the snow, and the crunch under her feet. It soothed her soul. When she was outside and the flakes fell slowly, like tonight, she would pick one out and follow it all the way to the ground. There was nothing to think about. Nothing to worry about. Just follow that one little, crystallized pillow of frozen water until it became one with the others. Rinse and repeat. The world disappeared for a while. That was good. Sometimes, there was *nothing* better.

From a very young age, Jo discovered making the world go away—if just for a little while—allowed you to come back to it. It wasn't always a place she *wanted* to come back to, but getting away from it—escaping into the snow—always brought her back a little bit stronger, a little bit wiser, and a lot more centered. It helped her deal with the crazies.

At least, it did until she'd found booze and drugs. When that happened, at least in the beginning, it snowed *every day*.

She made her way through the hush to the end of Essex Street. A lonely plow scraped the quiet from the street in front of her, then turned the corner and gave it slowly back. With peace restored, Jo made her way toward the Salem Common. The sight of the wrought-iron gates brought her another level of comfort. Her heart hummed with satisfaction as she stepped through the entrance and into the empty park. It was just her, the snow, the soft yellow lamps dotting the Common, and blessed silence.

Puffy flakes floated across shafts of golden lamplight. They reminded her of potato chips, and she said, "Betcha can't eat just one!" She laughed at her own joke and it echoed from somewhere in the vast park.

That was odd. Not only was there nothing for her voice to echo *from* in the huge and empty park, but the echo sounded nothing like her own voice. What returned sounded deep, dangerous... and male.

Jo stood still, listening. Her cherished silence tainted by fear and unease. She strained to hear... something. Anything. What moments ago was a blissfully silent and peaceful walk in the park had turned sour. Echoes of Armand Moreland's warning from the last time they'd gotten together at Wanda's Wicca'd Emporium played on a loop in her mind.

"Watch your back," he'd said. "Keep your guard up."

He had warned them that the children of the void would

come back for them. She felt the hair on her neck stand up. The park appeared empty, but she knew they were near.

Jo looked around, seeking a way to even the odds. A place she could give herself a fighting chance. She spied the gazebo in the middle of the park and sprinted for it.

It was fifty yards away and to her right. The first of them sprang from the dark, as if pulled from the blackness between snowflakes. It stood directly in Jo's path to the gazebo. Another warning from Armand flashed through her mind, although it wasn't as much of a warning as it was permission to act. He'd told everyone in the League of the Moon to defend themselves, "By any means necessary."

Bad news for whoever this shit bag was, or *used* to be. Jo never broke stride. She ran full tilt toward the entity as it raised both hands in her direction. Anticipating a magical attack, she beat the creepy bastard to it. Green fire exploded from her upturned palm, knocking the hulking entity flat on its back. It struggled to regain its footing and slipped in the snow. It would never get a chance to make another mistake.

Jo still carried the enchanted hunting knife she'd claimed from the demon Chesrule. She whipped it from the pocket of her peacoat, slid to a stop next to the massive entity, and drove it straight through its neck. A blinding flash of light, a wail of pain and frustration, and the entity was gone—sent to the nothingness from which it came.

As if ignited by the loss, five more entities apparated in the spot where the first perished. The initial attack slowed her, but she was quickly back at full speed. She sprinted toward the gazebo, sensing her only chance to defeat the odds was claiming the higher ground. Her arms and legs pumped in furious rhythm. Vaporous breath trailed her, pistoning from her mouth like steam from a train. The knife glinted gold in the lamplight, keeping time with her breath. She took the stairs two at a time, making it to the top in less than two seconds. Once there, she stood in the middle, knife out, readied for battle.

The gazebo had two sets of stairs, six steps to a side, and were wide enough to accommodate multiple tourists. If her enemies were smart, they'd come at her from both sides. Jo knew hoping for them to come at her all at once, and from one side, was wishful thinking.

They seemed to read her mind, pulling up short. Three split from the group and rounded the gazebo, taking position on the opposite side. Jo stood calmly in the middle, twirling the knife slowly in her hand. She turned toward the group of three. Her green eyes bathed the gazebo in emerald light. With the knife in her left hand, she beckoned them with her right. "Come get some."

At first, the entities seemed tentative in the face of such boldness from the witch with the green eyes. Then, they found courage. The first screamed with rage and charged Joanne. Exactly what she wanted.

Of course, the one that broke from the pack first was the biggest, but also proved to be the dumbest. It charged head down, like a bull. Jo dodged its attack, brought the knife down as it passed, and watched as he burst into pieces and then disappeared in a flash of light.

One down.

The others learned quickly from the mistake of their gung-ho counterpart. Jo looked from the couple on her left to the pair at her right. They were coordinating. *Telepathically.* They moved as one, taking each step on either side of the gazebo at the same time. She knew if she let them onto the platform all at once, she was a goner.

The pair on her knife side would have to die first. It was simple math, when you came right down to it. If she attacked first from that side, she'd probably save herself about a half-second. In a fight like this, it was an eternity. From decision to execution, less than a second passed. Her aim was true. The knife cleaved the head of the blackened shape of what used to be a man—*and was God knew what now*, Jo thought—turning it to dust after a blinding flash of light. The entity beside it froze in fear, and the bolt of green Jo shot from her hands sent it hurtling toward oblivion before it knew what happened.

Three down.

Jo never turned to watch the remaining pair. She leapt from the gazebo, flew over the steps to the snow-covered grass, dropped, and rolled until she reached the knife, popping up with it thrust forward. The entities were on her fast.

As Jo raised the knife, the one in the lead swiped at her arm, knocking it from her grasp. It flew high in the air, then tumbled through the night. Golden light from the Common lamps winked off the bright steel as it landed, point first, on the lawn. Jo made a move for it, but the second entity flanked her and kicked the legs out from under her. Jo landed hard on her back, the wind knocked from her lungs. The dark mass who'd knocked the knife from her hand was on her in a flash, and the one who'd swept her legs now lay across them, pinning her at the knees.

The entity straddled her stomach and stilled her arms with its knees. It leaned forward, placing the black mass of its face directly on Joanne's. Its breath was ice cold, its lips colder. They clamped over Jo's, and as it drank her life force, everything that made her who she was flashed before her eyes.

Jo tried to scream, tried to fight, but could only watch, helpless. Images of Henry and Delilah floated in midair, and were swallowed into the black mass pinning her down. They purred like lions at a kill, and it sickened her.

Memories, and the emotions attached to them, flowed from Joanne and into the children of the void. Tears fell from her eyes as the fullness of her soul was ripped from her body, and the essence of who she was drained into them, bit by bit.

Henry, Delilah, Wanda, Archie, Mercy. As their images hung in the air between her and the dark mass, Jo realized, to her horror, she was forgetting their names. Henry was now the handsome guy—familiar, but nothing more. *What a cute child. What was her name? I know that tiny woman in the purple cloak, or do I? Who's that guy with the ponytail and the hat?*

"Have you found it?" hissed the entity pinning her knees.

The dark mass on Jo's chest peeled its lips from her and hissed its reply. "Yesssss. They will be pleased."

Jo felt everything slipping away. All she was and all she'd been, in this life and others, and all she would ever be, was being devoured. There was nothing she could do to stop it. The children of the void had claimed the reward promised by the Red Witch.

Only one face remained with a name attached to it. But *that* was weird, because that face didn't hang in the air before her, like the hot guy, or the cute child, or the little woman in the purple cloak. It was *behind* the entity, hovering over it. Armand Moreland stood above them all, knife in hand, raised and ready.

What was his name again?

The well-dressed man slashed down brutally with the knife, killing the entity on her chest. Something flashed brightly in the air a few feet above her face. Before the entity pinning her legs could reach it, Armand Moreland opened his mouth and swallowed it down. Then the vampire whirled and executed the last of her enemies.

The darkness vanished. The pain of memories lost fled. Names she couldn't come up with moments earlier were back on her lips once again. Then everything went dark.

The next time Joanne opened her eyes, Armand Moreland was reaching a hand toward her. She took it, and he pulled her gently to her feet.

"What are you doing here, GQ?"

"I was about to ask you the same question, Joanne."

Jo was taken aback by his question. Not because it offended her, but because she couldn't remember how she'd gotten to the middle of the Salem Common.

Moreland watched as Jo turned in circles, a look of total confusion on her face.

"It will come back to you. Here, take my arm. Do you remember where you were headed?" asked Moreland.

Jo was still looking around, confused. "I think I was on my way to Mercy's house. At least that rings a bell. For what reason, I don't quite remember."

"Let's keep moving. We'll head to Miss Glass's. Maybe the walk will help. It will come to you. Just be patient."

Jo leaned her head on Moreland's shoulder. Moreland took this as a sign of trust, but also a sign that Jo hadn't quite gotten her memory all the way back. It had only been a month, and her distrust of him hadn't simply vanished. He knew this, but kept his silence. Once she realized fully who he was, and also why she was out here, her head would come off his shoulder soon enough.

They walked onward through the snow, and ever so slightly, her head came from his shoulder. He was smiling on the outside but felt some regrets. He'd hoped they would become closer. That she would learn to trust him. But it had only been a little over three weeks since everything went down with the Red Witch, and he knew it would take her more time.

Time was something Armand Moreland had in great supply. At least, at the time, it seemed so.

"So, Mr. Moreland. What the hell just happened back there?"

"Ah, good. You're remembering. Well, first off, you were just attacked by no less than six entities from the void. They surrounded you on the gazebo in the middle of the park. You killed four of them straightaway, but the other two got a hold of you. They were claiming your soul. Something promised them by the Red Witch."

Jo pulled her arm free from his.

"Are you serious?"

Moreland raised his right hand. "God as my witness."

Fear ripped through Jo. "Why don't I remember any of it?"

"You will. It might take a day or two, but it will mostly come back to you."

Jo nodded, but a look of skepticism hung on her face.

"I believe you were on the way to Mercy Glass's apartment. At least, that's what you told me. Shall we continue on?"

"I think I can find it on my own, thanks."

"Humor me," said Moreland. "I love a snowy night. Keep me company for a bit."

Jo shrugged. "Suit yourself."

The phantom intimacy of moments ago vanished. The true state of their relationship resumed. This saddened Moreland, but gave him something to strive for.

They walked on in uncomfortable silence. When they reached the edge of the Common, Jo sucked in a surprised breath.

"What is it?" asked Moreland.

Jo turned to him, shocked. "You just saved my life, didn't you?"

Moreland smiled.

vinci-books.com/envy

ABOUT THE AUTHOR

Robert Sanborn lives in north central Massachusetts with his wife, Diana, their sweet-natured dog, Coco, the Brussels Griffon, their psychotic black cat Luna, the Devon Rex, Jason, the extremely talkative African-Grey Parrot, Angus, the cranky Quaker Parrot, Artemis, the cute-as-hell Java Finch, and two Parakeets named Sweetie and Sunny. He spends a lot on pet food.

Oh, yeah. And a Crested Gecko Lizard named Gretel. Sheesh!

He is a survivor of Hodgkin's Lymphoma, diagnosed in 1993.

He has been clean and sober since September 24, 1991.

His first book, *In Your Dreams*, was written and published in July, 2020, during the event which shall not be named, and between making deliveries to health care facilities as part of his day job. Not nerve-racking at all.